Small-town life in Hazel Rock becomes a Texas-size crime scene when murder takes a page from Charli Rae Warren's book club's latest mystery...

Charli takes great pride in running one of the few independent, family-owned bookstores in small-town Texas. She vets everything carefully, with an eye to the eclectic tastes of the locals. That includes the Book Barn's weekly book club selection. This time out it's a mystery whose characters bear a striking resemblance to local citizens, including Charli's friend Sugar...who's the prime suspect when her real-life nemesis is found dead in the hotel's water tank.

With help from her pet armadillo Princess, Charli campaigns to clear Sugar's sweet name—literally—when the up-for-election mayor becomes a killer's next target. Murder and politics make scandalous bedfellows as Charli discovers that fiction may be fatal, but reality could be just as deadly...

The Book Barn Mystery Series
by Kym Roberts

Fatal Fiction

A Reference to Murder

Perilous Poetry

Lethal Literature

Killer Classics

KILLER CLASSICS

A Book Barn Mystery

Kym Roberts

LYRICAL UNDERGROUND
Kensington Publishing Corp.
www.kensingtonbooks.com

Lyrical Press books are published by
Kensington Publishing Corp. 119 West 40th Street New York, NY 10018

Special book excerpts or customized printings can also be created to fit specific needs. For details, write or phone the office of the Kensington Special Sales Manager:
Kensington Publishing Corp.
119 West 40th Street
New York, NY 10018
Attn. Special Sales Department. Phone: 1-800-221-2647.

First Electronic Edition: December 2018
eISBN-13: 978-1-5161-0659-2
eISBN-10: 1-5161-0659-8

First Print Edition: December 2018
ISBN-13: 978-1-5161-0661-5
ISBN-10: 1-5161-0661-X

Printed in the United States of America

For the characters who inspire the mystery

Acknowledgments

Thank you to the members of the Kensington team who have made this series possible. I am ever so grateful for their hard work and patience. Thank you to my editor Martin Biro, who is the brain behind several of my titles, including *Killer Classics* and the man who made the series possible. I would be remiss to forget Penny's line edits—whew! She worked hard! Thank you to my agent, Kim Lionetti, who has been with me from the beginning—pushing me and my work to make it the best it can be. Keep pushing, Kim! But most of all, thank you dear readers. Y'all have made my Book Barn Mysteries a fun and joyous adventure. Without you, there would be no Princess or Team Mateo.

Chapter 1

"Sugar did it."

Sugar's mouth dropped open, and her eyes nearly popped out of her head at Reba Sue's accusation.

"Sugar didn't kill anyone," Leila argued. "The woman traps scorpions at the bar and releases them outside." Leila shuddered, her round body jiggling from head to toe. "Stupid critters belong under a boot heel."

Reba Sue, however wasn't backing down. "We're not talking about Sugar killing a pest that could sting her," she insisted. "We're talking about a gold-diggin' woman dying after she made a move on Sugar's man. I'm telling you, any woman would kill Maddie after what that good for nothin' tramp did. And Sugar is no different."

My best friend Scarlet joined the argument. "As usual, you're barking up the wrong hemline, Reba Sue. Liza Twine killed her." Scarlet ticked off the points of her argument on two well-manicured, red nails. "She had motive and opportunity."

Liza Twaine scoffed. Her purple nails drummed on the surface of the hand-milled, ten-foot-long table the women of the Mystery Moms Book Club were gathered around. It was like a personal nail war going on between the two of them. "What could I possibly have against Maddie?"

The rest of the book club members in the loft of my family bookstore, the Book Barn Princess, began arguing back and forth. More names were thrown into the hat as potential suspects to the murder.

Rolling my eyes, I put my index finger and thumb together, raised them to my lips, and let loose a whistle loud enough to bring the rafters down. The argument stopped cold turkey. All twelve women turned as one to look at me.

"May I remind y'all that you're talking about characters in a book—*not* our very own Sugar who is sitting right here."

Sugar's lips pursed, and her chin bobbed toward her chest in a silent thank you for me giving her redemption.

"And..." I raised my hand to Maddie sitting on the opposite side of the table. "Sugar brought Maddie as a guest to our book club today. I hardly think they're at odds."

We all looked at Maddie, who had the same features as Sugar. Both in their twenties with blue eyes and long, blond hair, the two could have been sisters. Instead, they had both fallen for the same man, five years apart. Maddie was the ex-wife in the relationship, while Sugar was the current girlfriend.

"I would hope that Sugar or Liza Twaine wouldn't dream of trying to kill me." Maddie flipped her blond hair over her shoulder.

Daisy coughed and said something under her breath that wasn't fit for print. "Well, I've finished the book, and I can tell you that—"

Every member of the Mystery Moms Book Club's voice rose to stop Daisy, our eldest member, before she could give away the plot. Most of the women hadn't finished the book since I'd just sent out the recommendation the previous day. In fact, we weren't even supposed to be discussing *Woman Scorned* until next week. Yet the book had grabbed their attention, and their responses had been passionate. Between the loud noises, squeals, and inappropriate phrases, I truly hoped we didn't have any tourists shopping on the lower lever of the store. Any outsiders would think we were plum crazy. Anyone who lived in the tri-county area would know it was just book club Wednesday.

Daisy's husband Jessie cleared the air of animosity. "That's my wife," he said with sarcasm dripping off every word.

All the women began to laugh...with the exception of Daisy. Her scowl deepened as she directed it toward Jessie. She obviously didn't care for her husband talking about her in that tone. Especially when it was so close to the line she was famous for using when talking about him. *That's my husband* was the most commonly used phrase in Hazel Rock thanks to Daisy, and it had multiple meanings. It could mean, *get your grubby paws away from my man*, or *this old coot is going to get an earful when I get him alone*. The possibilities were endless—until Jessie applied the phrase to Daisy.

I was betting that would be the first and last time he tried it.

"Doesn't anyone else find it creepy that the author used real people from our town to write a murder mystery?" I asked.

Reba Sue dismissed my concern. "He changed the names."

"Changing Sugar's name to Candy isn't much of a stretch," I argued. "Not to mention killing off Maddie—I mean Pattie, isn't very nice if he's angling it about real people." The author had changed Maddie's name, to Pattie in his book and her death hadn't been pleasant.

"That's because he was smitten with Sugar. The way my husband used to be with me." Daisy glared at Jessie sitting across the room reading a copy of *Rodeo Times*. As a retired rodeo star, Jessie loved to catch up on what was going on throughout the circuit with the monthly newspaper.

Jessie lowered the paper and winked at Daisy. "I still am, darlin'."

Daisy's frown disappeared, and a twinkle appeared in her eyes.

"Nathan Daniels wasn't smitten. He was obsessed with Sugar," Leila interjected.

"What do you mean?" I asked.

"He came into the bar every night and watched her. If Sugar wasn't scheduled, he'd turn around and head out without having one beer. He claimed she was inspiring his next best seller." Leila's nose scrunched with distaste. "I think he was one creepy man."

Mateo Espinosa, the county sheriff who'd kept silent throughout the entire meeting while he leaned against the railing with his chiseled arms folded across his chest, frowned. His brown uniform wasn't the most appealing, but the body that filled it out made up for the putrid color. Tall and muscular, he had dark hair and dark eyes that put him in the Sheriff McDreamy category. "Why didn't someone say something to me?"

Leila shook her head, her curls jiggling in time with her body. "Sugar never complained. Not once. She said it was fine if he looked, as long as he didn't touch. I had Joe watching him whenever he came into the bar."

Joe and Leila Buck owned the Tool Shed Tavern. It was where everyone went on Monday, Thursday, and Sunday nights during football season. When it wasn't football season, they offered the only live entertainment in town every Friday night. The bar had been a staple in town long before my family had moved to Hazel Rock, Texas.

Mateo looked at Sugar. "You should have said something."

I knew Mateo better than most people in Hazel Rock. He was irritated that he missed something everyone else knew about. I could tell by the creases forming in his brow. Right now, he wasn't happy with the possibility of someone stalking Sugar.

And, like Mateo, I wasn't comfortable with it either. "Changing the name of the Tool Shed to the Tool Shack for his novel wasn't exactly a stretch of the imagination," I said.

"Nor is Eliza Blain that far of a stretch from Liza Twaine. From what I've read so far, he's depicted me as a desperate reporter who'd stop at nothing to get a story. Including murder."

No one argued with Liza. If anything, a few heads nodded in agreement with the author's description of her. Which was enough to tick Liza off from here 'til Tuesday.

"Whatever." She huffed. "I have a deadline to make." Liza got up and stomped down the steps in her four-inch, purple stilettos.

"See you next week!" I called down to her. Her response was mumbled too quietly for me to hear before she disappeared behind the swish of the sliding front doors.

Daisy continued the discussion. "Luckily, Nathan Daniels doesn't write true crime stories. If he did, his book would have left one of us dead, one of us widowed, and one of us locked up. The last thing we need is trouble."

"This town could use a little trouble," Jessie said from behind his newspaper.

The silence echoed as we waited for Jessie to explain himself. Even Daisy seemed shocked by her husband's comment. The sound of Daddy ringing up a sale downstairs traveled to us, and I felt momentary relief that at least something was going right this morning, since the book club was turning out to be a bust. When Jessie let his comment fester as he turned the page of his newspaper, his wife finally responded for all of us.

"You've done lost your mind Jessie; none of us are young enough to stir up anything anymore."

Several of the mystery moms nodded in agreement, but Mateo just grinned and looked in my direction.

"I know you're not thinking that I'm a troublemaker," I leaned over and whispered in his ear.

"I'm thinking your name is synonymous with trouble."

Before I could respond my daddy made his way up the stairs. In his late fifties, he was lean and fit with enough gray in all the right places to make him look distinguished. His plaid shirt, jeans, and cowboy boots were pretty common in Hazel Rock, especially for the men of his generation.

"Has Cade moved in?" he asked me. "His stuff is scattered everywhere."

Mateo's left eyebrow rose a quarter of a centimeter. No one noticed it. Except me.

Jessie laid his paper in his lap. "And the trouble begins."

Daisy smiled at her spouse as she swiped the air in his direction. "That's my husband."

I laughed at my father's question, but it sounded more like a nervous cackle. "Don't be ridiculous."

The members of the Mystery Moms were intrigued. They saw the opportunity to get the answers to a question that had plagued the citizens of Hazel Rock for over a dozen years. Would the town princess and her hero, Hazel Rock's current mayor, get back together, or not?

We would not.

Mateo uncrossed his legs as he leaned against the post at the top of the steps. We'd been quietly dating for the past several months. For a small town, it was amazing that our relationship had never filled the rumor mill with yards of material. No one teased us, and no one asked us about it. They just let us be, and that was the way I liked it. But it looked like Daddy had opened a can of worms that was going to start the rumor mill grinding at full speed.

Mateo snuck a peek in the opposite direction of the front door. Again, no one noticed his reaction to the conversation. But I'd recently found I could read him like a children's novel, and by turning his back away from the front door, Mateo's actions told me he was more than a little bit interested in where Cade Calloway had left his "stuff." Mateo always watched the front door. The last thing he was comfortable doing was turning his back to any door, yet apparently not knowing about Cade's things sprawled across the tearoom downstairs made him even more uncomfortable.

The wicked woman in me took pleasure in his insecurity. It was the biggest reveal to date as to how much it would bother him if Cade and I got back together.

Which we were not doing. Cade was my ex-high school sweetheart, for Pete's sake. There were too many years under that particular bridge. I glanced at the boxes of Cade's stuff that had overflowed into the loft. Hopefully everyone would continue to think they were used books I needed to put out for sale. Cause if they didn't...

"Can we talk about this later?" I asked under my breath as Daddy approached me and gave me a kiss on the cheek.

"Is that why we had to meet up here instead of in the tearoom?" My best friend Scarlet asked.

Scarlet was the last person I expected to lead the charge into private matters of my heart, or to stir up the trouble that was beginning to brew. My best friend knew what the women were like when they smelled blood—they'd grab hold of the gossip, shake it one way, and if nothing came out, they'd shake it the other way before tossing it in the air for the next mystery mom to try her luck at ferreting out the answers.

"I saw them huddled together at the back door of the Barn this morning. They were real cozy-like," added Reba Sue. She'd had her eye on Cade for the past several years, but a couple months back she'd realized she didn't stand a chance. It wasn't my fault. Reba Sue lost Cade to the same woman everyone lost Cade to—his career.

Unfortunately, I was pretty sure she hit record on her phone to get the scoop on the town mayor. I had no doubt this conversation was going to make it to Liza Twaine's in-box at the local TV station. Cade was not going to be happy.

"It's not true!" I screeched with a nervous look in Mateo's direction. His brow was wrinkled, but he didn't say a word, and his dark Latino eyes lost their expressiveness.

Fuzz buckets. I couldn't tell what he was thinking now, but I knew it couldn't be good. The problem was that I'd been sworn to secrecy, and breaking Cade's trust was the last thing I wanted to do.

"Let's get back to the reason why we're here—we were talking about next week's mystery, *Woman Scorned* by Nathan Daniels," I said.

Daisy Mahan rescued me. "I knew the killer from page one."

"So did I," added Scarlet as she reached for the pitcher of tea in the middle of the table.

"You haven't even finished the book," Reba Sue protested. Tall with a little too much makeup, her complaint was loud and impatient. She rolled her eyes when everyone looked at her. "What? She hasn't. None of us have."

"Well, I have, and I didn't know who the killer was until the last chapter of the book," added Jessie.

"Of course, you didn't," Reba Sue mumbled. "But you're not a member of the Mystery Moms, are you?"

Daisy bristled, sat up a little straighter, and glared at Reba Sue. "That's. My. Husband," she ground out between her dentures.

Reba Sue ignored her. "I'm telling you, Sugar killed her."

Jessie rolled his eyes at her accusation. "You make it sound like the victim died of diabetes, not a bullet in the head."

"And you make it sound like a joke," Reba Sue accused.

Reba Sue and I had never been friends, and like Jessie, my eyes rolled when she compared the killer in Nathan Daniels latest mystery novel to our very own Sugar McWilliams. Sugar was as sweet as her name implied and worked as a waitress at the Tool Shed. In her spare time, she worked part time at the Barn. She was responsible. She took care of her boyfriend's children better than their moms. Sugar was *not* a killer...and we were arguing about a fictional murder.

"Good grief, Reba Sue. You sound like you really believe Sugar killed someone," Leila said.

Reba Sue began skimming through the book in front of her. "Listen to his description: A voluptuous blond, Candy's breasts were the size of—"

It was my best friend who shut her down this time. "We get the picture, Reba Sue. We're all reading the novel." Scarlet Jenkins could have been the voluptuous killer Nathan Daniels was describing in his book, except my best friend barely reached five foot, and she had a shimmering flow of red hair, not "sun-kissed blond tresses cascading over her shoulders to tickle the tops of her..."

If someone described Scarlet like that...bless his heart, because it wouldn't be beating in his chest for very long.

"You're right. I don't know why I didn't see the similarities between Candy and our Sugar before now," said Betty Walker, the owner of Bluebonnet Quilt Shop. Betty wasn't the eldest of the group, but her blue hair which looked like a helmet sitting on top of her head, didn't quite go with her skin tone. It made the veins in her face more visible, and I suspected her bobble-head effect was just one of several identical wigs she chose to wear in public.

"Of course, there are similarities, that's what Nathan Daniels is known for—creating characters who are relatable and believable." Scarlet took a sip of her sweet tea and looked around the table, daring anyone to argue.

This was the wrong group to dare.

"So, you agree that he based the characters on the real people of Hazel Rock?" I asked as I moved to the table and sat down across from Reba Sue.

"There's a baker named Hans, for Pete's sake," Betty chimed in.

"He makes wedding cakes. Does your Franz make wedding cakes for people around the globe?" Scarlet asked.

"No, but he makes world-renowned pastries," Betty argued.

Franz made some mighty fine goodies, but I hated to tell Betty that her beau wasn't world renowned.

Daisy wasn't about to be left out of the argument. "The name of the town is Greenstone and the mayor's name is Wade. Did you guys know our mayor was stepping out with Candy...I mean, Sugar?"

Maddie's head swiveled in Betty's direction.

Sugar had had enough. "I am not!"

"Lord have mercy, you ladies have lost your minds in this heat!" Daisy's husband sat in the corner fanning himself with his cowboy hat.

Daisy gave another eye roll. "That's my husband."

The women started arguing across the tables, each with their own opinion about Nathan Daniels's fictional town mirroring our own Hazel Rock. I leaned toward Scarlet. "Cade's not seeing Sugar, is he?"

She gave me a look that said I had gone plum crazy if I believed that.

Daddy chose that as his cue to exit and headed for the stairs. He hadn't planned on staying longer than an hour while I managed the book club meeting since it was his day off. I had no doubt there were a few fish with his name on them waiting for him in the river.

Reba Sue took offense to Jessie's interruption. "Hush up, you old coot. This is serious business."

Every other word being hurled across the table dropped to the floor in one beat of silence. The Mysteries Moms looked at Reba Sue who had no clue she'd just committed a crime against society. Specifically, we all knew better than to insult Jessie Mahan in front of his wife, Daisy. And Reba Sue had done it several times.

Reba Sue looked at all the women staring at her. "What?" she asked. "He's not even a mystery mom."

All eyes darted to Daisy, who slowly stood up, every joint in her body creaking in slow motion as it echoed throughout the loft.

Jessie was the first to recognize the threat. "Now, Daisy. She didn't mean nothin'." His knees groaned as he got up and approached the table, but no one paid him no mind.

Especially Daisy. She was too busy seeing red—or in this case, blue—the blue blouse that was showing off Reba Sue's cleavage.

"That's. My. Husband."

Everyone but Reba Sue winced with each word. She was oblivious to the threat standing before her in the eighty-some-year-old body. She dismissed the elderly woman as easily as if she were a just another woman trying to get some attention.

"Daisy, you know darn well the man is a menace," Reba Sue said, and then took a sip of her tea like she'd made a comment about the weather.

And just as I thought Daisy was going to reach for a handful of Reba Sue's perfectly coiffed blond hair, Reba Sue let out a horrible noise that could compete with a herd of screeching cats on a hot tin roof. She pushed her chair back from the table with so much force, the table drove into Daisy and knocked her back into her chair. Reba Sue went the opposite direction, but our store had old wooden floors that had seen more than a little wear and tear through the years, and Liza just happened to find a divot in one of the planks with the right back leg of her chair.

Her legs flew up in the air, and her frilly skirt had a new hem length... at her waist as the contents of her glass went directly in her face, and she crashed against the floor.

Her screeching came to an end as Daddy ran back up the stairs.

"What in the—?" His mouth gaped for just a fraction of a second before he choked down a laugh and moved to help Reba Sue, who was sputtering and spitting tea from her position flat on her back with her legs up in the air displaying a pair of...granny panties.

Mateo was right there with Daddy to help Reba Sue get upright and decent, and despite Reba Sue's harsh words directed at the town's octogenarian rodeo star, Jessie ran over to assist her any way he could. Most of the women, however, wore smirks or giggled. I picked up the glass before someone stepped on it. It was only then that I caught sight of movement on the floor scurrying behind Scarlet's legs.

"Someone kicked me and knocked me over!" Reba Sue yelled as she pulled tea-drenched hair out of her eyes and yanked her left arm then her right away from Daddy and Mateo.

All eyes turned toward me. I'd been sitting directly across the table from Reba Sue.

Fuzz buckets. Trouble *was* synonymous with my name—my nickname, anyway, which was Princess. But it wasn't me who had knocked Reba Sue on her back. It was our pet pink armadillo who just happened to be named Princess as well.

I saw the real culprit make her way downstairs as her toenails clicked on the stairs all the way down to the first floor. She'd committed her crime and made her getaway without anyone being the wiser.

Chapter 2

Mateo stuck around after my daddy and the others left. There wasn't much to pick up, but I was avoiding the tearoom, the boxes in the corner, and any conversation they might inspire. Mateo was clearly waiting for the right time to bring it up. I was hoping that time never arrived before I had Cade's permission to talk about the reason the tearoom was closed for business. I'd done a pretty good job of deflecting Mateo's attempts at an interrogation for the past twenty minutes. Except now the loft was back in order, and we were alone.

Mateo reached around me and took the book from my hand, placing it down on the table. Then he pulled me back against him and nuzzled my neck as his arms wrapped around my midsection. I couldn't resist holding them in place.

"Do you realize that none of your friends know we're dating?" he asked.

"What are you talking about?"

"You haven't told a single person that we are dating."

I spoke up without hesitation. "That's not true." I turned around in his embrace and looked him in the eyes. "Daddy knows, and Scarlet knows. Everyone else would have to be blind not to know."

"And yet not one of them felt uncomfortable talking about you getting back together with Cade in front of me."

I heard the front doors open and glanced down to see who was coming in the store. When I saw her signature purple clothing, I sighed. Liza Twaine was back. I squirmed in Mateo's arms. His gaze followed mine, and he tightened his grip. "If she sees us together, she won't bother you about Cade."

I pulled away. "If she sees us together, the gossip will be like wildfire. That's not the type of PR we want for the store."

Mateo looked skeptical.

"Besides, I don't think that's type of PR you want either, going into your next election."

Mateo didn't have a chance to respond before Liza Twaine's heels clicked up the stairway. "There you are. I was hoping to get a quote about your relationship with Cade Calloway for the evening news. I understand the mayor's moving in with you?"

I groaned as Mateo picked up one of the boxes I didn't want him to notice. I saw him frown as he stared at the shipping label.

Fuzz buckets.

Liza didn't seem to notice since she was on a mission. She stuck her phone in my face, and I could see a voice recorder app ticking away the time. Even Liza would have had more tact then to blatantly accuse me of infidelity in front of Mateo...if she knew Mateo and I were dating.

I glanced at Mateo. He was wearing an I-told-you expression. Drat the man.

"Mayor Calloway moved some of his belongings"—Liza moved her phone closer to my mouth as I spoke—"from the old barber shop down the street into our tearoom. He's remodeling the building and needed some storage space. We were more than happy to help him out after everything he's done for the Book Barn Princess and the town." To finish my interview, I turned toward Mateo and put my arm around his waist after he set the box down on the table. Although his grin was barely visible, his arm snuck around me. My silent announcement of our relationship squelched any questions he had.

Liza took notice, then turned the direction of her interview. She moved toward Mateo with her purple phone. "Did Mayor Calloway apply for permits to remodel the building, or is it another behind the scene private negotiation between friends like what he did with the Enchanted Inn?"

Mateo's smile disappeared. His arm dropped. "Don't move, Liza."

"I hardly think my question rises to the point of being bullied, Sheriff. The people have a right to know if the businesses of Hazel Rock are making deals under—"

"Liza, if you know what's good for you—"

Liza sputtered. "Are you threatening me, Sheriff?"

I looked at Mateo wondering what the heck he thought he was doing. She was recording for Pete's sake! Mateo, however, wasn't looking at either of us. Nor was he focused on her phone. He was looking at Princess who had just arrived at the top of the steps with a friend—her friend. Not mine. And her friend didn't talk, it waddled like her. But her guest wasn't another armadillo. It was a skunk.

"Holy schnikes. Shut up, Liza," I whispered.

Liza was about to argue until I pointed behind her.

"Don't move." Mateo inched away from me and reached for the box he'd set on the table. The box was filled to the brim with stuff I didn't want anyone to see. Especially Liza. Nor did Cade for that matter. Besides, dumping the box without spooking the skunk was next to impossible.

"Not that box," I ordered, but Mateo ignored me.

To make matters worse, Liza had never listened to anyone telling her what to do a day in her life. As a former kindergarten teacher, I knew exactly which kid she would have been in my classroom—the one who wreaked havoc during nap time. Reading time. Game time. Liza Twaine was that one kid who was the bane of existence to all teachers. As an adult she continued to challenge authority, much to Mateo Espinosa's chagrin. And mine.

Liza turned around, took one look at Princess and her new friend, and screamed. The skunk perked its ears, twitched its nose, and chattered as it lifted its tail and stomped its feet in response. Liza ignored the warning. Again, I pictured that kindergarten student who just didn't know when to quit. Liza shooed with both hands, and the skunk lifted its back legs in what looked like the most threatening handstand I'd ever witnessed. Liza saw it as a bigger target for a field goal between the two handrails of the steps and cocked her purple pump. The skunk was going to be her football.

I yelled, "Liza don't!"

Mateo forgot the box and turned his attention toward Liza to stop her. Or maybe, it was to save her. I'm not quite sure. Princess however, decided to attack her. She rammed her little head into Liza's support leg. The only leg the reporter had planted on the floor. It didn't succeed in knocking her off her feet. It just knocked Liza off balance, and her purple phone went flying in the air as her kick went wide, and Mateo tackled her. I had a split second to grab Princess before she ended up beneath the pile, and as I reached for my pet, the skunk turned around.

It was one of those slow-motion moments in life. Liza's garbled cussing filled one ear as she and Mateo hit the floor, while a distressed squeal from Princess filled my other ear as we saw them land precariously close to Princess's friend.

I wouldn't say it was an accusatory look Mateo gave my retreating form, but it was definitely one that I'd remember for a long time. Liza's phone hit the skunk on the back, and it was done being patient. I heard a distinct hissing sound, like someone decided to spray several aerosol cans at once as I ran for the door that connects my apartment to the store.

Liza screamed again, and Mateo, bless his heart, let loose a trail of Spanish words I was unfamiliar with, though I could guess their meaning.

I looked back to see Liza crawling in my direction, Mateo dumping the box on the floor while rubbing his eyes, and a faintly yellow mist in the air. Liza reached toward me, but I was not exposing my apartment to that odor. I closed the door, locked it, and jammed a towel at the base of the door. Then Princess and I ran around to the other entrance. I made it down the stairs and to the front of the bookstore just as Sugar came running outside. She didn't seem to be wearing any new form of perfume in the scent of eau de skunk.

She stopped me from going inside. "Mateo said to keep everyone out."

"He's going to need my help."

"He said he would take care of it."

I was afraid of what that meant. Did it mean he would kill the skunk, whom Princess had somehow lured into the Barn? Or did it mean things were so bad, he didn't want me to be anywhere near my store? Or did it mean something else altogether?

I didn't have time to think about it before the front door to the Barn swished open, and Mateo came out with a box in his hands. His new cologne reached us before he did, and I hate to say that Sugar and I took a step back.

Mateo's eyes were red and running. He squinted and rubbed his left eye on his shoulder as he held the box out in front of him. We all took another step backward.

He looked completely distraught. Hopefully he couldn't see my reaction, but I seriously doubted that he missed it.

God in heaven...he stunk.

"I've called animal control to relocate our delinquent," he said.

Princess squealed at his feet and then pawed at his combat boot.

"I think that's her friend."

"You want him?" He took a couple of steps in my direction.

"Don't you dare, Mateo Espinosa!" I warned as I backed up into the street.

He smirked. At least his sense of humor hadn't failed him.

Princess followed him and began chatting up a storm. The box answered. It wobbled in his grasp. A violent struggle for freedom ensued. Mateo hugged the box as the weight shifted, and Sugar and I ran behind the police car. Mateo lost the battle and barely got the box near the ground when the skunk escaped through the top and ran for the back of the Barn with Princess on his tail.

Fuzz buckets. She was going to smell worse than ever when she came home. Just like Mateo.

"You lost your man," I said.

Mateo scowled in my direction. He looked as if he wanted to respond, but Liza exited the Barn.

She didn't look bad. Just a little rough around the edges with a scrape on her knee. Her body spray, however, could have been named Eau de Salaud. Aromatic Stinkard.

Liza eyed the onlookers who weren't about to approach her. Then she spotted me behind Mateo's unmarked patrol car and stomped in my direction. As she moved closer, Sugar went the opposite direction I did, and one thought came to mind: Liza's scent wasn't light like an eau de toilette. It wasn't even in line with an eau de parfum. Liza was wearing the strongest variety of heavy-oiled perfume money couldn't buy. She smelled even worse than Mateo.

I grimaced and moved around the cruiser. Sugar decided it was time to get the heck out of Dodge. Her blond ponytail bobbed along with her across the street.

"This is your fault!" Liza accused as she followed me around the car.

"It was an act of God." It wasn't like I had control over the skunk entering the store.

"Your *pet* led that thing right to me!" Liza continued to stalk me.

"But you're the one who tried to kick it and threw your phone at it."

"It was going to spray me!" she sputtered. "And I wouldn't have thrown my phone if it hadn't been for someone kicking my foot out from under me!" Liza's face was pinched. For a pretty woman, she was rather unattractive when she was angry.

As she rounded the passenger side of the car, Mateo stepped in front of her. "I told you not to move," he said.

"I thought you were denying the freedom of the press!"

Mateo winced at the high pitch of her voice. He held her back as he shot me a warning with his eyes over the top of his car.

"I'm sorry you got sprayed, Liza. I wouldn't wish that on anyone. If you'd like, I've got a bunch of leftover tomato sauce that wasn't used at the spring picnic. You can use our outdoor shower at the back of the Barn."

Liza's eyes bulged into saucers, then turned to slits as her voice filled with indignation. "Your outdoor shower!"

My hands rose in surrender. "Sorry, I just thought you wouldn't want to go home smelling like..."

Liza tried to step around Mateo, but he blocked her path once more.

I'd offered enough help for one day. "I'm just going to go check out the store," I said and made my escape.

The moment I walked in the front door of the bookstore, however, I was hit with remnants of Princess's bad choices in friends. The entire store reeked of skunk. I coughed then coughed again. Airing the store out was going to be brutal. I flipped the sign to closed and propped the doors open. I pulled my shirt over my nose and mouth and made a beeline for the tearoom. I didn't want to open the side door and let anyone wander inside and see Cade's stuff, so I opened the two windows and headed for the back door.

"O.M.W.," Scarlet gagged. "I ran into Liza and Mateo, but I had no idea they'd had an encounter *inside* the Barn." Scarlet was holding her beauty shop apron over her face. She had on a one-piece, sleeveless, summer pantsuit that hugged all her curves, and her ginger-colored hair fell in loose ringlets over her shoulders, accentuating her rosy complexion.

"You may want to go back to the beauty shop," I yelled to her as I made my way to the back door and propped it open.

"I have an industrial fan if you'd like to use it," she responded.

I coughed as I passed the loft. "I would love it, thank you."

"I'll be right back."

An hour later, Scarlet's fan was clearing the air, and I was boxing up Cade's signs that had spilled all over the floor in the loft. Sugar had volunteered to help, but she was working at the Tool Shed that night, and I honestly didn't think it was fair to ask her to stay. No one would tip a waitress whose hair smelled like skunk. She was better off staying away.

The buzzer sounded at the front door, and I looked down to see Mateo enter the store. He looked tired and frazzled. If I wasn't mistaken, the scent of skunk got stronger the closer he got.

"I thought you'd be up here," he said as he came up the stairs.

"You haven't showered yet, have you?"

He shook his head. "Nope."

I backed up. "Don't you think you should?"

"I lost my sense of smell almost an hour ago. It doesn't really bother me anymore."

"Too bad all of us aren't so blessed."

"Are you saying that I stink, Charli Rae?"

"You've smelled better."

He stalked me, and I put the table between us. "We haven't reached that place in our relationship where I can embrace the type of stink you're emitting." I wasn't sure I'd ever be able to get past that odor—even if my own child wore it. Which was a sure sign of me not being ready for parenthood.

Mateo stopped. "I'm not sure I'd be able to handle it if you smelled like Liza Twaine did this morning."

I laughed. "At least we're on the same page. Would you like to use our outdoor shower?"

"That's why I'm here. It's either that or my office, and I'd rather not go there. I've received enough ribbing over the radio to last through the rest of my career."

I grinned. "Daddy called and said he'd heard it over the scanner."

Mateo groaned as we headed downstairs. I grabbed the tomato sauce before we went out the back of the store. All the businesses on Main Street had backyards butting up to the Brazos River. The Barn had a privacy fence on two sides, so the yard was only semiprivate. We used the shower fairly often after kayaking, but I never stripped down naked when I used it despite the small wooded enclosure surrounding it. Mateo, on the other hand, wasn't afraid to get down to his birthday suit.

I handed him the first jar of tomato sauce, and he dumped it over his head and worked it into his hair.

"You wouldn't look half bad as a ginger."

Mateo peeked with one eye. "You want me to dye my hair red?"

"I didn't say that..."

"Dios mio, you're a fickle woman." He continued to scrub his head with his eyes closed and held his hand out for another bottle of sauce.

"Excuse me? Did you just call me fickle?"

Mateo's lips were pressed together in a firm line. With his palm open and his fingers arched, his arm bounce on top of the wooden shower wall, punctuating his impatience for the next bottle. The jar opened with a pop, and I poured it over his head and waited in silence for him to respond.

He didn't. Possibly the wisest decision he could have made. I took pity on him and decided he'd had a bad enough day without me compounding it. After all, the man now smelled like a skunk bathing in tomato sauce.

"That's not working," I said.

"I'm well aware of that," he ground out. "Have you used it before?"

"No."

Mateo glanced up at me, his face and arms tinged orange. "I thought you knew what you were talking about."

"They say to bathe in tomato sauce."

His hands stopped scrubbing and dropped to his sides. "Who's they?"

"Everyone."

Mateo closed his eyes and sighed heavily before asking in a controlled voice, "Could you Google how to get rid of skunk scent?"

I looked it up on my phone. "Oops."

Mateo froze. "What do you mean 'oops?'"

"It says that tomato sauce doesn't work. It just turns your hair and skin orange."

He shoved his head under the spray of water and began rinsing his body without looking at me. The only sign of his irritation was the force he used to scrub his head. I needed to find the right recipe—fast.

Chapter 3

The Tool Shed Tavern should have been packed. Instead it was uncharacteristically empty. Granted it was a Wednesday night, but what the heck else was there to do in Hazel Rock, especially when Joe and Leila held an extra-long happy hour for hump day? My daddy didn't work most Wednesdays, so I usually opened and closed the bookstore. Today, however the store had closed so early, and I'd been stuck dealing with cleanup instead of customers all day. A little downtime with Scarlet was well deserved.

Sugar walked up with margaritas and put them on the table in front of us. "This day started out as a stink bomb and is going to end the same way."

"It couldn't be any worse than this morning," I said.

"Oh yeah? Look who's sitting at the bar...with her paws on Dean."

Scarlet and I turned and looked at who had Sugar's flowing blond tresses all knotted up.

The woman sitting next to Sugar's boyfriend could have been Sugar's twin, or older sister. She had the natural beauty of a California Barbie and the pleasant smile to match. Unlike Sugar, however, Maddie MacAlister had perfect teeth. But it was the imperfection in Sugar's smile that made her beautiful. Plus, she had an angelic personality—that disappeared when Maddie rubbed her chest on Dean's arm.

"That does it," Sugar exclaimed. "I don't care if she's the mother of his child! I am tired of trying to help that woman. I've invited her to events, I've tried to be a friend to her, but she's got no desire to be my friend. She wants Dean back. That's her number one goal. That woman has pushed me too far, and I am not going to tolerate her moving in on my man like that." Sugar stormed off with her tray under her arm and the angry swagger of a woman scorned.

Woman scorned.

I thought about Nathan Daniels's book and the conversation in the Barn with the mystery moms that morning.

"Sugar is not Candy and Maddie is not a victim," Scarlet assured me, as if reading my mind.

"The similarities are beginning to freak me out," I said. I watched as Sugar and Maddie squared off, their expressions anything but friendly, while Dean hunkered down lower into his beer.

"He should put a stop to that," Cade Calloway said as he walked up to our table. The mayor was one of the best-looking men in town—next to Mateo, of course—and at his height, he was hard to ignore. But I wasn't taking my eyes off the trio who looked like they were in the middle of a love triangle.

Dean didn't want any part of the argument brewing between the two women. Maddie was his ex-wife, and Sugar was his girlfriend. No matter what he did, he would lose.

I looked up at Cade. "You better go over there."

Cade's hazel eyes turned toward me, and he grimaced. "This day is just going to keep getting worse and worse, isn't it?"

I nodded. There was no reason to argue a moot point. I got up and followed Cade just in case he needed my support.

"Sugar McWilliams, you got no right to interrupt my conversation with Dean. Do your job and bring me another drink." Maddie turned and ran her hand up Dean's arm. She was wearing a white sleeveless blouse with a tight, red, leather skirt that showed off her shapely legs. The hemline had creeped up to an almost indecent height, but Maddie didn't seem to mind in the least. She wiggled her foot that was clad in red-and-black suede ankle boots against Dean's thigh. The blatant suggestion wasn't missed by many.

Dean winced, pulled his arm back, and scooted off his bar stool, but Sugar only saw the too familiar way in which Maddie was handling her man. She didn't like it one bit. Sugar leaned between them and grabbed a set of keys from the bar then shoved them into the half apron she wore around her waist. "I'm cutting you off, Maddie. You've had too much to drink. I'm calling you a cab."

Maddie whipped around, her blond hair flying like a model in a hair commercial—it was too bad Scarlet hadn't recorded it to use for her salon.

"Don't you—"

"Ladies, please." Cade's tone was gentle. Too gentle. Neither one of them heard him.

Maddie grabbed for Sugar's arm, but I slid between them as Cade pulled Sugar away.

"We've got this, Sugar. Why don't you call Maddie a cab?" I asked.

"I don't need no stinking cab!" Maddie yelled. "You may have taken my man, but you ain't taking my keys!" Maddie's words slurred as she lunged toward Sugar and knocked me back into Cade.

"I'm not going to let you drive when you have a baby at home." Sugar jutted her chin out in defiance.

Finally, Dean stood up and paid attention to what was really happening. "I'll take you home," he said. His forty-something face was pinched with worry. Worry that Sugar wouldn't understand and worry that Maddie would read too much into his offer. But most of all, worry for his child who might end up being a victim to Maddie's overindulgence and drinking and driving.

Maddie beamed while Sugar scowled.

Dean held his hand out for Maddie's car keys, and for a moment, it looked as though Sugar was going to smack his hand away. The pleading in his eyes, however, changed her mind, and she slammed the keys into his palm before stomping away.

"Do you want me to take her?" Cade asked.

I looked at him like he'd lost his mind. The last thing he needed was to get in the middle of this drama. Maddie had a well-earned reputation as a woman who always had a bank account within her sights, and Cade had the biggest bank account in town. Besides, we had enough drama of our own going on.

Dean shook his head and grabbed Maddie's arm as she swayed toward him. "No. I got her. This is my mess to clean up."

Maddie's brows drew together, but despite the consternation in her words, her tone was frisky as all get-out. "Are you saying I'm a mess, Dean MacAlister?"

Dean gave his ex-wife a sad grin. "I'm saying I'm the mess darlin'. Not you, and certainly not Sugar."

I didn't hear Maddie's response as they made their way to the door, but I saw the anger on Sugar's face. She was one unhappy girlfriend.

When I'd first returned to Hazel Rock, Sugar threw a beer in my face because she thought I was making a move on her man. Tonight, I had to give her credit. If anyone deserved to wear the beer sitting on Sugar's tray, it was Maddie Macalister. Yet, as they walked past Sugar, Dean tipped his ball cap in her direction, and Sugar held her tongue.

"Why haven't you returned my calls?" Cade asked, interrupting my observations.

I turned and looked up at him. "Why didn't you return my call?"

"Look at your phone. I've called you multiple times since six o'clock."

"I've been in here since six. Why didn't you call earlier?"

"I was catching a flight back home."

"Oh. I didn't know you were out of town. You should have told me."

We worked our way back to Scarlet, who had already finished her margarita and was working her way through mine. "I ordered you a double. I figured you could use it."

Scarlet was the best friend a woman could ever have.

Cade pulled out my stool for me and joined us. After Cade placed an order with another waitress for a beer he leaned over and asked, "How much damage did you sustain today?"

"Most of the books on the second floor are a total loss. Luckily, they're all used books."

"Was anything else damaged?" he asked.

I knew he was referring to his boxes we had stored in the loft and the tearoom. "The two boxes we put in the loft are a complete loss."

Cade sighed. "I suppose the boxes were spilled open and were quite a mess to clean up, huh?"

Cade wasn't necessarily concerned about the physical mess, he was worried about the fallout from his stuff being in the Barn. He was a politician through and through.

"Mateo knows...everything."

"That's it? No one else?" he asked.

"That's it. Liza Twaine was too busy worrying about the smell of her clothes. And her hair. And skin."

The Cade I knew and loved grinned and began laughing, until the politician in him took over and covered up his smile as he tried to wipe it off his face. The rumble of humor escaped between his fingers.

"What was in the boxes?" Scarlet asked.

"Nothing," Cade and I said in unison.

Scarlet raised her eyebrows and looked as if she was about to call us out, but Cade steered the conversation in a different direction.

"You're going to recycle those books, aren't you?" Cade had run his campaign with the slogan: *A greener Hazel Rock, a greener Texas.* Considering our town was mostly brown, it was an appealing promise.

"Do you think I could?" I asked.

Cade nodded and took a drink of his beer that had just arrived. "Go see Dallas Dover at the recycling plant. He's a little crude, but he knows how to get the job done. We gave him the city contract eight months ago. I'm sure he can help you out."

Finally, a solution to my problem. I could get rid of the books that smelled worse than roadkill.

* * * *

The next morning, I borrowed my Daddy's truck at the crack of dawn and made my way to the recycling plant located off County Road 57. A couple of trash trucks were in line to turn onto the dirt road that led to the facility on the other side of the hill. It was one of the reasons the people of Hazel Rock had approved the permit for the business. They didn't particularly want a trash collection site in their neck of the woods—no one did—but Bin Dover Recycling was out of sight and out of mind. It didn't get any better than that.

After a guy in a company shirt unhooked a chain from across the drive and waved us through, I followed the two trucks into the lot with a third one behind me. As I passed, I returned the friendly gesture and proceeded down the drive to where it opened up on the backside of the hill into a parking lot. I parked in front of a tan mobile trailer that had two small windows. The backside of the hill had been excavated sometime through the years and the office sat in front of the off-white cliffs. There was no grass around the office, nor were there any bushes. Just the sand rock cliff, the gravel driveway, the parking lot, and huge bins for customers to deposit their recyclables. Two pickup trucks were parked in the lot that I assumed belonged to employees.

Directly opposite the office sat a large metal building with several large garage doors that led to the sorting area for the recycling. I waited for the trash trucks to park in front of the bins marked glass, paper, and plastic then made my way up the metal staircase of the trailer. A picture of white cliffs with a large green bin sitting in front them was painted on the front of the door of Bin Dover Recycling. It was the same logo they used on their trucks.

I tried the door, but it was locked, and then noticed the hours of operation sign down below the window.

Fuzz buckets. They didn't open for another two hours, and I needed to get back to the Barn. Scarlet and I had a book art class scheduled and were going to teach seven women how to make book wreaths that I needed to reschedule for the next day. I could not be late. Yet I didn't want to bring back the smelly books in the back of the truck either. The odor was overwhelming.

I approached one of the trash trucks and knocked on the driver's door. He jumped and grabbed his chest before rolling down his window.

"Sorry, I didn't mean to startle you."

"No worries, darlin'. I was just waiting for the boss to show up."

"Do you mean Dallas Dover?" I asked.

"That's right. In fact, that's him coming across the lot now."

I turned around to see a lanky man wearing jeans, a plaid button-down shirt, and a black leather belt with a silver buckle that had two old Mexican coins adorning the front. The black cowboy hat he wore had feathers plastered across the front. The whole outfit showed off his long dishwater-blond hair and a goatee. A pair of dark wraparound sunglasses hid his eyes and reminded me of biker goggles, but he wore a wide, friendly smile as he pulled off his leather gloves.

He glanced at the trashman and shook his head. "I'll be with you guys in a minute." He turned to me and grinned even larger. "How can I help you ma'am?"

"Are you Dallas Dover?"

He nodded and led me toward the trailer. "Yes, ma'am. But we're not open for business yet. Gary at the gate should have told you that."

I thought about the man who'd let me in the driveway. Maybe he'd been trying to wave me back. "Sorry. I thought he was just being friendly."

Dallas laughed. "I suppose I can't fault him for that, now can I? Since you're already here, what can I do for you?"

"Mayor Calloway sent me to see you."

"The mayor's a good man."

I nodded in agreement. "Yes, he is."

As we approached the back of my daddy's truck, Dallas got a whiff of the books and began looking around for the culprit.

"That smell is my problem. I own the Book Barn Princess in Hazel Rock and a skunk got into the store and sprayed the books."

Dallas chuckled. "I was afraid my breakfast burrito was coming back to haunt me in front of a customer."

I smiled but thought I was going to die of embarrassment for him, but Dallas didn't seem to mind talking about bodily functions with a complete stranger.

"I hope that's all it sprayed," he continued. When I shook my head, he grimaced.

"That couldn't have been good."

"You have no idea. Can I show you what I have?"

"Sure thing."

As we reached the tailgate, Dallas lifted his shirt and covered his face. "Are you sure it wasn't a whole herd of skunks?"

"No, it was just one very aromatic male. He wasn't happy."

"I'd say he sprayed more than once."

I hadn't thought about that, but remembering Mateo and Liza on the floor, I had no doubt the skunk probably had. I pulled a box toward the back of the bed, but Dallas stopped me.

"I'm sorry but I won't be able to help you."

"What?"

"We can't take these in the center. My employees would quit."

"But...but...what about the bins outside?" I pointed to the bins where the three drivers waited patiently inside their trash trucks for Dallas. "Or the trucks. They could go directly into the trucks."

"I'm sorry, miss, but those are trash trucks. They take what we can't recycle."

I looked over at the trash trucks and saw the different logo on the side. They had two large letter *C*s with *Waste Services* printed below them.

Fuzz buckets. I wasn't sure how I'd missed the Coleman County logo. "But you can't recycle these. Couldn't they take my boxes?"

"I would be in violation of the contract I have with them. We aren't supposed to accept trash here, it's only the trash we inadvertently pick up. If I took this in front of the drivers...

I can't break the contract, but you could put them in the trash or take them directly to the dump."

I thanked Dallas for his time and got back in my daddy's truck. I'd already thought of his suggestions and decided against them. They weren't viable options. For one, my trash pickup was Wednesday morning. It was Thursday. Where in the world would I put these boxes for the next week? I'd also thought of taking them to the dump, but a "green" candidate couldn't have his name associated with such a move, and Cade's stuff couldn't be handed off to dump personnel to go into a landfill. Nor could books stamped with the Book Barn's trademark tiara stamp. We were located in his town. We were his friends. We, namely I, could be a blemish on his career. The last thing in the world I wanted credit for was being the boil that busted his career.

I backed up and drove past the trash trucks raising the recycle bins to empty into their beds, but all I could think about was what I had to do. It was the last thing any bookstore owner would even consider. Yet I had no choice.

I had to burn the books.

Chapter 4

After leaving the recycling plant, I immediately called the sheriff's office and advised the dispatcher that I was going to be burning debris behind the Barn. It was a lie, and I felt sick about my blatant disregard for the law and the environment. The dispatcher, however, told me I had to wait twenty-four hours. It seemed Mother Nature didn't particularly care for my decision to have a book burning. She'd kicked up the winds to stop me.

The entire rest of the day I pouted. I unloaded every stinky box of books from daddy's truck by myself before anyone else caught wind of what I was doing and carted them into the middle of the backyard. Once there, I cussed them and arranged them neatly into a symmetrical pyre that would ignite easily. Then I hauled branches that had fallen off the trees in the last wind advisory to the pyre. Daddy normally took them to the county's recycling center. Not this time, though. They were the camouflage for my crime.

Which spoke volumes to how low I'd sunk.

I'd also cleaned the Barn and used the skunk scent remover on the floorboards, shelves, and tables in the loft. The wood on the tables survived the onslaught. The old wood floors and the shelves, however, were going to need some TLC. Instead of sorting through the books and taking the titles out of inventory one stinky volume at a time, Sugar had suggested taking photos of them and using the photos to delete them from the program. It worked like a charm, and three hundred and sixty-one books were wiped out of inventory.

The number alone was staggering. The value to the Barn was worse. Yet it couldn't be helped. If I looked on the bright side, only used books had been damaged. The new books were on the lower level and although some of the scent went downstairs, the inventory downstairs had been protected from spray and residual fog by the shelves of books that were destroyed in the loft. Still, taking that quantity of books out of our inventory made me ill. To top off my really bad day, Princess didn't want my company that night after my second chemical shower. She wanted to go out and stay out. She never stayed out overnight. It seemed her new friend was more appealing than me.

When I lay my head on my pillow and closed my eyes, I thought the nightmare would finally be over. It wasn't. All night long the smell from the pyre in my backyard wafted in through the deck doors to my bedroom. I had dreams of smelling like skunk for the rest of my life with Cade opening a skunk perfume store and Mateo giving me a bottle of skunk perfume for my birthday.

I welcomed the obnoxious bell of my alarm clock the next morning and immediately called the sheriff's dispatcher to let her know I'd be having a fire the first thing that morning. She'd taken my information and address and the fire was set for eight o'clock.

I took yet another shower and headed to the store. The first thing I did when I opened the door was take a deep breath. Peroxide and soap hit my senses.

I smiled and savored the new scent. Today was going to be a good day.

I made my way downstairs and started my daddy's coffee. Normally, I would have made sweet tea for our customers as well, but the tearoom would be closed for three more days thanks to Cade's boxes filling every table and chair. He'd promised to move all of the boxes out by Monday, and I was going to hold him to it.

Princess came in through her pet door at the back of the store, and I immediately looked for her cohort. Thank God, he hadn't followed her. As she approached, however, I could smell his cologne.

"He's a bad influence. You know that, right?"

Princess looked up at me with innocent eyes.

"Do we need to have a talk about you staying out all night long?"

Princess snorted and headed for her bedazzled dog bowl for breakfast. She wasn't going to be happy with the healthy meal that awaited her.

"I never thought I'd have a teenager at thirty!" I yelled, but she ignored me completely and disappeared behind the pink curtain to the store room.

Her bowl shuffled across the floor and from the sound of it, Princess was none too happy about the dried mealworms I'd put down for her. I hid a smile only a parent trying to get their kid to quit eating junk food would understand. While she ate in a huff, I prepared a bath that would do away with the scent of her new boyfriend. I knew I wouldn't have to coax her into the water; after being out all night, Princess was going to relish rolling around in one tub and then the next. It was her favorite thing to do. Just having her home eased my mood. Her nose pushed out from under the curtain. It twitched as she stood there and smelled the scent of her bath. She knew something was up, but the draw of her favorite pastime caused her to come out and make a dash for the tubs. Seconds later, she was rolling around in the de-skunk water and then rinsing in the second tub. I sat down and watched her frolic in the water and just enjoyed the moment.

When she finished, we both relished the time together as I toweled her off, rubbed her belly, and scratched her ears. Our favorite nighttime routine wasn't too bad during the morning hours either.

I looked at my phone and realized I needed to get busy. If I didn't get the fire going, I wouldn't have it almost out by the time we opened the store at ten.

I gave Princess a final pat and said, "Mama's gotta go to work."

Princess shook her body like a dog would after a bath, her little tail shaking last. Then she headed for her bed under the register. I had no doubt she'd sleep the day away.

I grabbed the lighter fluid and matches I'd purchased and headed out the back of the Barn. As I approached my pyre, that same feeling of dread came over me that I'd had all day the previous day. There was something about burning books that just didn't sit well with me. It was bad enough that I was breaking the law by burning something that the trashman would take, but voluntarily burning books was just wrong on so many levels. I knew the books couldn't be saved. I'd created a business of selling used books and creating art out of those that were too damaged to resell, but these weren't good for resale or book art, and because of that, I was stuck with no other recourse. It still didn't make me feel any better. Today's task was the greatest sin a bookseller could commit.

I kicked the boxes at the bottom of the pile, then reached through to rattle the boxes on top as I yelled to make sure no critters had decided to nest in them overnight. When nothing scurried out, I sprayed the lighter fluid in between to make sure the bottom boxes were saturate. I bent down to light the pages I'd curled up for kindling around the base.

"There she is!"

I didn't recognize the masculine voice coming from the other side of the fence.

Holy schnikes, what if a child had hidden in the middle of the boxes! I quickly shook out the flame that had leapt to life on the end of my match and stood up.

"Are you missing someone?" I yelled over the fence.

A camera appeared in response.

Fuzz Buckets.

A picket sign appeared next. Bobbing above the privacy fence, it read: *Censorship is un-American*, written in bold red letters on a large white poster board. A second sign appeared: *The Book Barn Princess dictates what you can read.* It was written in cursive and was a little hard to read, but its message got across loud and clear. Especially when it was accompanied with a chant that was getting louder by the moment. "Stop the Book Barn's Book Burn!"

My heart raced. This was a nightmare. How had anyone found out about my plans? As the chants grew louder, I could only see two choices in front of me. I could abandon my plans and wait until they went away. Or I could get it over with and destroy the evidence. If I waited, the crowd could grow. Cade would hate that, and Mateo would be ticked off.

I struck the match and lit the pyre in multiple places. It was in a full blaze when my daddy walked out the back door of the Barn. The crowd on the other side of the fence sounded like it had grown to around fifteen people from what I could tell by the volume of the voices and the number of women sitting on shoulders yelling obscenities at me.

"Please tell me you're not burning the books," Daddy said.

I looked at him and a tear slipped down my cheek. "Burning books is the last thing I ever thought I'd do. But I didn't have a choice." My voice hitched, and Daddy put his arm around my shoulder.

"It'll be alright. This will blow over."

No sooner had he said those words than Liza Twaine came around the end of the fence down by the river with a cameraman. His camera was on his shoulder, and a red light at the base of it was blinking a warning in our direction. He was documenting every last moment for the local news. Daddy tried to push me behind him, but I wasn't about to let that happen. I moved up next to him to let the world know we stood together.

"You're on private property, Liza Twaine," I said.

"Why are you burning books at the Book Barn Princess?" Liza held a large microphone in her hand and turned her best side to the camera. She hadn't been accompanied by cameraman for a long time. Not since she'd broken into Scarlet's trailer to get the scoop on a story. That crime had gotten Liza in trouble with the law and the local townspeople. Since then she'd been demoted to her cell phone for interviews. Unfortunately for us, it seemed she'd gained back her status at the television station.

Dagnabit! This day had started off so good. Now I knew what being a criminal was really like.

"You're trespassing," I said. My tone was cold and my eyes squinty. I could blame it on the morning sun backlighting her, but I hoped she saw warning behind my expression.

If she did, she ignored it.

"Our viewers would like to know what drives a bookstore owner to burn literary works of art?" Fate screwed with me at that moment. It was almost as if it was thumbing its nose at me for comparing Liza to an out of control five-year-old the previous day. A box tumbled down from the top of the pile, bypassing the branch that was meant to hide it, and several books spilled out at the base of the pyre.

"Why would you burn *The Catcher in the Rye*, *Huckleberry Finn*, *Wuthering Heights* and *Jane Eyre*?" Liza directed the cameraman toward the classics catching fire.

"You know good and well why we're burning these books, Liza Twaine." Daddy chastised Liza, and I thought for a moment she was going to quit. Her shoulders slumped ever so slightly in her sleeveless purple blouse. But fate was on her side today. A box on the outside edge began burning and revealed the contents no one was supposed to see.

Liza leaned closer and her eyes nearly bugged out of her head. "Is it true?" she asked. Frantically she waved the cameraman in the direction of the forbidden box. The cameraman moved for a better angle, and her assistant turned the lens to zero in on his target.

I quickly stepped in front of him. "That's none of your business, Liza." I pointed back at the fence where they'd come in and where some of the braver protestors were starting to come around. "You need to leave." I addressed the picketers. "All of you need to leave. This is private property."

Liza, however, had found the bloody trail to another story, and she wasn't going to let it go. She went to the other side of the fire and began pulling a box from it. That was such a bad idea, I couldn't begin to fathom how stupid she was being.

The fiery pile wobbled. It's neat cone shape giving way on Liza's side. Daddy ran and pushed her back, but the damage was done. An avalanche of boxes and books scattered across the lawn. I ran for the hose that I'd laid at the ready in case something went wrong. I never dreamed it would be like this.

Liza didn't miss a beat. "Cade Calloway is running for the Senate?" she asked.

But all Daddy could give her was a blank stare. He didn't know. He hadn't seen the posters. He'd assumed the stuff in the tearoom was for Cade's next mayoral race. And I'd let him believe it. He looked down at the posters. Flames licked at Cade's political campaign slogan: *A Greener Tomorrow with Cade Calloway.*

Fuzz buckets. Cade's dreams were slowly ebbing from existence as the fire devoured his posters and the camera recorded every last bit.

Chapter 5

"It made the national news." Cade scrubbed the back of his neck as he paced back and forth in the tearoom. It'd only been forty-five minutes since Liza had blown the whistle on my crime, but the damage was done. The pile had continued to burn rapidly with the exception of two boxes I doused that had fallen out of the pyre.

"I'm sorry."

Cade didn't say anything as he continued to pace the tearoom filled to the gills with boxes upon boxes of his political campaign advertisements. He ran his fingers through his hair, a habit he'd had since high school. According to Cade, he'd refrained from doing it for twelve years—until I returned to Hazel Rock and drove him back to the habit that was going to make him bald by forty. He only did it when I frustrated the heck out of him. Like now.

With his hair short, Cade didn't seem to get as much of a release out of the act as he used to when his hair was longer. After having it singed off when my truck exploded several months ago, he'd worn his hair high and tight like a military man. He'd saved my life that day, and he had the scar on the back of his head to prove it.

"I'm sorry, I-I didn't mean—"

Cade turned and looked at me. His warm hazel eyes held a look of defeat that I'd never seen in them before. "I don't blame you, Princess. I just think it's time I rethink my political career."

"But this was your dream," I argued.

"The Enchanted Inn is packed with protesters. They're staying there and spying on the staff to make sure it is as green as the hotel claims to be."

"Do they know what the Inn was planning before you stepped in and made them see the potential of going green?"

Cade shook his head. "They don't care, Princess. None of that matters. What matters is that I claim to run on an environmental platform, and I didn't recycle the very things I'm pushing every other business to dispose of in a way that is good for the earth."

"What about the solar panels on the roof of the hotel? The built-in containers for hair products and soap in all the bathrooms that reduce the amount of waste, the recycled furniture and LED light fixtures in every room? What about the stone, metal, and wood fixtures throughout the hotel that are all recycled? Do those count for nothing?" I was on my soapbox now, standing up, pacing as he had while ticking off each point as I went. I stopped with my biggest point of all. "What about the low-flow showerheads and toilets and the huge water tank sitting on top of that tower attached to the hotel that is collecting rain water? Do they know the expense the hotel went through to meet the demands of our mayor? I can't believe they even considered it without legislation; Hazel Rock is not a booming tourist center! What about the recycling center you brought to town? We are producing a quarter of the trash we used to!"

I took a breath and waited for Cade to respond. He of all people knew how much work he'd put into convincing the hotel and the town to help with the expense of renovating the hotel in an eco-friendly manner. He'd been the talk of the town and the state for his success, and there was expansion in the works to have all the businesses use the Enchanted Inn as a model for future renovations and building projects. It was one of the reasons Cade had been chosen months ago by some bigwigs in DC to be groomed for a bigger role in the political machine.

"The protestors seem to be multiplying," my daddy said as he walked in with some pastries from the bakery across the street. "There's more outside the Barn."

Mateo followed him in wearing a frown the size of Texas.

I didn't wait for Daddy to set down the box. I grabbed it instead, took out a bagel, and shoved it in my mouth without putting cream cheese or butter on it. I held out the open box for everyone else. Cade and Mateo declined the offer. My daddy took a croissant and pointed it at me. "Liza Twaine would like a statement."

"Liza Twaine can stick her interview where the sun doesn't shine," I said through my mouthful of bagel.

"I thought you'd say that. So, I handled it."

"What'd you say?"

"I told her she knew exactly why we burned those books, and I expected her to do an honest report."

I took another bite of my bagel. I wasn't sure how Daddy could possibly think Liza wouldn't turn this into an opportunity to give her career a facelift. It was her big chance to redeem herself as a reporter and nobody was going to stop her. Not even the truth. Nathan Daniels had pegged her personality with his copycat character in his book.

"Unfortunately, I'm here for the same reason," Mateo said as he walked over and opened one of the boxes of political signs.

I swallowed the bagel too soon. It stuck in my throat and refused to go down. Cade patted me on the back.

Daddy set his croissant down without taking a bite. "This isn't a social call to check on Princess?"

Mateo shook his head. "This is an official visit."

Fuzz buckets.

"Who's responsible for the fire?" Mateo asked.

"I—" Daddy started to take credit, but this wasn't his doing; it was mine.

I cleared the bagel from my throat. "I did it," I blurted out with a rasp. "It was my idea."

"Charli, don't say another word." Cade forgot about his political troubles and dropped back into his attorney role.

"No one helped? Or added items to the pile?" Mateo's fingers grazed another box with Cade's name plastered on the front.

I shook my head and put up my hand in a gesture to stop Cade from trying to take the blame. "This is on me." I lifted my chin. "No one else participated."

"That's a misdemeanor in Texas. You told the dispatcher you were burning yard waste, not trash."

I gulped.

Cade took over. "As your attorney, I advise you not to say another word." He addressed Mateo. "This is a signature bond, Sheriff."

"Perhaps."

Mateo looked at me with all kinds of disappointment written on his face. Because I broke the law, he was here. Mateo. Not a deputy, but my boyfriend and he didn't like Cade stepping up to help when he was trying to do his best to take care of me.

I wanted to tell both of them I was a grown woman, but to be honest, I was humbled by their desire to help me out of the corner I'd put myself in.

I heard the front buzzer ring and looked at my phone for the time.

Fuzz buckets. It was time for my book art class with Scarlet. We had seven women signed up to create wreaths out of book pages. Luckily for us, the old, damaged books we'd saved for the class had been sealed in plastic storage bins when our visitor opened a can of stink-butt on the entire loft. But now...

The significance of Mateo hauling me to jail hit me like I'd been slapped across the face with a copy of *The Count of Monte Cristo.* "I have to go. My book art class with Scarlet is about ready to start."

Mateo stepped directly in front of me as I tried to walk out of the tearoom. His eyes held an apology I didn't want. "I haven't prepared anything yet," I tried to explain. "Scarlet can't do the class by herself..." Who was I kidding? Scarlet could give the class with her eyes closed.

"Can she turn herself in this afternoon?" Cade asked.

Mateo hesitated, and I knew he was thinking about the repercussions of him walking out of the Barn without an arrest by his side. The protestors wouldn't like it. Liza would undoubtedly ask if he was giving preferential treatment to his girlfriend. He shouldn't let me go. I deserved to be booked for illegal burning.

He gave one curt nod: his eyes never leaving mine. "What time?" he asked. He wasn't expecting an answer from me, but rather from my attorney who'd advised me to keep my mouth shut. Yet Cade needed to know how long I would need.

"Our class ends at one."

"I'll be here," Daddy assured me.

"Can she be at the station at two o'clock?" Cade asked.

With another terse nod Mateo said, "I'll be back at two."

"That's not necessary. As her attorney, I'll have her at the station at two." Mateo wouldn't stand for it. "I said I'd be back here to get her at two."

I turned toward Cade. "It's okay. It's best this way considering everything. But I want you to know, I'm really sorry. I know that doesn't mean much right now, but don't give up on your political aspirations. You will make a great senator." I walked back to him and kissed him on the cheek.

Then I turned around in time to see Mateo's jaw clench. I wasn't sure how to address him since he was going to arrest me in a few hours. I couldn't exactly kiss my jailer. I settled for a nod in his direction and said, "Sheriff," before I exited the tearoom.

Our class went without a hitch. Each member of the group had a choice of creating a round or a cross-shaped wreath. The ladies followed Scarlet's lead and rolled their book pages into cones that looked like mini megaphone then dipped the wide end into glitter glue. The narrow end was stapled onto the cardboard backing. The cones were then layered systematically to the fullness each student desired. Once the backings were filled, everyone watched as I showed them how to make roses out of additional book pages. Initially, I had them cut out three six petal flowers from my templates. On the first flower, I demonstrated how to cut a line to the center. The second flower, I had them cut out one petal from a point at the center like a slice of pizza. The third flower they removed two petals in the same manner. Each petal was then covered with Mod Podge or the edges were tinged with an ink pad and then allowed to dry as we had sweet tea and pastries.

Several of the women tried to get me to talk about the book burning during the break, but Scarlet quickly changed the subject to ribbons and burlap. Once the flowers were dry, we rolled the edges of the petals downward, glued the flower pieces into individual cone shapes, overlapping one petal on each flower piece. When they were done, each student had five mini flowers that were then glued one on top of the other with the last cone being the single petal to create the center of the rose. Most of the women had created three to five flowers total to decorate their wreaths, and when they were complete, the flowers, ribbons, and burlap were placed on the wreaths and crosses.

They turned out beautifully, and I was glad I'd gotten a little funky with my wreath and made it out of old, chewed-up Marvel graphic novels. It was perfect for the door on the kids' book stall in the Barn.

But the sound of protesters outside the store put a damper on the mood. Sugar, who'd made the best cross wreath of the class, with red glitter accentuating the dainty folds of the roses, was quiet throughout the entire class. Her bubbly personality was decidedly missing from the hushed conversations. It seemed no one wanted to ask the difficult questions about what started the influx of loud and obnoxious people raining down on Hazel Rock. They all knew I was responsible; who else could cause that much uproar in town?

Everyone left with their new piece of home decor except Scarlet and Sugar.

"Is everything alright, Sugar?" I asked as we finished storing away the books for more projects.

Sugar's eyes rimmed with unshed tears. "It's Dean."

I dreaded what was going to come next. It'd been a couple of days since Dean had walked Maddie out of the bar, and I could tell it was still taking its toll on my friend. "Did he…"

Sugar immediately shook her head. "I don't know." She sniffed, picked up her cross, and headed for the steps. "I haven't seen him since Wednesday. He's been too busy working."

I walked her and Scarlet to the door, and we stared out at the picketers. Not one was a resident of Hazel Rock. Mostly in their twenties, they wore T-shirts with hip slogans, jeans, shorts, and tennis shoes. They wore their hair long and draped across their faces. A few wore bandanas to hide their identity.

"O.M.W. I never thought I'd see the day that the Book Barn Princess would warrant such ugliness."

My head snapped in Scarlet's direction, causing my curls to brush against my face and tickle my jaw. "Warrant, as in *deserve*?"

She shrugged her shoulder. "If you look at it from their perspective, you burned books, plain and simple."

"And if you look at it…realistically?" I asked with more than a tinge of irritation in my voice as I pulled my hair back and trapped the unruly strands into a ponytail.

"Realistically, you've got your backside in a sling and your feet in the fire."

I snapped my hair tie one last time. "Okay. That's it. They can go get heatstroke somewhere else."

I marched outside with Sugar and Scarlet scurrying after me, but the arrival of a loud motorcycle captured the picketers' attention more than my appearance. It was one of those large motorcycles that every middle-aged man in the country wanted to own, with a rumble to its engine that shook the ground under our feet. We couldn't see it over the protesters, but from the looks on their faces and the sound of the engine that sent a shiver traveling from the ground through my body, it had obviously slowed to a crawl and was working its way into the crowd. The protestors parted and a man in his late thirties with a bandana around his head and a braid falling down his back parked the machine at the curb. He eyed us and sneered. Sugar took a step backward, and I somehow knew I needed to protect her from this man.

I moved in front of her and pulled Scarlet with me as he swung his leg over the seat. He pulled up his jeans that wouldn't raise above his belly and caressed the two-foot chain hanging down from his handlebars. He looked up at us with his sneer firmly in place. His cheeks were ruddy from the wind and the sun and his eyes were deep set in his face. He spit, and a large juicy wad of tobacco hit the dirt and splattered. Several protesters moved back as they wiped at their legs. He didn't seem to care. He slipped the back of his hand across his chin and took one step up onto the boardwalk. I straightened my back and stood taller. Scarlet did the same and linked her arm with mine. He was well over six foot with a girth that made the boards creak beneath him. His dingy T-shirt was covered by a leather vest with patches I didn't recognize.

"Is there something I can do for you?" I asked while praying the quiver I heard in my voice was only noticeable to me.

"I'm not here to buy *Moby Dick*. I'm here to talk to her." He pointed a beefy hand at Sugar, between Scarlet and me then waited for a response.

"May I ask what this is regarding?"

"It's a private matter." His gravelly voice held a threat that made my knees want to shake, but I wasn't about to let that happen. I lifted my chin.

"I'm sure anything you have to say to Sugar can be said in my company."

Scarlet agreed. "Mine too." Her voice was stronger than mine and gave me the confidence I needed to bolster through this no matter what.

He took one fast step in our direction and stomped on the wooden planks. His fists whipped straight out to his sides, and I truly expected some kind of blade to appear out of nowhere and into his hand. It was one of those Hollywood moves you see in the movies but not in real life. It was meant to bully and intimidate.

I hid my fear by releasing all my pent-up emotions in one large sigh that actually worked to help me control the adrenaline dump he'd caused.

"Look, mister—" I paused for him to fill in the blank.

"Tiny."

"Mister Tiny, we don't want any trouble."

"It's just Tiny. No mister."

I nodded in acknowledgment. "Tiny, we don't want any trouble. We can all go to the courtyard and have a seat at the fountain." I didn't want to leave the store but there was no way I was going into the store and let this guy pull out a weapon. If he was going to try to kill us, he was going to have witnesses.

"Fine." He leaned down and got in my face. The smell of the tobacco on his breath was so strong and pungent, it was as if I could taste it in my own mouth. Then Tiny leaned around me and spoke to Sugar. "Where's that sleazeball boyfriend of yours?"

Sugar didn't hesitate to defend Dean. She pushed forward between us and got in Tiny's face. "My *fiancée* is working, unlike some people I know." Her eyes washed down him with disdain.

Her scorn ticked Tiny off even more, and by the look on his face, we were all going to be road pizza within minutes.

Tiny didn't wait for us to move toward the courtyard between the Barn and the antique store next door. His lips rolled in on themselves and his nostrils flared. "Where's my sister?" he demanded.

I looked at Scarlet to see if she knew who he was talking about, but she shook her head. Whoever Tiny's sister was, I hoped for her sake she got the good genes in the family. Being Tiny's female twin would be hell.

"I don't know where she is. I haven't seen her," Sugar answered. "Maddie missed our mama's birthday yesterday, and she didn't show up for work today."

Sugar's emotions tracked from her forehead to her chin like a slow trickle of water washing away the dirt inch by inch. Sugar hadn't seen Dean since Wednesday, and now we knew Maddie had been missing as well. Had the two run off together?

Sugar's chin quivered but she lifted it to Tiny and denied any wrongdoing on Dean's part. "Dean is working. Maddie probably found another man and will show up when she tires of him." Despite all her bravado, it was obvious she didn't believe Maddie had found herself a new man. Nor did she want to believe what we were all thinking.

The whelp of a police siren separated the crowd of protestors who'd become more interested in our conversation than yelling obscenities in our direction, and Mateo maneuvered his unmarked police cruiser toward the Barn. Tiny took one look at the navy-blue charger and shoved his finger in Sugar's direction.

"You tell Dean to call me," he ordered then got on his bike and started it. He walked it backward through the crowd that was looking a little green after a day of picketing in the hot sun and took off down the street. His bike kicked up dust on the picketers who looked as if they'd suffered enough for their efforts and began dispersing.

I wasn't sure what had caused them to give up, but in the last fifteen minutes, they'd lost their exuberance to tell me how communistic I was.

Liza Twaine came running out of the Hazel Rock Diner with her cameraman in tow yelling at the protesters, "You can't leave! You were paid to be here for the day!"

"You *paid* them?" I asked.

Liza didn't miss a beat. "Of course I didn't pay them. Someone else did. They're professionals. Don't you know anything?" She chased after her retreating story.

Apparently, I didn't know anything. My mom had told me about the marches her parents had done during the sixties. She'd been a young child, but she remembered the racial tensions and the hatred that was tossed around like it was acceptable to hate her for her darker skin tone. I'd always been proud of the stand my grandparents had taken during a tumultuous time in our country's history. But this was different. These people didn't stand for anything but the dollar. What did that say?

Scarlet returned to where Sugar and I stood. With Mateo's arrival, the crowd was now nearly gone, walking down the street with their signs dragging on the ground.

"Sugar, don't you go questioning Dean's loyalty. You *know* him," Scarlet said as she climbed the steps.

But Sugar wasn't listening. Her head was bent over her phone, and her fingers were flying across the screen. Her anger was completely gone, and the worry for Dean had returned. "I blew it. I let my temper get the best of me with her the other night, and I blew it. He's gone back to her. They have a kid together. They have history. What was I thinking?" Her pretty blond hair fell in front of her face as she stared down at her phone, hoping for a reply.

Nothing came, and Scarlet wrapped her arm around one shoulder, and I wrapped mine around the other. There was nothing to say, because Sugar knew Dean's track record with women. She knew the man. And if she didn't trust him right know, how could we?

Mateo sauntered up the steps, his uniform hugging all the right spots as he casually took off his sunglasses and hung them from his shirt pocket. His brow was drawn, but he wore the comfortable expression of a man who wasn't about to put me in shackles and deliver me to jail. I looked down the street where Liza and her cameraman were trying to turn the picketers around.

"It looks like she missed the real story," I said, happy that she wouldn't see Mateo arrest me.

"Looks like we caught a break. Are you ready?"

"Are you going to put me in cuffs?"

Scarlet's head whipped around. I hadn't told her about the charges I faced. "What for?" she asked.

Sugar joined in. "You wouldn't dare!"

Mateo held up his hands in supplication. "I'm just giving her a ride to Oak Grove."

He wasn't fooling anyone. The county jail was in Oak Grove.

"For what?" Scarlet asked from her position on his right. She looked like she was about to hold her own protest.

Mateo threw the ball in my court by looking in my direction and lifting his left brow.

"I have some business I need to attend to," I said.

Sugar looked doubtful, and it was clear that Scarlet also didn't believe a word I said.

Mateo gently took my arm and led me to his car. "'Sorry, ladies. I don't have time to sit around and chat. The health inspector has been ordered to the Inn. It seems a large percentage of their customers have come down with some kind of illness." He didn't wait for their response before opening the passenger side of his car and tucking my head down as he helped me inside.

I hated when he did that. Granted, he'd only done it once before, but still.

I waited for him to walk around and get in the car. I looked at the protestors entering the Inn. "What do you think is making them ill?"

Mateo clicked his seat belt in place and started the car. "I wouldn't begin to speculate. I'm just hoping you didn't burn something hazardous."

"I would never!" I exclaimed.

"I never thought you'd sacrifice yourself for Cade either."

I looked over at the man I'd been dating for several months, and for the first time, I saw real insecurity. Jealousy, even.

"I didn't do it for Cade." *Did I?*

"I can't see where you benefit from not throwing those books and posters in the trash," he said.

"It would have been a week before they came to get them!"

Mateo shrugged. "You have a huge backyard."

"I made a promise to a man who saved my life."

"A man who wants you…" He let that comment hang in the air as my mouth fell open.

"Are we having our first real fight as a couple?" I asked.

"I believe we are."

Silence filled the car, and I realized I might not be sitting next to my boyfriend anymore…but I was definitely sitting next to the sheriff.

Fuzz buckets.

Chapter 6

I hadn't expected Mateo to walk me through the process and take me back home...but I had hoped. Instead, when the desk sergeant pulled him aside and whispered something in his ear, he disappeared with an apologetic look over his shoulder.

Drat the man.

It was hard enough being booked in for a crime, but to not have the support of your boyfriend? Well, that stunk more than the stupid skunk that had caused this whole mess. Except, it wasn't really the skunk's fault. It was Liza Twaine's with her stupid purple pumps and purple telephone. And I was pretty sure Princess wouldn't appreciate me calling her new beau stupid, who hadn't done anything but try to warn away his foes and protect himself.

If I as being honest with myself, I couldn't even blame Liza. I was the one who lit the fire.

I sighed as one of the new deputies, who couldn't have been much over twenty-one, with his baby fresh complexion and chin that couldn't sport facial hair if he skipped shaving for a month, held my fingers down over the electronic fingerprint machine. The small box looked like a dated piece of electronic equipment from the 1970s that you would find in a garage sale. The image it displayed of my fingerprints on the computer screen, however, displayed how high tech the system was. It also made the procedure all that much scarier knowing that my fingerprints were permanently imaged into the legal system's internet skyway. With a click of a button, Moscow could probably have my identity.

Would they take my DNA too? I thought of those spy movies where some innocent shmuck was framed for a crime he didn't commit with files hacked out of systems like this one. Then I reminded myself that Mateo had taken my fingerprints once before when I was suspected of murdering my real estate woman. If I was going to be framed for the fall of democracy, that ship had already sailed well before today's pleasure cruise.

The next step was to fill out some paperwork and sign my name on the dotted line promising to show up for my appointed court date in four weeks. I walked out the door the deputy held open to the lobby and found Cade sitting on the bench in his lawyer attire. His tailored suit fit well and didn't hold any creases when he abandoned the bench, stood and held his arms open wide.

I didn't hesitate; I took the hug he offered. He at least knew me well enough to know that despite my lifted chin, I was more than disturbed by this whole ordeal. Jail was not my favorite place to be.

"It's going to be alright," he said as he kissed the top of my head.

Mateo chose that moment to walk out the same door I had, and he stopped and looked at us. I immediately pulled away, but it was too late. The hurt in his chocolate eyes was caused by me. I hoped he saw the same pain in mine.

He glanced around at the empty lobby and desk clerks sitting behind the bulletproof glass before he approached us. "The deputy told me you were done."

"Yeah," I responded.

Mateo nodded and rubbed his chin in a manner that said he was debating whether to say something. He dropped his hand and said, "I suppose you heard about the health inspector going to the Enchanted Inn?" When Cade nodded, Mateo continued, "They just found the cause of their guests getting sick."

Wanting to be a part of the conversation, and not be ignored, I asked, "What was it?"

Mateo looked at Cade and then answered my question, "They found a body in the water cistern on top of the Inn."

Cade's eyes closed as if the worst possible news had slapped him in the face, and he was afraid to hear anymore. Not only had someone lost their life, but that hotel was his baby. His pride and joy. His political hothouse of success…that had just crumbled to the ground.

"In the water cistern?" I asked, thinking about the rainwater collection system Cade had sold to the hotel owners. He didn't have a direct link to the actual sale, but he'd pitched the idea to the Enchanted Inn's owners and was trying to use it as a selling point to other businesses in town. Collect rainwater and save on your water bill. It was instrumental in his push to make the town have a smaller environmental footprint.

"Yeah. The body has been in there a couple days." Mateo spoke to Cade, as if I hadn't been the one to ask the question. I didn't get angry. I was surprised he was giving as much information as he was. Although I suspected it was because the town's mayor standing at my side deserved more information than a small business owner who had a propensity for ending up in the slammer.

"Who was it?" I asked as a sense of dread washed over me, and I thought of Tiny's accusing finger pointing in Sugar's direction.

"There's no ID on the victim yet," Mateo responded, yet something in his eyes told me that despite the lack of ID, Mateo knew exactly who the victim was.

"But you know who it is," I said.

"We have an idea. According to the Texas Missing Persons Clearinghouse there are only five women who have disappeared in the past few days throughout Texas."

My eyebrows shot up. "*Only* five?"

Mateo gave me a sad smile. "There's a reason I worry about you. Most of the victims have high-risk lifestyles though. We're working with Oklahoma too, just in case we don't identify the victim, but I think we will."

I asked the question he was evading, "Are any of the missing women local?"

"One."

"You're not going to tell us who it is, are you?"

Mateo shook his head. "Mayor, I'll update you when I get more information. I'm heading out there now."

Cade shook Mateo's hand. "Of course, Sheriff. Thank you."

"Can I come?" I asked. I knew it was a harebrained idea, but I needed to know the identity of the victim. Not for myself, but for Sugar. I had a feeling Tiny and his family weren't going to take the news well.

Once again, Mateo gave me a sad smile. It was a smile I didn't like very much. "No." He turned to walk away and then hesitated. "I can drop you off at the Barn, if you'd like?"

Cade interrupted before I could answer. "That's not necessary. As her attorney, I'd like some time to talk to her. I can take her home."

Mateo nodded as he and Cade had some type of silent male-to-male eye conversation. I had no idea what was said, but they each gave a short nod at the end. Mateo hesitated, and I thought he was going to lean forward and give me a kiss, at least on the cheek. He'd announced to Liza that we were a couple by putting his arm around me. Surely, he'd do it with Cade too.

But if he'd been considering it, he changed his mind and said, "Make sure her doors are locked," as he walked away.

I turned all my pent-up frustration on Cade. "I don't need anyone to check my doors. I can check them myself."

"I know you can. Come on, I'll take you home."

"I'm not going home," I told him.

"Princess." His voice held that *don't get yourself into any more trouble* tone. He sounded too much like my daddy. It was creepy.

"Don't 'Princess' me. I have a vested interest in finding out who died at the Enchanted Inn and so do you."

"I think I can wait until the sheriff tells me," Cade argued as he led me across the parking lot to a brand new, very sleek, black, four-door sedan.

"Who does this belong to?" I asked.

Cade opened the front passenger door to a dark interior with white leather seats and black wood-grain trim. "I bought it."

"You sold your Camaro?" Cade had had his vintage Camaro since he turned sixteen. It was his baby. The thought of him selling it seemed almost sacrilegious.

He pulled at the collar of his shirt. "No. It's at home in the garage."

I looked at the manufacturer's symbol I didn't recognize as I got inside. "What is it?"

"It's a Tesla," he said as he closed the door. The airtight seal gave a soft thunk, much different from the sound of the doors on my daddy's three-year-old truck. The smell of new car enveloped me in the luxurious interior. I'd always known Cade had money. He came from money. Made big money in the NFL before he injured his knee. After that, he'd made good business decisions, and still did. He may not have owned the Enchanted Inn, but he was a major investor in the finished product of the quaint hotel that was making a name for itself as the greenest hotel in Texas. The Calloway name was synonymous with deep pockets and power. But when we'd dated as teenagers, we hung out at the Barn, not the Calloway Estate that made the Ewing spread on the television show *Dallas* look like a ranch hand's bunk house. He always drove his truck or his Camaro, which was in great shape, but it was old when we were kids. It was ancient now.

This car meant a level of money that I couldn't relate to.

"What made you buy this?"

"I thought it was time to get something grown-up." He turned on the vehicle, and the engine didn't make a sound. No rumble. No purr. The exact opposite of his Camaro.

I grinned. "You got it because it's electric."

Cade tried to hide his embarrassment, but I saw the slight shade of pink touch his ears. "That was one of the selling points."

Then I remembered why having an environmentally friendly car wouldn't matter as much today as it did yesterday. "I'm sorry. You've been doing everything right to advance your career, and I screwed it all up in one morning."

"There's a dead body in the cistern of the hotel I funded. I don't think a few posters are going to matter after that. Especially since a whole group of protesters became ill from the water."

"How could someone have dumped a body in the cistern?"

Cade glanced at me as he maneuvered the vehicle through the streets of Oak Grove. "Mateo didn't say it was a homicide. He said it was a dead body. For all we know someone got drunk and decided it was a perfect place to go swimming."

I didn't think there was a positive spin on this scenario, but Cade made it sound less sinister. Even if the woman had decided to go swimming... her body had been there long enough for the officers not to be able to identify her, and her remains floating in that cistern was the source for the numerous people becoming ill. I thought about what that meant. It wasn't the most pleasant thought to have racing through my head.

I shuddered.

Cade talked about my charges and his strategy for defending against them during the rest of the way back to Hazel Rock, but I could tell he was worried. Worried about the victim's identity and if it was someone we knew. Worried about the hotel and its guests. And to round it off in a great big bundle, was his concern for his career. Life as the mayor of Hazel Rock wasn't as easy as it appeared.

The Enchanted Inn had been a major part of his success. It'd been recently renovated and had only reopened about a month ago. The owners and Cade had given a tour before it opened to showcase not only the design, but the energy efficiency of all the fixtures, windows, appliances, and the water saving features. It was the tallest building in town and had state-of-the-art technology with an old-world charm. The top three floors we're made of brick, but the first floor had a concrete facade with arched openings leading to a paved courtyard and the front doors. The back of the building had a branch coming out to form a *T* that had been added in the early 1900s.

Before the renovation, the Inn had been an apartment building and had shown its age. Since the renovation it looked brand new. The floor-to-ceiling windows on the second and third floors mirrored the arches to the courtyard and were a main draw to most visitors. The views of the Brazos River from the front and Hill Country in the back, were spectacular. When the sun set, they were a sight to behold.

Even the water tank located on the back wing of the hotel didn't detract from the charm the Enchanted Inn possessed. The tank had been designed with the same charm as the rest of the building. Except now, as we approached the scene, emergency responders and the Medical Examiner's Office personnel could be seen on top of the roof. The water rescue team had been called in to retrieve the body, and even though we couldn't see the solar panels on the roof, it was obvious that everyone was having to work around them.

Police tape was replaced with temporary barriers keeping hordes of reporters back as the police filtered hotel guests toward a bus that had been brought in to transport those individuals who weren't seriously ill. The entire scene looked macabre with a crowd of onlookers watching and being interviewed by news sources from across the state. Among them I recognized Scarlet with her arm around Sugar's shoulder.

Cade winced as we drove by. Even the local reporters didn't recognize his new car, which had windows tinted so dark, they couldn't possibly see us inside. It gave Cade a break that would allow him time gather information before speaking to them. I didn't envy the job ahead of him.

"Where are we going?" I asked.

"I thought I'd park down at the Barn, make a few phone calls, and head down to the Inn once I had a little bit more information." He grabbed his phone from the dash and made sure Bluetooth was turned off. He wanted privacy, and I was going to give it to him.

"Thank you for the lift. I appreciate all your help."

"I know you wouldn't be in this mess it wasn't for me. We'll get through it together." Cade smiled but it wasn't real.

I could've said the same thing to him, but I didn't. Instead I opened the door and headed toward the crowd where I'd seen Scarlet and Sugar standing outside of the hotel. I squeezed my way through some of the same people who had been protesting outside the Book Barn earlier that day. Apparently harassing me had become low on their list of priorities.

I approached my friends and noticed that Scarlet looked like she'd just come out of the beauty salon as a customer. Sugar, on the other hand, didn't. Her makeup was gone, and even though she was a beautiful woman, tears and stress had taken a toll on her complexion. It was blotchy, and her nose and eyes were as red as Mateo's had been after being sprayed by a skunk. She saw me approach and immediately wiped her eyes and nose.

"Have they identified the victim yet?" I asked.

Sugar tried to respond but couldn't. Only inarticulate noises escaped her mouth as she broke into a fresh set of tears. Scarlet handed her a tissue from a pack she had in her hand.

"Sally Ferguson just told me the victim was wearing a red leather skirt, a white sleeveless blouse, and one red-and-black boot. She had blond hair, but the body was too decomposed for anyone to get a positive ID. The ME will have to obtain that."

Sally Ferguson was the deputy with the Coleman County Sheriff's Department. She was also a good friend of Scarlet's and a major source of information when it came to which men in town were good candidates for boyfriend material. Granted she couldn't tell us which guys had jerk genes in their DNA, but she could tell us we didn't want to date those who had criminal records.

I wondered if I'd just earned myself a spot in the do-not-date column in Sally's book of eligible singles, and if I'd also reclassified myself as ineligible to Mateo. Then I remembered what Maddie was wearing in the bar on Wednesday night and refocused on what was important.

I looked at Sugar, whose face crumpled before my eyes. I said the only thing I could think of, "I'm so sorry," but my sympathy caused more tears to flow down her face. My words seemed inadequate and a little inappropriate. Sugar and Maddie weren't friends. They didn't even like each other, but Sugar loved Maddie's little boy, and that boy was without a mother.

No child should lose their mom. I knew that better than most. I'd lost my mom to cancer at the tender age of ten, and Maddie's four-year-old wouldn't begin to understand why his mom disappeared.

"How is Dean supposed to tell his son that his mom is dead? He won't understand, and he'll want to see her even more." Sugar blew her nose.

"Where is Scotty?" Scarlet asked.

"He's with Dean's parents. I'm supposed to pick him up after my shift at the Tool Shed." Sugar's eyes widened. "I don't want to be the one to tell him." She grabbed Scarlet's wrist. "I can't tell him," she insisted.

"It may not be her."

Sugar shook her head. "Everybody knows it's her. She was last seen wearing a red leather skirt and white top and—and—" She hiccupped. "She has blond hair. Blond hair." Sugar pulled her hair to emphasize the color and enunciated the words one by one as if we didn't know the details of the description.

"But as long as there's a smidgen of hope, you can't tell Scotty that his mom is dead."

Scarlet agreed, "Charli's right. You can't take away his hope that his mom will walk through that door. Not yet."

"But what will I say? She was supposed to pick him up tomorrow morning." A fresh batch of tears streamed down her cheeks. "She won't be there tomorrow morning."

"But Dean will," Scarlet reassured her.

As if we somehow cast a spell and conjured him up, a tow truck screeched around the corner and came to a stop in the middle of the street. Dean MacAlister jumped out of the vehicle and ran to Sugar's side. She threw her arms around his neck, and he held her tight. What they had was special, and I wasn't sure either one recognized just how precious it was.

Dean pulled back and looked Sugar in the eyes. For a man like Dean, who had always worn an easygoing smile, it was strange to see anything but his boyish grin plastered on his face. He'd reached middle age without most of us noticing. The string of exes he left behind was a mile long, and what he owed in child support was probably more then I earned in a month. But he was a good dad and a Southern gentleman, provided you weren't married to him. Maddie had been his third wife, and after her, he'd vowed to never marry again. As much as Sugar wanted to change that, I didn't think Dean would ever take the plunge again. Especially now.

Detective Youngblood approached us with a look that we all recognized. He had bad news, and he had questions that he wanted answers to.

Dean didn't beat around the bush. He turned toward Detective Youngblood and asked, "Is it Maddie?"

"We don't know for sure but…"

"But I reported her missing," Dean said.

We all look at Dean. Not one of us had been aware that he'd reported Maddie missing. Even Sugar was shocked by the news.

Detective Youngblood nodded. "Yes, she's the only female to be reported missing in the county for the past several weeks."

Sugar began sobbing and pressed her face into Dean's shoulder as he held her tight.

"Does the clothing description I gave you match what you found tonight?" Dean's question was worded slowly. Softly. Carefully. As if he wanted to make sure he didn't say anything wrong.

Sugar looked up for a moment and saw Detective Youngblood nod. Then she closed her eyes and snuggled into Dean a little tighter, but her tears were gone. Dean absently kissed the top of her head before looking up into the sky. I wasn't sure if he was praying or saying goodbye to the mother of his child.

Detective Youngblood opened his steno pad. "You said that Maddie had a room at the Inn the last time you saw her. Is that correct?"

Dean stiffened. Suddenly he looked extremely uncomfortable holding Sugar, and she no longer felt the need to hold on tight to her man. She stepped away, creating a gap that couldn't have been more than a foot, but appeared as big as the Grand Canyon.

"Yeah. The management team was allowed to use one of the rooms in the back of the Inn. The only time it was booked by guests was when the Inn was totally full."

"So why wouldn't it have been booked last night when the protesters arrived?"

Dean shook his head, honestly perplexed. "I have no idea. That's something you'll have to ask the hotel. All I know is that I walked her in and she spoke to the desk clerk and I walked out. That's the last time I saw her."

"You didn't walk her to her room?"

Dean hesitated. It wasn't long, but it was long enough to create doubt about his answer. "I walked her to the stairwell, and I got a call that someone needed a tow. I left her there."

Dean wasn't telling the truth. It was obvious to me, and I was pretty sure it was obvious to everyone in our little circle. Including Detective Youngblood. The reason for Dean's deceit stood right next to him staring off across the street at the Brazos River as the sun set in a beautiful mixture of colors only found on an artist's palette and the Texas sky.

Sugar swallowed hard, as if she could make Dean's grizzly secret disappear without anyone being the wiser. But secrets were never secrets in Hazel Rock, Texas, and I had no doubt Dean was going to learn that the hard way.

"I'd like for you to come down to the station and give me a statement, if you don't mind," Detective Youngblood said. He may have worded it like a request, but he expected Dean to comply.

Dean didn't hesitate. "Sure thing." He touched Sugar's shoulder, but she flinched out of his reach. "Could you pick up Scotty on your way home?" he asked.

"You know I will," Sugar replied. "I'll talk to you tomorrow, Charli."

Dean waited for her to look at him, but when Sugar walked away, Dean looked like a man who'd lost his best friend. Maybe he had.

He and Detective Youngblood walked toward their cars. I thought it was a good sign that the detective allowed Dean to drive his tow truck to the station.

"He's lying," I said.

Scarlet hustled me by Cade and Mateo who were giving a press conference to a horde of media gathered in front of the hotel. Liza Twaine was in the front row proving exactly what kind of pain in the rear she could be. Scarlet ignored the reporters and was walking faster on her four-inch heels than I could in my tennis shoes.

"Are you telling me you don't think he was lying?" I whispered.

Scarlet turned and grabbed my forearm, dragging me into an alcove for the bakery. The ground to ceiling display windows were full of everything I loved. But what caught my attention, what drew me in faster than a moth to a flame, were the cupcakes Franz had on display. There must've been five dozen decorated all the same: deep chocolate cake rising above metallic pink cupcake tins and smothered in white creamy icing with one square of dark chocolate sticking out from the middle of each cupcake. It was like that chocolate had my name written on it.

My stomach growled, and I realized I'd missed lunch, and it was well past the dinner hour. I would kill for a cupcake. But the bakery was closed, and I was already facing one misdemeanor charge. I didn't need another for burglary.

"You look like you're about ready to commit a B and E," Scarlet said.

"I'm hungry, not stupid."

"You could've fooled me."

"What's that supposed mean?" I asked.

"You got caught *burning* books." When I looked at her, Scarlet tore into me like never before. "Never, in all my days, would I have thought that Charli Rae Warren would burn books. And if that wasn't bad enough, oh no, you didn't do it for yourself. You weren't trying to cover up for your dad. You weren't even trying to save a little money. You did it for Cade. Cade!"

I scowled at her as I looked back at the reporters, hoping they didn't hear her tirade.

"And you got caught by Mateo," she said. "Are you trying to ruin the best thing that has happened to you since you came back to Hazel Rock?"

"I hardly think the best thing that has happened to me is a man. I have my daddy back in my life, and no one is going to take that from me ever again."

"I love you too, Princess, but I happen to agree with your friend."

Scarlet and I jumped at the same time. She let out a little squeal, and I released a grunt. Together we sounded like a baby pig having a nightmare. Daddy just laughed.

Scarlet grabbed her chest. "O.M.W. Bobby Ray Warren you are worse than your daughter!"

"I should be. I've got a twenty-five-year head start." Daddy leaned over and gave me a kiss on the cheek. "What are you two doing over here whispering in the corner? You look like a couple of teenage girls conspiring to do something they shouldn't."

This time I could plead not guilty, because we hadn't got to that point yet. If he'd come about five minutes later, we would've been guilty. As it was, Scarlet and I had just been bickering.

"Scarlet was lecturing me."

Daddy looked to Scarlet to explain.

"She's ruining a good thing, Bobby Ray. I'm trying to stop her from making a mistake she's going to regret."

"You must be talking about Mateo."

I rolled my eyes. "Not you too."

"It seems to me, that you have a good friend here who's trying to give you a good piece of advice. I suggest you listen to her, Princess."

I agreed, so I could get the two of them to change the subject. "Of course, Daddy." We had more important things to worry about other than my love life. "Did you hear what they found at the hotel?" I asked.

Daddy nodded. "Detective Youngblood spoke to me and Joe over at the Tool Shed."

I was all ears. I wanted to know what the detective knew before he approached us, but I didn't want Daddy to know that I planned to put my nose where it didn't belong. I didn't need lecture number two for the evening. "What was he wanting to know?"

"He was looking into the disappearance of Maddie MacAlister. He wanted to know the last time we saw Maddie and who she was with. I wasn't much help since I wasn't at the bar Wednesday night. The last time I saw Maddie was Wednesday morning at the Book Barn for the Mystery Moms Book Club meeting." Daddy shook his head. "I'm afraid I wasn't much help. Joe was able to give more information."

"What did he say?" Scarlet asked.

Despite all the bad stuff going on, inside I was smiling. Scarlet had joined my quest for the truth—through my method of *meddling*.

"He described what Maddie was wearing Wednesday night and said that Maddie got into a verbal altercation with Sugar. But Dean took her home." I winced. That statement didn't look good for either of them. Sugar looked like she had motive, and Dean looked like he was the last one to see Maddie alive. Both of our friends were in trouble.

I wasn't sure what else we could do, especially when I saw Detective Youngblood talking to Dean at his tow truck, and his partner stopping Sugar before she got in her car. The two detectives may have had small-town experience, but they knew their job well and had a drive for justice just as strong as Mateo did. They would get their man—or woman.

I just had to make sure it wasn't Dean or Sugar who ended up spending the rest of their life behind bars.

Chapter 7

I met Scarlet at the Hazel Rock Diner for breakfast before the store opened. She had the day off and was ready to get down to business. We didn't know the cause of Maddie's death, but the Inn had been closed for business, and the police were at the scene that morning. Not only was that bad for Cade, it didn't bode well for Dean and Sugar either. If Maddie had been on the clock and had gone to check the tank for some reason but fell in, the police would have cleared the scene. As it was they didn't look like they were going to be clearing out anytime soon.

"Did you hear from Mateo last night?" Scarlet asked me.

"No, I'm sure he's still working."

"You're sure?"

I took a bite of my French toast and ignored the question. Heck no, I wasn't sure. But I was pretty sure we were just fine. The fact that he hadn't even texted me didn't sit well, but the man was dedicated. That had to be the reason for his lack of communication.

The front door opened, and Reba Sue entered with Liza, Daisy, and Betty. All four were wearing their black T-shirts that had *Mystery Moms* imprinted on the front in pink letters. They looked around, saw Scarlet and me seated in the back of the restaurant, and headed our direction.

"That can't be good," Scarlet said into her coffee cup.

"It's too early in the morning for this. Maybe if we ignore them, they'll leave us alone." I dug into my scrambled eggs with catsup. Scarlet took a bite of her yogurt.

It didn't work. The ladies approached our table, and Liza slammed a newspaper down. "Have you seen this?"

We looked at the paper. *The Dallas Morning Daily*'s headline was an eye catcher. "Life Imitating Art" was plastered across the front page in bold script with a picture of the Enchanted Inn's water tank.

"O.M.W.," Scarlet said.

"How is it that I was out-scooped by a Dallas newspaper?" Liza complained.

I ignored Liza's complaint and scanned the article as the women pushed their way into our booth. Luckily it was big enough for four comfortably, six if you wanted to squeeze in together. We were crammed in together, and somehow, I'd drawn the short straw and had Liza crowding my immediate space. The woman had a spine stiffer than Princess's shell. I would never have dreamed of throwing someone under the bus one day and then cuddling up in a booth with them at the local diner the next. There was a steak knife at my disposal, for Pete's sake.

Scarlet saw my eyes stray toward the utensil and kicked me under the table.

I took a deep breath and returned my attention to the article, well aware that Liza was working the Mystery Moms angle to her advantage. I wouldn't put it past her to have a wire on under her clothes and a van parked at the curb listening to every word we exchanged.

Everyone waited patiently for me to finish the article about the body being found in the water tank being eerily familiar to the murder plot in Nathan Daniels's book *Woman Scorned,* and how it was the second time in recent history that Hazel Rock had been the scene of a serial copycat killer. It was an unfair comparison to an earlier murder mystery we'd had in our town. Unfortunately for Cade and Mateo, they pointed out that each crime wave—they actually called them crime waves—occurred while Cade was mayor and Mateo was sheriff. They went on to state that the dedicated duo would be better suited for the television show *America's Sexiest Catch* than civil servants.

"Holy crap."

"I take it you got to the part about Cade and Mateo?" Liza said as she grabbed a biscuit from my plate and took a bite.

I wanted to hit her. I just wasn't sure if it was from her casual tone or because she stole food off my plate. "Yeah." I didn't finish the article. I'd seen enough.

"What'd they say about Cade and Mateo?" Scarlet asked.

I handed the newspaper to her.

"What are we going to do about this?" Reba Sue asked. I had no doubt she was anxious to be Cade's hero.

Everyone looked at me for an answer, and I found myself in the role of leader of the pack. Mateo wouldn't like it.

"Where do you think they got the information?" I asked.

"If you read on to page two, you'll see that the reporter interviewed Nathan Daniels."

Scarlet flipped to page two and showed me a picture of Nathan Daniels. He wasn't a bad-looking guy, a little on the nerdy side with messy brown hair, glasses, and a bow tie. He appeared to be around forty, wore a tweed suit jacket, and a serious expression—no smile for the camera.

"I thought he was from Nevada," Scarlet said.

"He is," answered Reba Sue. "I don't know what he's doing in Dallas."

I swallowed a bite of eggs. They didn't want to go down, and they no longer tasted good. The catsup that had topped them off perfectly a couple minutes ago now seemed to dominate the flavor. "He's obviously capitalizing on Maddie's death."

"Have they identified it as Maddie?" Daisy asked.

"Yes," Liza answered. Then we all waited for her to explain how she knew that. "The crime beat reporter got the information this morning. They identified her through dental records and Mateo notified the family last night around midnight."

That explained why I hadn't heard from him. He'd apparently contacted Dr. Applewood and obtained Maddie's dental records after hours. It made a regular dental visit sound pleasant.

"Did they say what the cause of death was?" I asked.

"Mateo said the ME would complete the autopsy today," Reba Sue added.

Reba Sue was the last person I expected to have information from Mateo. Scarlet shared my shock. "When did you talk to Mateo?"

Reba Sue grinned. "I have my ways."

I leaned forward and stared her down, but Reba seemed oblivious to the stink eye I was giving her. "Who's going to go to Dallas and talk to Nathan Daniels?" she asked.

Daisy shook her head. "Too far from my husband for me to go."

Liza scoffed.

Daisy eyed her the way I'd eyed Reba Sue. "What's that supposed to mean?"

"Jessie is a grown man. He can take care of himself. You can have a life away from him you know."

"That's the problem with your generation. You want separate lives. I married Jessie when I was eighteen because I wanted to share my life with him. We do our own thing, but at the end of the day, I want my husband in the bed next to me."

It was obvious Liza didn't understand. I wasn't sure I wanted the type of relationship Daisy and Jessie had, but it worked for them, and I respected that.

Betty spoke up. "I think Reba Sue and I should go. She's got no ties here, and Franz will understand me going on a girls' trip. Besides maybe it will make him realize how much he needs me."

I wasn't sure how old Betty and Franz were or how long they'd been dating, but they were definitely old enough to have grandchildren, if not great grandchildren.

"How are you going to find Nathan?" Scarlet asked.

Reba Sue and Betty just looked at her. Each blinking with a blank expression.

"I'll go with them. I can use my connections and get the Dallas reporter to tell me what hotel Nathan is staying at."

Volunteering for a road trip didn't sound like something Liza would do. "Why wouldn't you want to stay here and get the ME's report?" I asked.

Liza took another bite of my biscuit. Just watching her eat my food was enough to stir my dander.

Scarlet kicked me under the table again. She seemed to be the only one in tune with what I was contemplating.

"I didn't get the story."

"Excuse me?"

Liza grabbed for my tea to wash down my biscuit, and I smacked her hand away.

"I didn't get the story, okay?" she said. "They gave it to the crime beat reporter."

I wanted to laugh but knew that would be in bad taste. I took a drink of my tea instead.

"Would you look at that?" Reba Sue said.

We all followed her gaze to the front of the diner. Sugar walked in with Dean on her heels. It was obvious that she'd seen us but considering most of us were wearing T-shirts that advertised we were getting ready to meddle in her life, Sugar decided to take a seat at the bar with Dean. Both of them still had on the same clothes they'd worn last night, and I got the impression they'd never slept.

"We should go offer our detective skills to them," Betty said as she started to get up.

Scarlet reached across the table and grabbed Betty's hand before she could tip her blue wig in their direction. "I don't think that'd be a wise decision."

Thank God for Scarlet.

Daisy agreed, "If Sugar wanted our help, she would have come back here."

"It's because Liza is with us. They saw how Liza raked Princess through the coals this week," Reba Sue stated.

Scarlet nodded, along with Daisy and Betty.

Liza growled. "I was doing my job. I report the news."

I took a drink of my sweet tea, savoring Liza's discomfort, and the women putting her on the defensive. "You could have reported the truth. That the books had been sprayed by a skunk."

"That doesn't bring ratings," she argued.

"When did reporting the news turn into ratings?" Betty asked.

Before Liza could answer, the front door of the diner burst open and slammed against the doorstop. The leather strap of bells hanging from the handle clanged violently against the door. Every single person who had been enjoying their breakfast suddenly turned silent. Forks froze midway to mouths. Waitresses' pens stopped scribbling, and newspapers stopped crinkling. Every gaze turned toward the large man storming inside cloaked in rage.

Kitchen noises could be heard along with a cook yelling, "Order up!" But not one of the diners said a word. All eyes rested on Tiny, his fists clenched, his chest heaving like he'd just run a marathon, and his eyes boring holes in Dean's back.

Dean looked up from his cup of coffee and saw the barely contained rage. I thought he would stand up and confront Tiny, but he didn't. Despite the animosity flowing from Tiny, Dean held only sympathy in his expression. Which seemed to anger Tiny even more.

"What did she do to deserve that, Dean?" Tiny's voice boomed the accusatory question in Dean's direction.

"Nothing. She didn't do anything to deserve that. No one deserves that," Dean responded in a soft voice. It almost sounded as if he was talking to his four-year-old son. Trying to explain the horrors of death without going into too much detail.

"Then why'd you do it? Why'd you kill my baby sister?"

Dean flinched with the accusation. He looked around the diner to see if others believed he was capable of murder, and I got the distinct impression he didn't like what he saw. I scanned the restaurant and saw that several people wanted an answer to the same question. I wasn't sure how they could possibly think that of Dean. Dean was always there with a helping hand. He loaned cars for a minimal fee or for free to the residents of Hazel Rock who needed them. He offered free tows to those in need. He was always there with a smile on his face and a helping hand held out.

Tiny reached for his waistband, and a collective gasp echoed through the diner. Sugar stood up and would have moved in front of Dean, but Dean stopped her and held her back with one arm. Tiny took one look at Sugar with her blond hair and looks so much like Maddie's, and his bottom lip quivered. He couldn't take his eyes off her.

"Let me out," I whispered to Liza who at some point had pulled her cell phone out and was recording the confrontation. She was more than happy to elbow Betty to stand up and let the two of us out of the booth. It gave her a better vantage point for the action.

I scooted across the seat and slowly made my way toward the bar that was lined with stationary stools made from saddles. The entire diner had a Western feel, and the standoff between the two men seemed to transport us back to an age where a saloon shoot-out was eminent. I could picture round tables being tossed over on end for concealment. They certainly wouldn't be any good as cover if bullets began to fly.

I prayed that didn't happen.

What did happen was the last thing I expected. It was the last thing everyone expected. Including the hostess at the register standing two feet away from him when Tiny reached for the display case and grabbed a pie from inside. It was as if no one could possibly understand what he was thinking about doing with that pie. No one would choose a pie when a shoot-out was called for. Cowboys didn't meet at sundown on Main Street to draw pastries from a gun belt.

But that's exactly what Tiny did. He cocked that pie back and released it with so much force, whipped cream flew off the sides before it hit Dean in the chest. Dean blinked but didn't say a word, until Tiny grabbed another one.

"Tiny, that's enough. We can take this outside," he said as he stepped forward.

But Tiny wasn't listening. He was driven to destroy Dean the only way he could in a diner full of witnesses—with baked goods. He grabbed a lemon meringue pie next, but Dean ducked, and it hit Sugar in the face. Everyone froze.

Sugar scrunched her eyes and wiped the meringue off in scoops.

That's when a little ten-year-old boy decided it looked like too much fun to be left out. He grabbed a handful of grits from the bowl in front of him and flung it at Tiny with everything he had. The grits hit Tiny on the side of his head and ran down his ear. Tiny never saw who threw it; he just reacted on instinct. He grabbed a third pie and whipped it across the diner. It hit Mr. Draper, a ranch owner with a team of ranch hands who'd been calmly eating their breakfast before all of us had arrived.

At that point, things erupted into a full-blown melee.

Food was tossed from every angle. Eggs, oatmeal, more grits, and juice. A pancake slapped my cheek and stuck with syrup. I pulled it off and tossed it back where it came from as I tried to make my way up front. I slipped on something slimy and thought I was going to crack my head open like the over easy egg that hit Dean on the face. There wasn't a full plate in the house when the shrill of a police whistle filled the air.

Once again, the restaurant grew quiet with the arrival of another customer. At the doorway with a look of total disbelief on their faces, stood Mateo and Cade. Both were still in the same clothes from the previous night, yet both were cleaner than every person inside the Hazel Rock Diner.

"I'm not sure I'm in the right town," Mateo said.

"I'm not sure we're in the right universe," added Cade.

"What the Sam Hill is going on?" Daddy asked as he poked his head inside the restaurant.

Princess waddled in at their feet and began licking coconut cream pie from the floor. Unfortunately, she'd decided to have the same guest join her for breakfast that she'd invited into the bookstore. It was only then that I realized Princess's boyfriend had become her prince.

Mateo froze. Cade did a little jig to get out of the way, and Daddy stood at attention.

"Do not move, people," Mateo ordered. "Anyone who does, I'm going to arrest on the spot."

"I know how to handle this," I told Mateo.

"Charli, for the love of God, don't..."

He was too late. I was on the move. I grabbed the pie tin that had held one of the pies and scooped up as much of the banana cream pie I could find. It was Princess's favorite, and if I could get Princess to follow me, I was betting her prince would do the same.

If he didn't, it wouldn't be the first time I'd been in trouble with the law, but it was working. Sorta.

Princess totally wanted the banana cream pie. Her prince, however, wanted to scrounge through everything. He picked up a tomato and rolled a sausage. It was as if he was in the grocery store and shopping for the best produce, the sweetest syrup, and softest eggs.

I moved closer and waved the pie in front of his nose. He paused his perusal near ten-year-old Jimmy's shoes and nearly gave Jimmy's mom a heart attack. Not because Prince did anything, but because Jimmy thought it's be cool to pet a skunk.

Prince arched his back like a cat and his tail went straight up in the air as Jimmy ran his hand down the length of his black-and-white fur.

It was only when Jimmy's mom whispered loudly, "Jimmy!" that the skunk became alarmed. He lifted his head and looked straight at the woman. Her face paled ten shades and Jimmy giggled.

"Skunks carry lice," I told Jimmy as he reached to pet him again.

His hand froze. Whether the boy had experienced lice before or not, I had no idea. He did know enough to know he didn't want to get them now. He pulled back his hand, and I waved the pie in front of Prince's face again.

We progressed toward the front door with everyone standing or sitting still, the only noise was coming from Princess and the skunk. They chattered, their nails scratched the floorboards, and Princess's tail dragged behind her. At one point, Princess became impatient for her treat and reached up and clawed the pie tin. She nearly knocked it out of my hand, and I grappled with it. I made too much noise and moved too quickly for Prince.

He raised his head and stamped his feet. A collective gasp went through the restaurant as everyone waited for the inevitable.

Nothing happened. I readjusted the tin so that it was balanced between my hands and forearms to ensure there was no way Princess could knock it out of my grasp and continued backing up toward the door. Just as I edged toward the last booth, I saw Liza standing at my side with a muffin in her hand.

I thought about her news broadcast and paused.

"Charli," Mateo warned. He dragged my name out like he was riding a rollercoaster. His tone held all kinds of secret meanings. Like, *don't do it, you'll just get yourself in trouble*, and *you're better than her.*

Except I wasn't. The woman told lies about my bookstore on the news. She'd damaged our reputation beyond anything I would've dreamed she'd be capable of. In the past twenty-four hours we'd received nasty emails and one death threat. I questioned whether or not we'd have one legitimate customer in for business that day. The only thing that had slowed the backlash from her story was the tragedy that followed it.

"Charli." His voice was soft, and the warning was gone. He was just letting me know he wasn't going to abandon me as he stood at the door holding it open for me, Princess, and the skunk to exit. Princess immediately followed me out the door as I backed up past Mateo. Her boyfriend was a little more hesitant. He'd hit a gold mine for breakfast. Banana cream pie was just icing on top of a banquet for royalty, and he wanted his due.

"Someone needs to kill that thing," said Liza.

"I won't be there to save you this time Liza," Mateo said.

She pursed her lips and didn't say another word.

The skunk finally waddled out the front door and Mateo closed it behind him, leaving me outside with Princess and her man and a pie tin filled with the sloppy remains of a banana cream pie. I walked across the street with the two of them following, then led them to the backyard, and set the pie tin down by the river.

"Princess, you cannot bring him into town," I warned. "You're special. People tolerate you. They're not going to do the same thing for him."

Princess looked up with whipped cream on her snout. With each of them on one side of the tin facing each other, they reminded me of a young couple eating dessert together at the diner. All they needed was a couple of forks.

Prince took a swipe at the pie and lifted a glob to his mouth. I supposed claws worked just as well as a fork any day.

"I mean it, girl. He can't come into town. Not when everybody is ready to turn him into a winter cap."

Princess's ears twitched before she lay them down flat. I was pretty sure she got the gist of what I was saying. If she wanted Prince to live, she was going to have to keep him outside. She looked like I was making her choose between me and him, but that wasn't what I was doing at all.

"I don't want you to choose between us," I told her. "I want you to understand that your time together must be outside away from people."

Princess snorted and went back to her pie and her prince nuzzled her nose. I could've sworn it was his way of saying, *it'll be all right, babe*.

Then again, maybe that was wishful thinking on my part, and I wanted someone to tell me that.

By the time I made it back to the diner, most of the patrons had left, and Tiny was being lectured by Officer Sally Ferguson. His head was downcast, and his expression was sad and regretful. I grappled with the difference in his personality. Yesterday he had seemed like a barely contained wild animal. This morning he'd looked like he could have committed murder, but instead he'd thrown a pie. And now he looked ashamed.

If appearances were deceiving, then Tiny exemplified the true meaning of that statement. He was nothing but a big teddy bear.

Daisy was standing at the door holding a basketful of money. She wasn't about to let one person leave that restaurant without donating to the cleanup cause. And when someone didn't give enough, she wouldn't move from her spot in front of the door until they reached into their wallet and pulled out more money.

It was the people standing around gawking that really got my attention. In the midst of them was Liza filming the entire thing on her phone. Mateo was handcuffing Dean while Sally Ferguson turned away from Tiny and slipped the cuffs around Sugar's wrists. It was a nightmare.

I ran to where they stood at the end of the bar. "Wait a minute." My brain took a moment to process what was happening. All I could do was repeat myself. "Wait a minute."

"Don't interfere, Charli." Mateo wasn't looking at me when he gave the order.

"Don't interfere? Don't interfere?" Geez Louise, I needed to think of something more intelligent to say.

"That's what he said," Liza interjected.

I ignored her. "What are you arresting them for?"

"I'm trying to do this as quietly as possible."

"In front of the whole town and Liza Twaine?"

"If you'll excuse us." Mateo began to walk Dean toward the front door. I stepped in his path.

"Charli."

"Mateo."

"It's Sheriff Espinoza."

"Fine. Sheriff Espinoza. Give me a minute to talk to Sugar."

"I don't want to talk to you, Charli. Just let us go." Sugar was dropping tears across the floor. My heart nearly broke.

Dean interrupted, "Sheriff, if I could give Charli my keys, I need her to make sure the house is locked up. I left it open for a contractor who was coming out today to finish up on our remodeling."

Sugar looked at him like he'd done lost his mind. I wasn't sure I disagreed. Who could think about remodeling when they were faced with jail?

Mateo nodded and reached into Dean's pocket for his keys. I moved closer to get the keys from him, and Mateo lowered his voice to keep Liza from hearing him. "However, there won't be any contractors at the house today. We're going to be serving a search warrant this afternoon, and no one is getting in that house. Including you. But you can make sure it's locked up when we leave."

Tiny chose that moment to go after Dean…again. Mateo pushed Dean behind him as he tried to contain Tiny before things got completely out of hand. It was during that moment that Dean leaned over and whispered. "Sugar just told Mateo she lost her gun. That's not true. I saw it in our safe this morning, and Mateo is looking for a 9mm handgun. He's looking for *Sugar's* gun. You *have* to get to the house and get rid of it."

Holy crap. I looked toward Mateo and Tiny. They were nose to nose, and Mateo was saying something to keep Tiny from losing it. I'm not sure what he was saying, but I wished he was saying it to me. I was seriously close to dropping down on the floor, wrapping my arms around my legs, and rocking myself into oblivion.

Sugar didn't say anything. She just pleaded with her eyes for me to do something to make this all go away. Was she asking me to cover up a murder of an innocent woman like Dean was? Or was she wanting something else entirely? I couldn't tell.

Granted, Maddie wasn't the nicest person in the world, but her brother loved her, and I'm sure the rest of her family loved her. Surely, she had redeeming qualities, and even if she didn't, there was no way she deserved this. Could I cover it up if Sugar killed her?

Was that how she ended up in the water tank? Had Dean covered up Sugar's crime?

I nodded. Not sure what I was agreeing to, but by then Mateo had gotten Tiny calmed down enough for him to walk out of the diner with Dean and Sugar. He stopped next to me and searched my face.

I tried to hide the horror that was coating my insides with darkness, but he knew me. Probably better than I knew myself, and he could tell something was wrong. "Are you alright?"

I nodded, unable to talk. It was as if I was choking on my own guilt.

"Remember Charli. I don't want to see you at their house until after the search warrant."

I could tell Mateo wanted to ask me what was wrong, but now wasn't the time. It was never the time for us. Something was always getting in the way, and right now it was something very, very big. I prayed he wouldn't push it. I was grappling with something so huge, I couldn't quite fathom it.

Scarlet came to my rescue. She moved up next to me. The front of her seafoam green floral dress was stained with jelly from the food fight. Rarely did Scarlet look like less than a million bucks, so I had to give her credit for carrying it off with style. "No worries, Sheriff. We won't go to the house until you let us know we need to lock it up."

Mateo glanced at me one last time and led Dean out of the restaurant with Deputy Ferguson and Sugar following. Liza took up the rear, and I grabbed a handful of oatmeal without even thinking.

Scarlet stilled my hand. "You'll get Sugar too."

She was right, of course, but she still held my hand down just in case I lost control.

"What's wrong with you?" she asked.

"What's wrong with me?" There I went. Repeating questions again and unable to form a complete sentence of my own. "Nothing."

"I've already talked to Cade."

"Great." Except Cade couldn't help me. He could help Dean and Sugar down at the police station and in the courtroom, but he couldn't help me with what Dean had asked. No one could help me, because I couldn't possibly get anyone else involved in this disaster. "I've gotta go."

"Where are you going?" Scarlet asked.

Where was I going? I wasn't sure. I hadn't made up my mind. "I've got to take care of something."

I walked away from Scarlet without looking back. Tiny was picking up slapjacks and putting them in a plastic bin that the busboys used to pick up dishes. He looked up at me, but I couldn't look him in the eyes. Not with the task that Dean had given to me. The guilt was overwhelming.

I wiped my hand off with a napkin, pulled a twenty out of my pocket and gave it to Daisy, who said, "Reba Sue and Betty went to get cleaned up, and then they're heading to Dallas. Liza was going to meet them there."

"Liza isn't a part of the Mystery Moms," I said. "Liza is in this for the story."

Daisy shrugged. "I think it's a little bit of both. But we can use that to our advantage."

"How?" I asked.

"Who else do you think will give Dean and Sugar the airtime to gain public trust?"

"Liza won't do that."

"Liza will do it because of the publicity this case is getting."

Daisy had a point, Liza would love to sit down and interview the couple accused of murder. A murder author Nathan Daniels had predicted. He'd just gotten the story a bit wrong. Maddie's body hadn't ended up in the town's water tower like Pattie in Nathan's novel, but she had been found in the *hotel's* water tank. Dean also wasn't technically a widow since he and Maddie had divorced over three years ago. And one person hadn't been arrested for Mattie's murder, but rather two people were being booked in for the crime.

I needed to decide if I was going to be an accessory after the fact, or not.

Chapter 8

The last time I'd been to Dean and Sugar's house, it'd been a rental property, and the interior walls had been painted black. But that wasn't the most eye-catching quality the house had at the time. The black walls had actually been the canvas for beautiful works of art. The pièce de résistance was on the ceiling of the master bedroom—a painting of my best friend wearing a bustier and looking like a warrior goddess from another time. Dean and Sugar had decided to change the décor when they moved into the house, and Scarlet hadn't minded seeing her warrior goddess likeness painted over with two layers of Kilz paint and then a more conservative light gray finish coat. The transformation was dramatic. Dean and Sugar did, however, give Scarlet a professional photograph of the image that had been painted directly on their ceiling as a keepsake. The photograph currently hung in her office at Beaus and Beauties Salon.

Today, I snuck in the back door of Sugar and Dean's house while a deputy sat in his car writing a report in the driveway. I was shaking so badly, it took me three times to get the key in the hole. Once I was inside, I couldn't move. I was frozen to the spot. Leaning against the kitchen door, I tried to control my breathing, but it wouldn't cooperate. I was hyperventilating, and I knew it. I sunk to the floor and put my head between my knees.

I couldn't do it. As much as I loved Sugar and Dean, I couldn't steal potential evidence of a crime. I called Cade, the only person I trusted in this situation. He was my attorney. Everything I said was privileged information.

He answered on the first ring. "Please tell me you weren't stupid enough to go to Dean and Sugar's place."

My head popped up from between my legs, and I looked around for cameras. "How did you—"

When Cade replied, his tone was calm and controlled, even if his words came out from between clamped teeth. "Get out of there now."

I heard voices at the front door. "I'm not sure that I can."

"Why not?"

"Someone's at the front door."

"That's the mailman and the officer."

"How do you know that?"

"Because I just got done talking to Dean, and he told me what he did."

"You already talked to Dean?"

"I met him at the station when he and Mateo arrived. When he told me that he gave you his keys and sent you in search of Sugar's gun, I left. Right in the middle of talking to him because I knew I'd have to stop you."

"How did you know?"

"You try to fix everything."

"I do not."

"Says the woman who burned books and posters and got herself arrested all to keep the media from knowing about my campaign a few days early."

I didn't like his tone. "I thought it was the right thing to do."

"You always think it's the right thing to do."

"I'm starting to take offense."

"Get out of the house, Princess. Mateo is on his way with a search warrant, crime scene techs, and a bunch of detectives."

I hopped to my feet. "I'm going."

"Leave the back door unlocked."

"Why?"

Cade sighed, and I pictured him running his hand through his hair. "Because Dean gave his keys to you, and Sugar didn't have any. So, if you don't leave it open, Mateo will have to call you, or force entry. I'd rather he does neither."

"Me too. What about the gun?"

"I'm not worried about the gun. I'm worried about you."

"You're not worried about Sugar, and Dean?"

"Of course, I am, but there's more evidence linking them to this crime than there are cattle on my ranch."

Cade had a lot of cattle. "It's that bad?"

"Yeah."

"What other evidence does Mateo have?"

"Would you just get out of the house? The officer is back in his car." Cade cussed again.

"Don't cuss at me Cade Calloway."

"I'm not cussing at you. I'm cussing because Mateo just turned the corner."

"I'm going." I hung up my phone and stuffed it in my pocket as I ran out the back door. I didn't slow down until I made it to the next block where I'd parked my daddy's truck.

My phone buzzed, and Mateo showed up on my caller ID. My finger hovered over the button for three rings. On the fourth ring I took a deep breath and answered the phone.

"That wasn't your daddy's truck I saw parked a street over from Dean and Sugar's place was it?"

If it wasn't hard enough to breathe from running through the yards with an adrenaline dump, now Mateo had to up the ante. I was stuck in a situation where I could lie, and say it wasn't my daddy's truck. Or I could say I was sitting a block away waiting for him to be finished. Which wasn't a lie, at the current moment. I chose the second answer and tried to slow my breathing. "I'm sitting here waiting for you to finish your search warrant."

"The search warrant is going to take several hours, Charli."

"Oh."

"I didn't see anyone sitting in the truck when I drove by."

I cringed. "I'm not sure how you missed me. "

The silence on the other end made me wonder if Mateo was questioning his own sanity. Sanity for dating me, or if it was insanity to continue.

He changed the subject. "Are you working at the store today?"

"Daddy opened, and I'm supposed to close."

Mateo looked disappointed. "How about I bring dinner by tomorrow night?"

His question threw me off guard. I really thought his silence had meant he was going to break up with me. If I was in his shoes, I would. "Can you bring barbecue?" I asked.

"I'll be there around six with barbecue." He hung up without another word. I should've known he wasn't the type of man to break up over the phone. If Mateo was going to break up with me, he'd do it in person.

Fuzz buckets.

I drove back to Hazel Rock happy with my decision not to take Sugar's gun, yet angry that I hadn't done as Dean had asked. Another part of me was also angry that he'd asked me to do it in the first place. But I supposed if I was in love, I would sacrifice anyone to save my lover.

I didn't want to think about what that meant in regard to my relationship with Mateo. Was I willing to sacrifice everyone in my life for him? Would he ask me to?

I parked in front of the Barn, and Scarlet came running across the street. "Where have you been?"

"I went for a drive." Again, not a total lie.

You're lying to me, Charli Rae." She followed me through the courtyard and into the alley to my apartment. Princess came around from the back of the Barn, her boyfriend nowhere in sight.

"I have to say, I hope you ditch that man for good," I told her.

Princess snorted and hopped up the steps one at a time. Her kangaroo hops brought a smile to my face for the first time in several hours.

I unlocked the door and Princess scooted inside with Scarlet behind me.

Scarlet waited long enough for the door to close and then laid into me. "Please tell me you did not go to Dean and Sugar's house."

Why was everyone trying to get me to confess? Hadn't they heard of the Fifth Amendment? Unfortunately, Scarlet was not going to back down, so I told her the truth. "I did, but I changed my mind once I got there."

The last thing I was going to lay on her shoulders was that I actually had made it into the house before I changed my mind. It was my crime, not hers.

Scarlet crossed to my kitchen and poured two glasses of sweet tea. "Here, you look like you could use this."

"Thank you."

"Did you know you have syrup in your hair?"

I reached up and felt the remnants of that morning's food fight. It wasn't just one spot that had hardened. The entire left side of my head was stiff. "I forgot."

"I can only imagine what made you forget." She waited for me to tell her.

I turned toward the fridge and pulled out lettuce, tomato, and roast turkey. "You want a lettuce wrap? If you're like me, you didn't get much for breakfast."

"Sure, it will give us a chance to talk."

"About what?"

"The case."

"We don't have a case."

"Charli. You're not the only one invested in clearing Sugar and Dean. But I have to tell you, it doesn't look good."

"I know that. The two of them are in jail." I handed her a lettuce wrap, and we moved to the table to eat.

"The day manager for the Inn came in and got her nails done today."

I took a bite and was amazed that I could taste anything. "She didn't get sick?"

Scarlet shook her head. "She was skeptical of the filtration system, so she only drank bottled water. While Joellen was doing her nails, she found out that Detective Youngblood took a copy of the surveillance tape from the hotel."

I was beginning to hate all the cameras in our town. It seemed you couldn't breathe without being filmed. "What did it show?"

"Dean went up to the room with Maddie."

My lunch lost its appeal. I set it on the table. Why were all my meals being ruined with bad news? "It shows him going into the room?" I asked.

"No, it shows him going up the elevator with her and never coming down."

"He had to come down. Even if he spent the night, at some point he has to leave the hotel."

"According to the manager, you can go out the back door and never be seen on camera."

"Well, that's a crappy surveillance system," I said.

Princess came over and begged for my lunch. I unwrapped my turkey and gave her the lettuce and tomato. She seemed happy.

"It gets worse."

I was tired of things getting worse. Dean was the last one to see Maddie, and surveillance video showed he hadn't been honest about not going into the hotel with her. A lie like that could get a man hung by a jury. Especially, when we were talking about his ex-wife. "It can't be much worse for Dean, considering he was the last one to see Maddie alive."

"Except he wasn't."

"You just said—"

"Sugar entered the hotel and went up the elevator thirty-five minutes after Dean and Maddie went upstairs."

I nearly dropped my sweet tea. "What?"

Scarlet nodded. "I know. She was up there for ten minutes, and when she got off the elevator to leave, her hair was a mess. She looked like she'd been involved in a struggle according to the manager." Scarlet paused and said, "And she was crying."

"She never said a word."

"Which looks even worse for her."

"We need to tell Cade."

"He knows. He was there when they pulled the tape."

"Oh."

"The manager thinks Sugar killed her and Dean disposed of the body."

"They wouldn't do that."

"Are you sure? We're talking about a woman who spoke poorly of Sugar every time she had the opportunity, and Maddie was making a play for Dean at the bar that night. She could have lost control after finding them together."

"You don't believe that," I said, because despite everything I still could not picture Sugar killing anyone or Dean covering up for her by disposing of Maddie's body. Granted he'd asked me to hide Sugar's gun, but so far all we knew was that Maddie's body had been found in the cistern. She may not have been shot.

"Have you heard how Maddie died?" I asked.

Scarlet shook her head as she finished her lettuce wrap and answered, "No. The autopsy is being done today. The cause of death should be release to the media for the evening news. There's one more thing."

I rubbed my face not sure I wanted to hear one more thing. "What?"

"The manager seems to think Dean has been dating Maddie for the past month."

I didn't want to believe it. Dean had a reputation for being a player. It had destroyed his first two marriages. His third with Maddie however, had been what Dean called a turning point in his life. He had married Maddie and stayed faithful, working hard to create a family with his young wife and child. That time, however, Maddie had strayed at the first chance she had to make it rich with a wealthy man, and Dean and Maddie's marriage had fallen apart. The two had divorced when their son was barely a year old and had shared custody of Scotty since. But when Dean started dating Sugar, it had been Dean and Sugar who took care of Scotty ninety percent of the time while Maddie had been in search of one prince after another to ride into town on his white horse and saddle made of gold to rescue her from small-town living. She never found the prince she was looking for. She could have recognized that Dean was a better catch than she first thought. He had always been a hard worker and had a successful auto shop. Macalister's Auto Shop was the only one in the county that people used and recommended. He'd built himself a reputation of being a reliable mechanic, if not a husband. Until Sugar. He and Sugar seemed to be the perfect couple, despite their nearly twenty-year age gap.

I didn't want to believe that Dean had been pulling the wool over Sugar's eyes, and everyone else's at the same time. It just didn't fit the man who had a heart bigger than Texas when it came to giving to the community.

"Do you believe that?" I asked Scarlet.

She didn't hesitate. "No. I think that's what Maddie wanted her to think."

"Why? Why would Maddie want someone to believe she was back with Dean?"

"Only Maddie can answer that question and..."

And she was dead. But there was someone else we could talk to. It would be awkward, and we'd have to handle it delicately. "I think we need to go talk to Maddie's mama," I said.

Scarlet winced. "Do you think we should? It hasn't even been twenty-four hours since she found out she lost her daughter."

"It's time the Mystery Moms pay their respects to the family of our latest member."

Chapter 9

It was two o'clock by the time we drove north on Main Street and headed toward Oak Grove in Scarlet's little white Isetta two-seater. Maddie's mom lived on FM 103 in a rundown ranch on forty acres. Greta Geer had never married, and the house and property had been handed down by her parents. It had been her saving grace since Greta had never held a job in her life. She did have goats, though, which appeared to be her major source of income.

Scarlet pulled into the driveway that was at least two hundred yards long and blocked by a gate. "Do you think it's electric?" I asked.

"There's no solar panel, so I don't think so. You'll have to get out and see if you can open it."

I looked at the goats wandering around at the entrance. "I'm not good with farm animals."

"You have a pet armadillo."

"And she didn't like me when I first came to town. She tried to frame me for murder."

"Princess wouldn't do that." I didn't think Scarlet was giving Princess enough credit. She didn't see her knock Reba Sue over and expose her granny panties. Nor did she see her bring that skunk right up to Liza Twaine like she knew exactly how Liza would react. She could be diabolical.

Which made me love her even more. She got to do all the things I couldn't, and she got away with it.

"I didn't think Charli Rae Warren was afraid of anything."

"Now you're just playing me."

Scarlet grinned, and I got out of the car. She was right about the gate, not so much me. The gate was latched and had a heavy chain wrapped around it several times that I assumed was there to keep the goats in. I eyed the one closest to the gate.

It bleated in my direction and caused three more goats with large horns on their heads to walk toward me.

Fuzz buckets.

I glanced back at Scarlet and she shooed me forward. Her grin had grown. I took a deep breath and immediately regretted it. Goats stink almost as bad as skunks. I pushed the gate open and more goats started bleating. Across the field, I could see several begin to run in my direction, and I waved Scarlet through. She crept at the speed of a five-year-old riding a bicycle without training wheels for the first time.

Something tugged my T-shirt, and I looked down and found a goat chewing on my clothes. I yanked my shirt out of its mouth, but I was too late. A piece of pink material disappeared between smacking lips, and I watched as it gnawed on it like a little kid chewing bubble gum. I wouldn't be surprised if it blew a bubble and popped it in my face. It had a superior look in its eyes like it'd gotten one over on me. I glance down at my shirt and found a hole the size of the palm of my hand in the middle just below the advertisement, *Killer Classics at the Book Barn Princess*. In a matter of seconds, my shirt had been transformed into a rag.

Scarlet made it through the gate, and I closed it and wrapped the chain around the posts. Then I ran for the car and got inside before another goat decided my clothing looked like a meal.

"You should probably put my sweater on," Scarlet said.

"Why, because I don't want Mrs. Greer to know that her goats attacked me?"

"No, because I just realized your shirt is entirely inappropriate."

I looked down at the wording. "Oh yeah, you're right."

I pulled on Scarlet's fuzzy sweater that she kept in the car for when she opened the top late at night. During the heat of the day, the temperature was miserable, and I really hoped Mrs. Greer had air-conditioning. Scarlet drove up the driveway with a herd of goats following the car.

"They don't eat meat, do they?" I asked.

"They will try anything, even things that aren't good for them. They like to shop around."

"So that stupid goat just decided *hey, I want that shirt?*"

"Chances are it said *I wonder what shirt tastes like; it looks like a patch of flowers.* I'm sure it spit it out after you ran away."

"I didn't *run away.* I ran to the car because we're in a hurry."

"Un-huh."

By the time we reached the house the entire herd was following her car like it was a feed truck. Scarlet parked, and we approached the house together. Safety in numbers as far as I was concerned.

It was a traditional ranch with a few bushes around it that had been picked clean of leaves. The red brick on the front of the house had numerous white arcs from the sprinklers hitting it and mineral deposits changing the color of the brick from red to white. It almost looked like someone had painted rows of leaping white rainbows across the lower portion of the side of the house. It wasn't like Greta was watering the flowerbeds, I knew from experience the sprinklers were there to water the foundation and keep it from cracking in the dry Texas heat.

White square columns supported the porch that ran the length of the house. There were two white rockers separated by an antique painted milk can in front of a bay window that gave the mid-fifties home a cozy appearance. I could picture an older couple enjoying the sunsets together as they talked about their day. It made for a very peaceful setting.

Provided the goats didn't run up to gnaw the clothes off their bodies.

I knocked on the front door. A dog barked from within, and we waited for Greta to answer the door. We heard her yell at the dog to be quiet, and then the deadbolt tumbled on the front door. The dog barked at us from behind the glass storm door.

"Hush!" she told the scraggly white mop of a dog.

Dressed in navy-blue, polyester pants and a wrinkled floral blouse, Greta showed every one of her sixty-some years. Perhaps even more. She had been a pretty woman once. Her unruly curls of platinum blond didn't look like they'd had a professional set in a long time. Her skin appeared jaundiced, and her light gray eyes were glassy and bloodshot, a telltale sign of a serious drinking problem. Greta opened the door and had to hold her little dog back with her foot as the odor of alcohol made its way out onto the porch. "Can I help you?" she asked in a surprisingly sober voice.

Scarlet introduced us and offered the pot of flowers we'd stopped to pick up along the way. "We're from the Mystery Moms, a book club at the Book Barn Princess that Maddie had just joined."

Greta blinked. "I didn't know Maddie liked to read." Her brows drew together as if she was trying to remember Maddie's love of reading or if she'd ever seen Maddie hold a book in her hands. I was pretty sure she hadn't.

"To be honest Mrs. Greer," I said, "this week was Maddie's first meeting, but we felt the need to offer you our condolences."

Greta took the plant and smelled the hydrangeas then said, "Thank you." Her eyes were surprisingly dry for a woman who had just lost her only daughter. Then she set the flowers down on the porch.

They wouldn't last two minutes with her herd of goats.

"Maddie was a mystery to me. We never really connected. It's kind of ironic that she would be a mystery to her mom and join a group called the Mystery Moms." She stood back, picked up her dog who growled in my direction, and motioned for us to come in.

I was more than happy to go inside since the goats had made their way to the front flowerbed and were circling around like vultures after carrion. They were even pushing at each other and knocking their heads together. I wasn't going to let them get Scarlet's sweater. The front entry, which consisted of a three-foot block of tile at the front door, expanded out into brown shag carpeting of the living room. Scarlet's nose scrunched as she recognized the effects of a several pack a day smoker.

Her sweater was doomed no matter what I did.

The living room furniture was old with a yellow tint to the light tan upholstery from the amount of tar in the air. The coffee table was full of mail and magazines, and I couldn't help but wonder if they were *too contaminated* for Dallas Dover to take at his recycling facility. They would be if it was my business.

From the looks of it, Greta liked magazines about home improvement and raising goats. I'd never realized there were so many magazines about goats. Apparently, we needed to increase the amount of goat magazines we kept in stock at the Book Barn.

Scarlet and I sat on the couch while Greta took a seat in a wingback chair and put her feet on the ottoman. She took a drink from the tumbler sitting on the table that looked suspiciously like whiskey on the rocks, and not sweet tea. I suspected the living room may be the only clean room in the house—just to keep up appearances.

"I appreciate you coming by. I'm not sure what to think about the whole thing. Part of me thinks she's better off; the other part of me thinks she was too young to die."

I wondered what kind of mom would actually verbalize those horrible thoughts.

"Have the police said how she died?" Scarlet asked. I couldn't believe she got straight to the point.

"She died quickly. Someone shot her and threw her body into the water tank." Greta shook her head. "Why would anyone do that? Why wouldn't they just leave her be on the roof?"

That explained the search for Sugar's gun. The queasiness I'd experienced while sitting on her kitchen floor debating whether or not to steal it returned. Maddie hadn't accidentally locked herself in the tank and drowned. She'd been shot, and if Mateo found Sugar's gun...

I should have walked in that house, unlocked the safe and taken the gun.

"There's no telling what was in the killer's mind. When was the last time you saw Maddie?" Scarlet asked.

"She hadn't been home in almost a week."

We waited for Greta to continue. The ice in her drink tinkled against the glass as she took another sip. "I still can't believe Dean killed her. Every time I saw him he treated her with respect. What would make a man change like that?"

I didn't have an answer for Greta because I didn't think Dean killed Maddie any more than Sugar did. I tried to refocus Greta's attention on something that would help us find the real killer. "Who was Maddie seeing?"

Greta shook her head and petted the little dog now nestled on her lap. "I have no idea. Maddie always kept that information to herself. But her manager at the hotel seems to believe she was seeing Dean. What's to become of Scotty?"

"Where is Scotty?" I asked.

"Tiny wanted to bring him home, but I couldn't take care of him while Tiny was looking for a job. Even I know that. Dean's done a good job raising the boy without Maddie up until now..." Greta took another drink of whiskey and relit a cigarette that had burned halfway down in her ashtray. As an afterthought, she offered one to us. Scarlet and I politely declined.

"You make it sound like Maddie didn't have much to do with Scotty." I waited for Greta to defend Maddie. She did the opposite.

"That girl hasn't had anything to do with her son since he was six months old and she walked out on Dean."

"Didn't they share custody?" asked Scarlet.

Greta shook her head. "Legally, yes. In reality, no. But I think Dean and his girlfriend were trying to change that. They seemed like they were trying to help Maddie become a better parent the past couple months." She shook her head. "You never know about people."

"Will Scotty be put in foster care?"

Greta looked up at me like I'd slapped her in the face. "We would never let him go there. Dean's parents have him for now."

Scarlet turned the conversation back to Maddie's brother. "I thought Tiny had a job," she said.

"He did. He was working at the recycling plant, but he got laid off last week. Not enough recycling business." The cigarette burned down between Greta's fingers, and she didn't flinch. The red embers were growing, and I could have sworn I smelled burning flesh.

I looked at Scarlet. Her eyes were nearly bugging out of her head.

"Ah, Greta, your cigarette..."

Greta's dog jumped up and started barking at her cigarette.

Greta lifted her hand and looked at the cigarette burning into her. As if it didn't bother her in the least. She petted her dog with her free hand and flicked the tip of the cigarette off into the ashtray before stubbing it out. Then she rested her arm across the arm of the chair and didn't look at the blackened skin between her fingers again. I was pretty sure I was feeling the effects of that burn more than she was.

We left the house after Greta received a call from Tiny. He was the last person I wanted to run into. As we exited the front door, we saw what was left of our gift. The flower pot was knocked over, and dirt was scattered across the porch. I didn't see a flower in sight. Scarlet began talking to the goats like they were precious puppies, which only seemed to encourage their attention as we fought our way to the car.

I shooed one away that wanted to taste Scarlet's sweater. "They are not pets," I told her. "Stop encouraging them."

"Sure, they are. They're no different than Princess."

"Princess doesn't eat my clothes."

"No, Princess eats your books."

She had me there. Princess liked to eat some of the older books that came into the store. We'd never figured out why she chose some, and not others, but the ones she did decide to snack on and tear up, we used for our book art classes.

"Should we call someone about her hand?" I asked.

"I think her dog is the best caregiver she could ask for."

We got in the car, and I had to push one persistent goat back by his head. I kept waiting for it to bite me, but it never did. The door closed, and they immediately got out of the way of the car as Scarlet backed out of the driveway and onto the gravel drive. When she stopped at the gate for me to open it, I was more than willing to let her have the honors.

"If you'd like for me to drive, I can."

Scarlet laughed. "You're afraid of being alone with a few goats."

"I'm not afraid. I just can't read them."

"That's the same thing."

I refused to argue such a trivial point. "Fine. I'll get the gate." I took off her sweater and got out of the car. The goats were immediately on me. Nudging my hands and nibbling at my shoelaces. I should have worn my boots.

I opened the gate, and Scarlet drove through. I said goodbye to the goats, and one moaned. It stuck out its nasty black tongue and made this horrible belching sound as I got in the car.

"Remind me to never eat hydrangeas."

Chapter 10

The bookstore was dead. It was Saturday night, and I was wasting away with nothing to do. Our used book stock was incredibly low, and normally on weekends we'd get an influx of people wanting to sell their books. Not this weekend though. My reputation for being a book burner was hurting the store's profits, and there was nothing I could do about it.

I picked up my copy of *Woman Scorned* and began reading it. I wanted to have it finished before our next meeting, and I wanted find the part that Scarlet had said was too close to real life for comfort.

I wasn't sure how more uncomfortable things could get than having an author predict how one of our residents would be killed, until I read the excerpt about my mama's sign cracking the killer on the head. Another fact just too close for comfort. In the book, Sugar or Candy, ran out of the town tavern in pursuit of her cheating boyfriend. The bar's sign fell and hit her on the head. The concussion she suffered then changed her personality and Candy became maniacal—devious in ways Sugar could never be.

The problem with the scene was the lore behind the sign. The sign in the book didn't protect its patrons the way some say the sign leading to my apartment protected me. The wrought iron sign swinging above the alleyway to my apartment had my mom's name on it. *Eve's Gate* was said to be a guardian angel watching over me.

I wasn't sure where the real-life rumor started about my mom's sign, but it was a fact that the sign had fallen on several people—most of whom were up to no good—from Cade trying to get to second base in high school, to a killer trying to stop me from figuring out his crime.

Up until that moment when I read it in print, I found the thought of my mom watching over me via her sign like a gift. Nathan Daniels's book, however, portrayed the sign as an evil entity turning the innocent into the deranged. I didn't like the comparison or anyone making the link between fiction in print and the reality that was my life. Nathan Daniels's book made a comforting aspect of my life sound evil. My mama's sign wasn't evil. Yet again, I couldn't deny the disturbing similarities.

The front doors opened, and the bell rang. I immediately took my feet off the counter and closed the book. Dallas Dover walked in the store looking as lost as ever. He wore the same cowboy hat he'd on the first time I met him at his recycling plant. His fancy belt with the shiny belt buckle was wrapped around his waist, and his leather gloves were sticking out of his back pocket. I was beginning to think he never went anywhere without those gloves.

"Dallas, welcome to the Book Barn Princess," I said with a smile. It was nice to see something positive come out of my crime. Dallas had been running the recycling plant for eight months, and I'd never seen him in our store until that moment. Maybe something good did come from something bad.

Dallas smiled, and when he did, it changed his appearance. He wasn't a bad-looking guy, just not one that would normally catch my attention, but when he grinned he was full of a boyish charm I found appealing. I got the impression that he recognized that charm and knew how to use it too. He sauntered toward the register. "Just the woman I was looking for," he said.

"Oh?"

"I was wondering if you had that book that everyone's talking about. *Scorned Woman* or something?"

I pulled my copy out from under the counter. "*Woman Scorned?*"

"That's it. Do you have any more copies?"

"I gotta warn you. After what happened at the hotel, it's kind of creepy." He rubbed his beard. "And yet, you're reading it."

He had me there. But I was reading it because I wanted to see how so-called art had turned into life. "I am. Let's go back and check. If I've got any back there, it's only one or two copies."

We made our way to the mystery section and sure enough, we had one copy left. As I rang it up, Dallas asked, "Did you know Maddie?"

"Not well, no. She came to a book club meeting last week with Sugar. But that's the first time I'd talked to her."

"She and Sugar were friends?"

I winced. I didn't want to talk about Sugar. Not only did she work for us, but she was a dear friend in quite a pickle. A life and death pickle. "I'm sorry, Dallas. I'd really rather not talk about it."

Dallas didn't hesitate. "Of course. I didn't mean to pry. I…I actually didn't come by to buy the book."

"You didn't?"

Dallas gave me that boyish grin again as he tipped his head. "I came to ask if I could take you to dinner."

"Dinner?" My vocabulary seemed to have gone on vacation.

"You know the last meal of the day that most people eat right about now?"

I grinned. "Obviously, you didn't come in to buy a dictionary."

Dallas winked, and I could have sworn he was about to say, *alright, alright, alright*, but I was wrong. "No, ma'am. Something else entirely."

I let him down easy. "I'm sorry. I have to work."

Dallas looked around the store. "Are you here by yourself? That doesn't seem very safe."

"We are a small operation. Not a lot of cash flow and not a lot of high-end merchandise to interest a thief."

No sooner had the words left my mouth, then the doors swished open, and Tiny stomped into the Barn. Unlike Dallas, Tiny knew exactly where he was going. Dressed in a white shirt and overalls, he looked the part of an angry farmer-biker. Lucky for me, he embraced the more urban persona, otherwise the meaty hand he raised with abrasions all over his knuckles would have had a pitch fork in its grasp. Instead it was just an index finger calling me out. From my angle, Tiny's fist looked like one of those trick photography images I'd seen on the internet when a giant pinched a mere mortal's head between his thumb and index finger. Dallas's head was about to be smushed like a grape.

"You!" Tiny yelled. "What are you doing going out to my mama's house?"

Staring down an angry Tiny made me glad I had a counter and a witness between him and me. I prayed his arms weren't long enough to snatch me out from behind the counter.

"I just went out to offer my condolences to your mom. That's it. That's all I was doing."

Tiny reached the counter, but Dallas stayed between us. I was thankful for that. Tiny looked down at him like he could swat him away like a fly. I didn't think Dallas would be that easy, but he definitely wasn't going to be able to go toe to toe the way Mateo had.

Tiny's gaze returned to me, and I could have sworn there was pure evil lurking in his soul, just dying to get out. "Why?" he demanded. "You weren't friends with Maddie."

That was true, but I went with the line Scarlet and I had used at his mom's house. "She was a new member of our Mystery Moms Book Club. We wanted to offer our—"

Tiny's response was less than pleasant. In the middle of it was an accusation that I was just trying to get Sugar off the hook for killing his sister. Spittle hit Dallas's face. He flinched but stood his ground between me and the angry man that stood head and shoulders above the two of us. I thought of David and Goliath. Except I'd always dreamed I was David, and I certainly wasn't acting like him while hiding behind a customer and the register.

I threw back my shoulders and came around the counter. I approached Tiny with the backbone my mama gave me. "Tiny, I'm sorry for your loss. I know you're hurting in ways no one else can imagine. We meant no harm."

Tiny stared at me. His nose flared and stayed flared as he exhaled. A rumble from deep within his gut reverberated through his belly like a bass drum. "My sister left me a voicemail telling me she got in a fight with Sugar. It was the very last time she called me." His voice quivered. "I missed that call." Then he turned and walked out the door without another word. He was like a man whose emotions were ready to erupt at any given moment. I didn't know if he was like that before Maddie disappeared, but every time I'd seen him since, his temper had been volatile.

"That wasn't smart, Charli," Dallas said.

I looked at him and felt the adrenaline seeping out of my system and tingling in my fingers. "I've never been accused of making smart decisions."

Dallas got a kick out of that. He laughed, the sound a bit high for a man, yet manly because of his lack of fear to share it. "A woman after my heart."

"Ahh, you should never give your heart away so quickly. That's dangerous."

Dallas's expression turned serious. "I mean it, though, Charli. Tiny's not a man to mess with."

Dallas stared at me, and I could tell he wanted to say more but wasn't sure how much he could say until he finally just blurted it out. "He abused his sister, that's why I laid him off."

That was the last thing I expected. "Maddie?"

Dallas rubbed his hand across his jaw. "I shouldn't be saying anything, but you gotta be careful around him. His temper is more explosive than a stick of dynamite."

The doors swished open again, and we both turned around expecting Tiny to be back, but it was Cade. He looked tired and rumpled like his day had been way too long. I was feeling the same way.

"Tiny didn't do anything, did he?" Cade asked.

"No. Did you expect him to?" I hoped Cade's response would be something like, *Tiny would never hit you. He's a pie thrower, not a guy who would punch a woman.* Even if he had hit his sister and looked like he was going to remove my head and put it on a spike.

"I wasn't sure what to expect." Cade brushed his hand across his scalp. "Thank you, Dallas."

"For what?"

"For keeping Princess safe."

Dallas laughed but it wasn't full of humor like it had been. "I think you got things all wrong, Mayor. Charli is the one who handled Tiny. Not me."

Cade looked like he didn't believe him, and Dallas patted him on the shoulder. "You've got a lot to learn about this woman. I'll see you later, Charli."

We watched him leave, and Cade asked, "Am I missing something?"

Princess came out from behind the counter and snorted before she headed out her pet door in the back of the barn. Cade watched her leave.

"She thinks that was a rhetorical question."

I bit my lip and tried not to laugh. Cade was giving Princess more credit than most people would even dream of doing. Yet I tended to agree with him, and it was nice to be on the same page with someone for once.

"I just got the results of the search warrant they served at the hotel where Maddie was staying."

That wiped my smile away. "What'd it say?"

"They found blond hair and a fingernail that matches Sugar's in Maddie's room."

"I thought it took a while for DNA—"

"The shade of blond is the same shade that Scarlet uses on Sugar's hair, and the nail matches the manicure Sugar had done last week."

"But that doesn't mean—"

"Sugar admitted to getting in a fight with Maddie the night she disappeared. The DNA will come back as hers."

"Oh."

"Yeah." Cade looked around for something to do or something to talk about as the bad news sunk in.

"Do you want a glass of tea?" I asked.

"I could use a whiskey."

I gave him a sad smile. "Sorry, we're all out."

"Then I'll take that tea."

We walked back to the tearoom, and I opened the sliding stall door to where his election supplies were stored.

"I suppose I should recycle this stuff..." Cade's voice drifted off like a wistful dream lost forever.

"Don't say that."

"Charli—"

I shut him down before he could argue. "This has always been your dream, and everyone who knows you believes in you."

"I got hate mail today," he confessed.

It was the last thing I expected. "What?"

Cade moved into the tearoom and got the tea out of the refrigerator. I pulled down two glasses and we sat down at the only table without *Calloway for Senate* paraphernalia covering the surface.

"My political party's not sure they want me as their candidate, and I got a stack of hate mail big enough that the post office said they would have to make a special delivery."

"How do you know it's all hate mail if you haven't read it?"

Cade took a long drink of tea and set his glass on the table. "Even if it was fan mail, which I seriously doubt, I'm going to have my hands full defending Sugar and Dean. It's a capital case."

I did not want to think about what that meant for my friends. "How did the search warrant go?"

"They got Sugar's gun."

I suddenly felt the pressure of the world on my chest. "Is it the murder weapon?"

"We're still waiting on the autopsy report. The ME was at a conference but was due back this afternoon. He should have it to Mateo tomorrow."

"No matter what the report says, you know they didn't do it."

"Their statements sound like they did."

"How so?"

Cade looked down at his tea. He looked defeated. It was the last expression I'd want to see on my attorney's face if I was facing the death penalty. "I can't discuss that with you, Charli."

"Why not? You've told me about the other stuff?"

"I told you about the things that are public record. If I tell you about their statements, nothing will protect Sugar and Dean from you having to testify about the content of our discussion. My privilege won't extend to you in their case. It only extends to you in your burning charges."

I was glad he didn't say book burning. It sounded much better that way.

Princess walked into the tearoom with her boyfriend on her tail. Cade froze. He hadn't been at the bookstore the day we got skunked.

"No, Princess." I pointed back at the way she'd waddled in. My frustration was evident in my voice. I'd had it up to my eyebrows with things going south.

Princess ignored my correction, stood up on her hind legs, and waved her front paws at me like a dog begging for dinner. Her boyfriend did the same. Any other day, it would have been cute. Adorable even. Tonight, I was prepared to send her to bed with no dinner.

"No. You take that young man outside, and you leave him outside. He is not allowed in any more buildings."

Princess huffed and dropped down on all fours. The skunk sniffed and then followed, his tail hung low and tight against his body.

"I've never seen you be that mean to Princess before."

"And you've never had a teenage girl with a troublemaker for her first boyfriend."

Cade brought up the topic I thought he'd forgotten about. "You almost got caught at Dean and Sugar's place."

"But I didn't." I reached over and squeezed his hand. "Thank you for coming to my rescue."

Cade held my hand across the table. "Can you keep your nose out of any more trouble? I'd like to focus on Dean and Sugar right now. As it is, I'm probably going to be bringing in a team to help me prepare their case. The last thing I need to add to my plate is defending you against charges for hindering a murder investigation."

I pulled my hand away and laughed. "Mateo wouldn't arrest me for trying to help my friends."

Cade stood up but didn't join in my good humor. "He would if I reported you."

My mouth fell open as he turned and walked out the door. Cade had gone to the other side. Drat the man.

Chapter 11

My conversation with Cade kept playing over and over in my head. I hadn't convinced him to hold on to his political dreams, yet he'd sounded more like a prosecutor than my defense attorney. In the past, he'd left everyone else behind in pursuit of his goals. Today he was a different man being led by outside forces.

I had one customer the rest of the night, and I was beginning to worry about the Book Barn's future. I called my cousin Jamal as I locked up the store and asked if he'd seen any downward drop in the use of our Book Seekers app that he'd launched a while back.

"Are you stirring up trouble again?" he asked.

"What makes you say that?"

"You tend to call when there's trouble."

"I do not."

"Do too."

"You know you sound like you're in grade school," I taunted.

"If I do, so do you."

"I do not."

"Do too."

I was getting nowhere. My cousin was like a brother to me. Except he got his daddy's freakishly tall genes, superior mathematical mind which made up for his lack of athletic ability. I'd like to think I was a little on the tall side, athletic, and possessed half a brain that was enough to keep me alive.

But even that was questionable sometimes.

"I just need to know the app isn't spiraling into a black hole of the unknown when it comes to book apps. Otherwise the Barn may be in trouble."

"Does this have anything to do with you burning books?"

"You know about that?"

"The whole country knows about that. Change that to the whole world. Maybe the universe. I hear Klingons are ordering books off Amazon instead of beaming down to Hazel Rock for the latest bestseller."

"You're not very funny."

"Mom seems to think so."

"She gave birth to you. She's supposed to laugh at your bad jokes." My aunt Violet had finished raising me after I ran away from home at seventeen. She was my mom's twin, but not a lot like her, other than having a heart bigger than the state of Texas. Jamal and I had been raised like siblings.

"The app is fine. We had a small down-tick the day the story broke about the book burning, but it's leveled out again. I'm launching a new version this summer, so that will drive it upward again." Jamal started talking algorithms and computer mumbo jumbo and lost me.

The Book Seekers app was his baby, not mine. I did what he told me to do on the computer and benefited with the profits. If we hadn't been cousins, another bookstore would be benefitting from his genius instead of the Barn. We talked for a bit longer as I got ready for bed. He told me his mom was doing great, and he thought she had a boyfriend she wasn't talking about yet. It was a little good news in the midst of a rough week in Hazel Rock. Jamal said he'd come to visit soon to discuss the new app, and we ended the conversation.

I went around the outside of the Barn after I set the alarm and locked the door. Most of the time, I used the hidden door between the loft and my apartment, but tonight I needed the fresh air. I also wanted to see my mom's sign and get the bad vibes out of my head about its ability to make people evil. I didn't believe spirits or circumstances of life that involved the perfect timing of a sign falling on someone's head changed a person's soul.

I walked through the gate and looked up at the lone light bulb with a metal hood illuminating the wrought iron scrolls of *Eve's Gate*. That sign and the gate below had marked the entrance to my private life since I was eight years old. Very few people were invited to enter.

The man sitting on the steps, however, had a standing invitation. He just hadn't accepted it in a while.

"Fancy meeting you here," I said as jumped up and touched my mom's sign. It creaked in response as it swung back and forth.

"That's how you get it to fall on so many heads, isn't it?"

Even though he was cloaked almost entirely in darkness, I could see Mateo's smile. It was the first one I'd seen all week that didn't hold any stress on it. It was relaxed and comfortable, just the way I liked it. I walked up and kissed him. It'd been too long since the two of us had had a moment alone.

"Is this part of the lure?" he asked.

"What lure?"

"You know, loosen the sign, soften the prey, and lead him to his doom under your mom's sign?"

"That only happened once."

"Is that all?" He nuzzled my neck, and I moaned.

"I brought you dessert."

I pulled back and looked at him. "Really?"

"That little white bag on your steps has coconut tres leches cake inside."

"Mmmmm. That sounds wonderful. Where did you get it?"

"I made it."

"The sheriff of Coleman County bakes?"

"Shhhh, it'll be our secret."

"And if I decide to share that information with the local paper?"

"You'll never get another one."

"I think I'm going to like this secret."

"You have no idea how much you're going to like it." Mateo's lips found mine just as a woman yelled from the courtyard, "Charli, is that you?"

Mateo groaned and stepped back, his hands lingering on my waist just a bit too long as Liza Twaine's heels came to a stop at the gate. "Am I interrupting something?" she asked.

Only a fool would ask such a ridiculous question.

Mateo saved her from my wrath. "I just brought Charli some dessert, but I was leaving."

"You're leaving?" I asked.

"Oh, good." Liza came through the gate.

Mateo's upper lip quirked with humor. "Good to see you too, Liza."

Mine raised with distaste as he walked out of the gate. "What do you want Liza?"

The sign squeaked, and Mateo looked up at it and smiled. I could have sworn he tipped his head in greeting, but that would be silly. Still, it made me feel warm and fuzzy that he would pay homage to my mom.

Liza looked at Mateo as if she was trying to figure something out. "Is there really something going on between you two? Cause I thought he was just messing with me in the Barn the other day."

I ignored her question and turned toward my steps. "You came here for a reason?"

Her heels clip-clopped behind me on the brick pavers. I picked up my little white bag and opened it just enough to smell the cake inside. The scent was pure heaven, and my stomach growled. I closed the bag unwilling to share if Liza chose to follow me inside my apartment, which she did.

Once inside Liza pulled a stack of paper from her purse. She had on a purple pantsuit that displayed the wrinkles of a long day at work and a matching purse and shoes. Her makeup needed to be refreshed, and her hair had lost its curl, yet she didn't seem to care. Which was completely out of character. That alone sparked my interest.

"I have a copy of the autopsy report."

"Whose autopsy report?"

Liza rolled her eyes. "There's only one autopsy report we've all been waiting for." She waved the papers in my face, and I leaned back. "Maddie's report."

I'd never seen an autopsy report. I'd heard about them and had been told about some of the details, but seeing one in person was a completely different animal. Especially if it was for someone I knew.

"I don't want to read that. Just tell me what it says."

Liza heaved a sigh, grabbed my hand, and pulled me over to counter. She slapped the papers on the surface and pushed me onto the bar stool.

I glared at her.

"This information is key to this case."

"Mateo didn't say anything about having the report."

"That's because he doesn't have it yet."

"What do you mean, he doesn't have it?"

"Would you read the stupid report?" Liza poked the paper like it was a man's chest.

"How did you get this?" When Liza ignored my question, I asked, "Did you steal it? Did you break into the Medical Examiner's office the same way you broke into Scarlet's trailer?"

Liza's index finger pounded on the papers in front of me.

"If you don't tell me how you got it, I'm going to call Mateo right now." I pulled my cell phone out of my back pocket. Liza tried to grab for my phone, but I held it back out of her reach.

"Fine. I have a person on the inside, alright?"

She wasn't getting off that easily. "Who?"

"If I told you who, you'd get them fired."

"Darn tootin'."

"And I'd be out of a source."

"What they're doing is illegal!" I insisted.

"Only in the sense that I get it a few hours before everyone else."

"With absolutely nothing redacted," I pointed out. There wasn't a black Sharpie mark on any of the pages. "Please tell me there are no pictures."

Liza was growing impatient. "What kind of mystery mom are you?"

"The Mystery Moms are a book club!"

"Whatever. Just read the stupid report."

"You have more in common with Nathan Daniels's character Eliza Blain than you think," I muttered as I picked up the report and saw the decedent's name, Maddie MacAlister, scrawled across the top with a case file number and the date. In the center of the page were the bold words MANNER OF DEATH. Handwritten next to it: Homicide.

Fuzz buckets. I had truly hoped Maddie had been drunk and went for a swim, played Russian roulette…something other than homicide. People did stupid things when under the influence of alcohol, and Maddie had definitely been under the influence.

I skimmed through several pages of Maddie's organs being measured and weighed then looked at Liza. "I really don't need all these details. Besides I don't understand most of it."

"Go down to page thirty-one."

I flipped to the page that had a diagram of a female body. On the diagram there were Xs on her left shoulder and left cheekbone. It then described the injuries to these areas. Her shoulder had a bullet wound entry with no exit. The bullet had fractured her clavicle bone and ricocheted into her left lung where the round was recovered.

"They got the bullet!" A nervous giggle escaped from somewhere inside me. It was completely inappropriate, and from the look on Liza's face, even she thought my reaction was uncalled for.

"Don't you see? They can clear Sugar of murder! I knew she wouldn't shoot Maddie."

"Keep reading."

I read on. Maddie also had a fractured infraorbital foramen and zygoma. I looked at the diagram to see what the heck they were talking about, and it was the cheekbone underneath her left eye. "It says her cheek was shattered due to blunt force trauma."

"Yes, and Sugar got in a fight with Maddie the night she died."

I didn't know how Liza found out about the fight, and I didn't care. All I knew was that Sugar didn't kill Maddie.

"Sugar would have broken her hand if she'd hit Maddie like that. She wouldn't have just lost a fingernail!"

"A fingernail?"

Realizing I'd just released information that Cade had given me, I waved Liza off. "I just mean, Sugar would have done some serious damage to her hand."

Liza nodded. "Read the conclusion."

I continued through the narrative and learned that the decedent would have been unable to swim for very long due to a collapsed lung and loss of blood. Maddie's death was ruled a homicide.

Which didn't mean it was premeditated murder, just that someone had caused her death, and it wasn't Maddie.

Nor did I believe it was Sugar or Dean. It would have taken two people to get Maddie in that tank unless someone forced her to go in at gunpoint.

But it was the last line of the report that made up for me having to invite Liza into my apartment: Collected and released to Coleman County Sheriff's Department: .40 cal slug.

"Does Mateo have the round that killed Maddie?"

Liza shook her head. "It's in the ME's evidence locker waiting to be picked up."

"When will Mateo get this report?"

"Tomorrow morning after it's been typed up."

"What about Cade?"

Liza smiled like the Cheshire cat. It was not pretty. "Well, that depends."

I proceeded with caution. "On what?"

"On when you plan on calling him and telling him to get his butt over here for an interview."

There was always a cost to a good deed. I was willing to give up my integrity for Sugar and Dean. The question remained…was Cade?

I glared at Liza and pulled up Cade's number on the address book of my phone. He answered on the first ring. "What's wrong?"

"Nothing's wrong."

"Then why are you calling."

"Can't I call you just to chat?"

Cade's voice was loaded with sarcasm. "I hardly think the princess I know would want to 'chat' after I threatened to turn her in on hindering charges if she meddled in Sugar and Dean's case."

Liza became impatient and began rolling her hand forward in the air trying to make me get to the point.

I bit my cheek to keep from cussing. "That was uncalled for."

Cade sighed on the other end of the phone. "What do you need, Princess?"

"Could you come over?" I asked.

"You're calling me to come over to your place at ten fifteen at night?" His voice was laced with disbelief, and I immediately understood where his mind went.

"That's not what I'm calling for Cade Calloway."

"What?" His tone was as innocent as a little boy getting caught putting a frog in his sister's bed.

"Would you just get over here?"

"Princess, I have to get up early in the morning."

"You're darn right you do. You have work that is waiting for you."

"What's that supposed to mean?" he asked.

"I'm tired of going around in circles with you, Cade. Just get over here." I hung up the phone before he could argue further.

Liza's grin was back. "Was the mayor suggesting something naughty?"

I rolled my eyes and stood up to make sure she knew I meant business. "He thought *I* was suggesting something naughty, thanks to you!" I leaned over her and let her know just how unhappy I was. "And if you breathe a word of that outside this room, I will make sure you regret it Liza Twaine."

"Fine. There's no reason to get your panties in a bunch."

My panties felt like they'd been in a bunch for too long, but I saw comfort in my future once Sugar and Dean were cleared. Their seventy-two-hour hold was about to end early.

Liza asked to use my restroom, and I text Mateo while she was inside.

A copy of the autopsy report has been leaked.

Are you telling me Liza has a copy of the report before me?

I'm telling you that it proves Sugar and Dean are innocent. She's getting ready to rake someone through the coals. Cade's on his way over here.

Does he know?

He doesn't have a clue.

Thank you, Charli.

I sent him a kissy face emoji and got a thumbs-up in return. What the heck did that mean?

I grabbed the white paper bag with my dessert and looked inside. A clear Tupperware container with two pieces of cake looked back at me. Surely, he'd meant to share it with me. The man was just busy and since he was going to be busy, I had a piece for dessert and a piece for breakfast. I could live with that.

I listened for Liza in the bathroom but didn't hear anything, so I grabbed a fork and opened the container. Inside I found whipped cream with coconut sprinkled across the top. The side of the cake showed two moist layers with whipped cream between them. My mouth began to water. I took a bite and moaned. Mateo's cake was incredible. It gave the appearance of being light, but it was dense with sugary goodness I could get lost in.

I heard Liza turn on the sink, and I took one last bite before I quickly put it in the refrigerator. I was not sharing my cake with a woman I didn't like. Nope. It wasn't going to happen. If she'd been Scarlet...maybe. But Scarlet didn't eat sugary foods. Mateo didn't either, which made the fact that he'd baked me a cake that much more special.

I was going to remember the flavor of his cake, and that he shared a part of himself with me that no one else knew about...and I was going to forget all about his thumbs-up response to my kisses.

Chapter 12

Two hours and twenty minutes later, Cade was at my door. I rubbed the sleep out of my eyes and answered it. Liza's smile, although tired and worn couldn't have gotten any bigger. Until Mateo stepped into the doorway behind him.

She looked at me with an outraged gleam in her eyes. "Touché."

"You didn't really think I could go behind Mateo's back, did you? He doesn't want to hold Sugar and Dean any more than the rest of us want him to if they're not guilty."

Liza grabbed the report on the counter and shoved it in her purse. "Is that what took you so long to get here, Mayor?"

"I had some business with the sheriff I needed to handle first."

Liza glanced at Mateo. I got the distinct impression she was waiting for him to make a move with his handcuffs. "Oh?" she said.

"It seems the autopsy report is complete, and there's new evidence in the case. Mateo has his crime scene technicians working overtime, and I'm hoping to get their reports soon."

A bit of panic crossed through Liza's eyes. Word was bound to get out that the case was moving and moving fast. Currently, she wasn't the only one with the scoop, and she'd missed the ten o'clock news, but Liza was anything but a quitter. She was resourceful and intuitive. She knew how to make a story out of nothing, and she knew a good story when she saw one. "I'd still like to interview you, Mayor, if you have time."

Mateo looked at his watch. "It's late, Liza. Surely, your interview can wait until tomorrow?"

"Actually, I have some questions for Liza." Cade stepped in, and Mateo stayed at the door.

"Me? What kind of questions could you possibly have for me?"

Cade grinned. I coughed, and Liza glared.

"Sheriff, could you wait for us outside for just a moment?" Cade asked.

Mateo's eyes narrowed ever so slightly, and I realized Cade was going rogue. Whatever they'd discussed, this was not part of the plan.

"I'll be right outside if you need me," Mateo said.

"I'll join—"

"I need you to stay with us, Princess. If you don't mind?"

I shrugged, and Mateo walked out the door, closing it behind him.

"Why don't we have a seat?" Cade walked Liza to my couch where she and I had nearly dozed off waiting for them to arrive. This time Liza wasn't even close to falling asleep. She sat on the edge of the couch looking like she was ready to sprint for the door at any given moment. Except facing Mateo was even less appealing to her. I sat down in my glider that had been around since the days my mom rocked me to sleep and watched Cade go to work on Liza. He slowly pulled out his phone and opened it to a page of notes. "When did you get back from Dallas?"

Liza looked at me like I had a clue what Cade was fishing for. I shrugged. "About four o'clock."

He jotted down the time. "Are Reba Sue and Betty still there?"

Uh-oh. He knew about the mystery moms' meddling. Which meant Mateo knew as well.

Liza nodded.

"Did you meet with the author Nathan Daniels while you were there?"

Liza nodded again.

"Did you interview him in reference to the murder of Maddie MacAlister?"

This time Liza didn't nod her head. She stared at him with the wheels spinning around in her brain. I could see it just as well as if the wheels were on the outside of her face.

"Did you interview Nathan Daniels regarding Maddie's death?" Cade repeated.

"Yes, I did," Liza confessed.

Cade typed something into his phone. "Did you have your photographer present?"

Liza paused. She didn't want to answer the question, and bit off her answer. "No."

"No?"

"I just told you no. No means no, doesn't it?"

"Of course, it does." Cade's voice was deceptively soothing. "Did you record the interview on your phone?"

I swore if Liza didn't bite off her own tongue, it would be a miracle.

"I had Reba Sue record it using my phone."

"I see." Cade tapped his finger against his pant leg. "And do you have your phone with you now?"

"Yes, of course," Liza admitted, but she made no move to take her phone from her purse.

Cade looked her directly in the eyes. "I'm going to need your phone, Liza."

"When did you become law enforcement, Mayor? Do you have a search warrant?"

Cade smiled. It was soft and pleasant, but I wasn't fooled. He was going in for the kill.

"The sheriff has probable cause to believe that you've obtained an autopsy report without a court order, and since the judge granted a seal on all records on this case, I would hate to tell him he needs to pursue that matter."

Liza pulled her phone out of her purse. "I'll send you a copy of the interview."

"I'm afraid that won't work. If it's going to be used as evidence, I need it collected by the sheriff's crime techs to show that it hasn't been altered." The look he gave her was hard as steel. I'd never seen that look on his face. It was scary, but I kind of liked it.

"But it's my interview!" Liza argued.

"And I'm sure the sheriff will be more than happy to give it back to you after this case goes to trial."

"Trial? But he may not solve it for months! And a trial will take longer than that!" Liza's hands were wrapped tightly around her phone. She didn't want to give it up. The interview had to be a good one, and I wished I'd asked to see it. I'd been so focused on the autopsy report, I didn't even think about why she'd gone to Dallas in the first place.

Cade held out his hand. "Would you rather we discuss the autopsy report with the sheriff?"

"Of course not." Liza huffed.

"We'll let you keep the report, but there are certain things that cannot go public. Not yet, anyway."

"Such as?"

"Everything outside of Maddie being under the influence and drowning."

"But...but then it looks like an accident or a suicide. You're telling me I can't release the manner of death being a homicide, and that Maddie had been beaten and shot?"

Cade nodded. "Not yet."

"When?" Liza demanded.

"When the time is right, we'll let you know." Cade ignored Liza's huff as she stood up to leave. He held out his hand. "I'll need your unlock code as well."

Liza's expression became defiant. "What if I refuse to give it to you?"

"Then I'm afraid I'll be asking some questions that make both of us very uncomfortable."

Steam rolled off Liza like an old locomotive crossing the prairie, and I suddenly realized that Cade was getting payback for me. His methods were subtle, but he was dealing with the bully who had hurt my business in a manner that hurt hers as well. It was the ultimate payback. He was being my hero without anyone even knowing he was doing it.

"I expect to see you at the television station for that interview tomorrow afternoon at two o'clock. My access code is 5-4-9-2. L-i-z-a. Plain and simple." She tapped the unlock code into her phone and handed it to Cade.

"Nothing about you is plain and simple, Liza."

Liza wasn't sure if that was a compliment or an insult. I wasn't either, but I suspected it may have just been a statement of the facts. Plain and simple.

Chapter 13

"You blackmailed her into giving you that video," I said to Cade.

"I'd call it negotiating terms for my television interview."

I laughed. "You threatened her with jail."

"That's something that never leaves this room."

Mateo walked in, his gaze traveling back and forth between Cade and me. "What's never to leave this room?"

"You don't want to know."

"Dios mio. Have the two of you lost your minds? This was supposed to be about getting the autopsy report back, so the media didn't spread the cause of death out there to the public and ruin the case."

"But it became so much more," Cade said. Mateo joined us and took Liza's spot on the couch. When Cade handed Liza's phone to Mateo with the video up and ready to play, I got up and made Mateo move to the middle of the couch.

"Liza wanted you to have this," Cade said.

"Why didn't she give it to me?"

"You know Liza. She doesn't want people to think she would put justice before a story."

Mateo didn't believe that for a minute. He scrunched his eyes closed and rubbed his brow before opening them once again and pushing play on the video.

"This is Liza Twaine with ABN News. I'm in Dallas today with best-selling author—"

"When did he become a best-selling author?" I asked.

"He's not yet. Liza is projecting that he will become one because of the dramatic uptick in his sales since the story hit the news."

I rolled my eyes. "That's sick on so many levels."

"Welcome to my world," Mateo said.

Cade pushed play on the interview again. Liza and Nathan were sitting at a picnic table in what appeared to be a campground. How she located him there was beyond my comprehension. Liza went on with her introduction and talked about Nathan Daniels's background as a traveling handyman and part-time PI. For the viewers, Nathan Daniels would be an interesting character. For me, I understood why Leila found him creepy.

It wasn't that he was a bad-looking guy, it was that he lacked a connection when he talked to Liza. He could have been talking to the picnic table or the trees. He established eye contact with her, but his attention was elsewhere. He had shaggy brown hair with a matching beard and brown eyes. In his mid to late thirties, he had the lean build of one of those survivalists living in the woods. He wore a T-shirt and jeans and a pair of grubby tennis shoes. He obviously didn't dress up for the interview that was taking place in an RV park. He personified a drifter who didn't become invested in people.

He spoke of no family, no friends, no home base. Not even a phone. After all, who would he call? He lived minimally in his trailer that he pulled behind his truck. His one tie to society was his laptop. Yet somehow Sugar had drawn his attention, and he'd liked what he saw while he was in Hazel Rock so much, she became the lead character in his book.

Liza finally asked the question that was bothering me, "How do you keep in contact with your publisher?"

"I check in once a week from a cafe or a library."

"I call bull on that one. How did he learn about the murder so quickly? How did Liza find him in less than twenty-four hours? He's more connected than he wants anyone to believe. What kind of truck does he drive?" I asked.

"He's got a two thousand five Explorer Sport Trac he bought two years ago. It's registered out of Nevada." Mateo's answer told more than his facial expression. I couldn't tell if he had investigated Nathan Daniels when he first heard about his obsession with Sugar, or if he started looking at him as a person of interest for Maddie's murder. Either way, I was comforted by his investigation.

Cade shushed us and rewound the movie to Liza's next question. "Tell us about your latest book, *Woman Scorned*. Where did you get the inspiration for it?"

Nathan chuckled. "Why Liza Twaine, I think you know very well where I got my inspiration for the book."

Liza jumped on his response. "You admit that you based your characters in your book on the people of Hazel Rock, Texas?"

"Some of the more interesting ones, yes."

I snorted. I didn't even have an honorable mention in the book.

Cade and Mateo looked at me, and I was pretty sure they got a kick out of my response to Nathan's answer, and I felt the sudden urge to defend my outburst.

"I have an armadillo for a pet, and I live in a book barn. That makes me pretty darn interesting."

Mateo patted my knee and squeezed it. It would have meant nothing if he'd pulled his hand away. But he didn't. It was a defining moment between the three of us. I caught Cade looking out of the corner of his eyes at Mateo's hand. He didn't say anything. Neither did I.

I put my hand over Mateo's and held it in place. The triangle we'd been dancing around for so long was broken in one small gesture.

Liza's next question brought our full attention back to the video. "Do you have a psychic gift, Mr. Daniels?" Liza asked.

Nathan chuckled. Again. It was becoming annoying. Almost like one of those teenage girls who find everything a cute boy says as funny. It wasn't a funny question. "Are you asking if I have the gift of precognition or are you asking if I'm a prophet?"

"Aren't they one in the same?"

Nathan became serious, as if he knew a lot about the subject and was going to clue the rest of the mere mortals in on how his gift worked. Again, it all felt like hogwash, but Cade and Mateo were completely engrossed. They listened to every word like Nathan was giving them a lesson in spirituality. I was pretty sure I could get a better lesson from my grandfather, not that I was going to go in search of one.

The camera panned back to Liza. "If you are so gifted, Mr. Daniels can you tell us who the killer is in the real-life murder mystery that is happening right now in Hazel Rock, Texas?"

The camera zoomed in on Nathan's face, and it was as if he was telling the whole world, one individual at a time, who killed Maddie MacAlister. "That's quite simple. It's the person with the most to gain."

Liza capitalized on his response. "Wouldn't that be you, Mr. Daniels?"

Nathan stared into the camera with a blank expression on his face then he threw back his head and laughed. He laughed so long it became uncomfortable. When he was finally able to control his mirth, he responded, "Wouldn't that make a great mystery?"

Liza then thanked him for joining her for the interview and the video ended.

"Are there any more videos?" Mateo asked.

Cade scrolled through the camera. "No. Just the one."

Cade told Mateo the access code to the phone and handed it to Mateo as he stood up.

"I appreciate you getting this information. I will make sure Detective Youngblood gets it and has Liza in for a statement first thing in the morning. Now I suggest we call it a night."

Cade agreed, and I walked them to the door.

"Where's Princess?" Cade asked.

"She's been staying out late because of her new boyfriend."

"He's a bad influence. I would expect you to nip that in the bud," Mateo said.

"Do you have any suggestions how I'm supposed to do that, short of locking her in her room?"

"This conversation has gone from weird to ridiculous. You're right, Princess. You and Princess II deserved an honorable mention in Nathan's book." Cade turned and walked out the door.

"I'd give you more than an honorable mention. You'd be the star," Mateo whispered as he leaned in and kissed my cheek.

"If you're writing a mystery, can you leave me out? I'd rather not play a victim or a suspect."

"How about lead investigator?"

"I could do that."

"I thought so. Thank you, Charli. I appreciate everything you did tonight." He was about to say something more when he got a call on his phone. He pulled it out of his pocket and put it to his ear. "Sheriff Espinoza."

I could hear a dispatcher on the other end, but I couldn't tell what she was saying.

"Where's he at now?" Mateo asked. He nodded as she spoke. "I'll be there in twenty minutes." He disconnected from the call.

"What was that?"

"There's someone waiting for me at the station."

"Now? You're going back to the office now?"

"That's what I signed up for when I ran for sheriff."

"But it's late. You need your sleep." I'd also thought that he might stay.

"Crime and the needs of the citizens don't sleep."

"Surely this person could wait until tomorrow to talk to you."

"I made the decision to go in on this one. It's important."

"What could possibly be that important? You don't have another murder or a fatality accident, do you?"

"No. Just trust me. This is important." He gave me a quick peck that was less romantic than the kiss on the cheek he'd given me a few moments earlier, then he walked out the door.

"Lock up," he said as he closed the door behind him.

Mateo waited to see that I locked the door, winked at me through the glass, and left.

* * * *

I woke up to the sounds of something scratching at my door. I squinted at my clock and groaned. It was ten o'clock, and I needed to be at the store in an hour for our Classic Shoes book art class.

I was going to be decorating an old pair of combat boots with a torn-up version of Helen MacInnes's WWII espionage novel *The Unconquerable*. My mom had read the book to me as a young girl, and I'd dreamt of becoming a spy like Sheila Matthews. Not that her life was glamorous, but it had purpose. The version I was using on my boots had the original cover of a fist clasped around a Polish war medal. I wasn't Polish. I just like the way the gold cross and the red ribbon looked with my black boots. The version my mom had read to me had a newer cover and was in my personal library in my apartment—untouched by Princess's claws or teeth.

Scarlet was going to be doing a pair of high heels with none other than *Gone with the Wind*. Sugar had planned to decorate a pair of little boy's boots with *The Very Hungry Caterpillar*.

I slid on my slippers and made my way to the front door to let Princess inside. She had yellow pollen covering her shell.

"Sit," I said.

She listened as if she knew she was in trouble for staying out all night again.

"This has got to stop. There are all kinds of dangers out there for you at night. There are coyotes, dogs, bobcats, wild pigs, cars... I could go on and on about all the bad things that go bump in the night. My point is...I'm worried about you."

Princess blinked and bowed her head.

If I was a fool, I would take that as an apology, like, *I'm sorry. It won't happen again.*

I rolled my eyes and shuffled to the kitchen in my slippers to get the tubs for her bath. I returned with them full of warm water and soap in one, just the way she liked it. I put a towel on the floor and positioned the tubs just so. She was pretty picky about them being the right temperature and the correct number of steps apart so she could go from the soapy one to the rinse tub without cooling off too much in between. As soon as I had them in position, Princess was in the washtub rolling and splashing all over the place. It was like watching my kid come in from playing out in the Texas dirt. Princess brought a simple joy to my life no one else could.

I spent a few minutes drying her off and rubbing her belly after her bath was over. When she still wanted more, I scratched behind her ears and chin, but then I had to go. I was running late. I took my shower and dressed in my "I Found Mr. Darcy at the Book Barn Princess" T-shirt and some capri jeans. Fifteen minutes later I was down at the bookstore preparing for our class with Princess at my feet. It felt good to have her back, and by the wiggle of her tail, I was pretty sure she was happy to be back.

Scarlet, looking like a million bucks in a coral summer dress, was the first one in. I'd learned a long time ago not to compare myself to her. If I did, my curly hair would have straightening solution weighing it down, and my wardrobe wouldn't be near as comfortable. She was the yin to my yang, and we liked it that way.

"Did I see Cade leaving your apartment early this morning?" she asked.

"If you mean late last night, then yes."

Scarlet waved her index finger back and forth in my face while making *tsk, tsk, tsk* noises.

"It wasn't like that. Mateo left right after him."

Scarlet lifted one eyebrow and gave me a sly smile.

"You have been reading too many romance novels. Let me introduce you to some classics."

"A girl can dream that her best friend will find the love of her life, can't she?"

I grabbed the basket I'd filled with Mod Podge, scissors, paint brushes, and sponge brushes and headed for the loft. "We're not looking for the love of our lives, are we Princess?"

Princess huffed and then hopped up the steps in front of me one at a time. Hopefully, that didn't mean she'd already found hers.

"You can fool yourselves, but I know better."

I ignored her comment. "Do you have the shoes that Sugar was going to decoupage for Scotty? I was thinking about doing them for her."

The front doors opened and announced our first arrival. I looked over the railing and nearly dropped everything. Her wet blond hair was falling across her shoulders as if she'd just gotten out of the shower and headed to the Book Barn. She wore no makeup, but she never really needed any. She had dark circles under her eyes as if she hadn't slept in a month, but I was pretty sure it had only been days. She looked exhausted, and relieved that part of her nightmare was over.

"Sugar!" I set everything on the tables and ran down and hugged her tight. She returned the embrace as Scarlet joined in. It was one of those rare girl moments when there was no drama, no outside stresses. Just the three of us happy to be together...and free.

Freedom can never be overrated.

Princess pawed at Sugar's leg as if she wanted to get in on the moment, and Sugar obliged with a laugh as she picked her up. Princess snuggled under her hair and made Sugar laugh even more when she tickled Sugar by sticking her nose in Sugar's ear. I wasn't sure how she knew it, but Princess recognized how precious it was to have Sugar back in our store.

"Did Cade get you out?" I asked.

Sugar shook her head and continued to hug on Princess. "He was there to give us a ride home, but Mateo released us on new evidence they obtained last night."

I thought about the autopsy report and the interview Liza had with Nathan Daniels. Was Mateo focusing on the author? Was there more evidence I didn't know about that pointed the guilty finger in his direction?

"Was it the autopsy or the interview?"

Sugar and Scarlet gave me a look that told me I'd opened Mateo's evidence bag too soon. They didn't know. Fuzz Buckets.

"What interview?" Sugar asked.

"Liza interviewed Nathan Daniels about his book. It was really creepy."

"Creepy is the guy trying to come see me at the jail."

Scarlet sucked in a breath, but I was more vocal. "Get out! Nathan Daniels came to see you at the county jail?"

Sugar put Princess down. "Yeah, Mateo wasn't very happy when he heard about it this morning."

"He didn't know?"

"No. The desk clerk passed the information over to the deputy in the jail but didn't tell Detective Youngblood. Nathan left without anyone talking to him. But another witness came in overnight and gave information that cleared Dean and me. Although I don't think that was his intention."

We moved up to the loft and continued to set up the stations for our class. "What kind of evidence?"

"It was a voicemail that Maddie left for her brother the night she died. She told Tiny she'd gotten in a fight with me." Sugar's lips pursed. "I shouldn't speak ill of the dead...but that woman did everything in her power to make life miserable for us when all we ever tried to do was make sure she had a relationship with her son. I tried to embrace her as part of the family, but not once did she give Scotty the time of day. Her son doesn't even know that she was his mother. Yet just as she did in life, in death Maddie turned our lives into a nightmare." Sugar looked off into space as if she was reliving every horrible moment she'd shared with Maddie. Scarlet squeezed her hand, and Sugar gave us a sad smile. "If she'd known her voicemail would clear us of charges, she'd be furious, but instead, she clarified the time of events and cleared me of charges by leaving that lying voicemail."

I remembered Tiny coming into the Barn the night before and telling me that Maddie had left him a voicemail about getting in a fight with Sugar. At the time, I'd felt horrible and worried about the evidence stacking up against my friend. But between the autopsy report showing Maddie had been beaten, the recovered slug that wasn't the same size as Sugar's gun, and the timing of Maddie's voicemail to Tiny, no one could deny Sugar's innocence. I should have realized when Tiny told me about it that her message would clear Sugar. I should have been able to see that, but I'd been so focused on Tiny's anger that his words had seeped through the cracks as unimportant.

If Maddie had called to tell Tiny about the fight, Sugar couldn't have killed her. After their fight, Sugar had gone back to the Tool Shed Tavern and had never returned to the hotel.

"What did she lie about?" asked Scarlet.

"I didn't fight her. I went to her room because I thought—" Her voice cracked. "I thought Dean was with her. She and I argued, and as I was leaving, she grabbed me by the hair. I had to peel her hands out of my hair, and that's how I broke off my nail. I didn't punch her, and I certainly didn't break her cheekbone."

"You heard about that?" I asked.

"Yeah. There wasn't anything wrong with Maddie's face when I left the hotel. I would have noticed if she'd had that kind of injury."

"Do they know how she got on the roof?"

"Detective Youngblood asked me in my interview if I'd seen Maddie's room key, but that's all I know."

The bell at the door announced the arrival of another member of our class and soon the loft was full of people who were offering Sugar their support. It was heartwarming to see the women of town treat her so nicely, especially when it was obvious that they'd had an unwavering belief in Sugar's and Dean's innocence.

We were midway through our project when Daddy walked in with Dean and Scotty. The little boy was the spitting image of his daddy, wearing a plaid button-down shirt tucked into Wrangler jeans and cowboy boots. Their hair was wet and tousled, and they both wore their carefree attitude that had the ladies eating out of the palm of their hands.

Scotty ran up to Sugar with a bouquet of flowers hidden behind his back. The way he stopped in front of her with the biggest grin this side of the Red River brought tears to the eyes of all of us. Even Princess could be heard sniffing under the table.

"I missed you, Sugar," Scotty said as he eyed the comic books and boots sitting on the table in front of her.

"Don't you peek at your present, little man."

"I wouldn't do that." The little boy crossed his heart and peeked around Sugar.

Dean cleared his throat as he came to stand next to his son.

"We have something we'd like to ask you," Dean said.

The table grew silent. That wasn't the type of thing a man said while standing in front of his girlfriend with every other woman in town looking on. The sense that something very important was about to occur passed through every one of us.

Sugar seemed to have trouble finding her voice. "What is it?" she whispered.

Dean and Scotty knelt on one knee, and a gasp went up one side and down the other of the table. The weepy eyes filled, spilled, and refilled.

"I know there are quite a few years between us, and I bring with me an entire herd of kids."

Scotty giggled at his dad's comment.

"But I've loved you since the first day I saw you sipping sweet tea in the tearoom downstairs."

I looked at Daddy, and he read my thoughts. They'd met in the tearoom? Daddy shrugged as if he'd no idea they'd fallen in love right under his nose in our store.

"I've made my mistakes, and I've never been good at being married. After Maddie and I blew what we had, I didn't want to try a fourth time. I was content to live life without any permanent ties. But in this past week, I've come to realize I can't live like this. I'm a passionate man. I've lived hard. I've work harder, and I promise to love you with all of my heart for the rest of my days."

Scotty pulled a ring out of his shirt pocket and handed it to his daddy. "Sugar McWilliams," Dean and Scotty said as one, "will you marry us?"

Chapter 14

Sugar's "Yes," was celebrated with a loud *whoop* and plenty of hugs and kisses. The book art projects were put on hold for our next class, and the mood in town seemed to be celebratory. But Maddie's death hung over us. There was a killer somewhere in our midst, and despite all the happiness, the sense of loss dampened what should have been the best days of Sugar and Dean's lives.

I didn't see or hear from Mateo all afternoon which was disappointing but understandable. He had a murder case to solve and no suspects in custody. It wouldn't be long before people were complaining about a murderer walking the streets.

I was sorting through some used books that had come in that afternoon when Cade came into the store. He looked as tired as I felt. The only difference, Cade wore an air of defeat that wasn't in his nature.

"What's going on, Mayor?"

Cade smirked. "I didn't realize we'd moved to formal titles, Ms. Warren."

"I figured I'd better call you mayor since you won't be holding the title for long."

"What makes you say that?"

"Because it's only a matter of time before we address you as Senator Calloway. Isn't that the first step to the White House?"

Cade laughed, and I had to admit it was good to see it on him.

"Only you would put me in the White House, Princess."

I disagreed. "I think there might be a few more people who would."

"Actually, I came to clear my stuff out of the tearoom. I've arranged with Dallas to take it to the plant."

Cade walked toward the tearoom, and I blocked his path by standing in front of the stall door with my arms spread wide. "You are not throwing in the towel. This is not you, Cade."

"Princess—"

"You listen to me. I've known you a long time, and I know this isn't what you want to do."

Cade finally capitulated. "You're right. I want to run for Senate."

"Why?"

"What do you mean, 'why'? I think that's pretty obvious."

I didn't let him off the hook. I asked him again. "Why do you want to be a senator?"

"I want to represent Texans and give us a voice in Washington."

"And is there anyone else running that can do it better than you can?" I knew what Cade thought of the incumbent. He didn't like him and didn't believe he voted in a manner that was the best for the future of Texas, or our country. Cade sincerely believed the current senator voted in the direction that special interests groups wanted him to. He also didn't think anyone else could unseat him.

When he didn't answer, I asked the next question, "Who is going to unseat him if you're not running? Are you going to give up the fight because you're down in the fourth quarter by fourteen?"

"I hate when you use football analogies."

I grinned. Football got him every time. "That's because you know I use them well."

"I'm supposed to meet Liza for an interview in five minutes to tell her I'm not running."

"I suggest you change that to an entirely different type of announcement."

"But I originally scheduled that for tomorrow."

"Let's make it today."

"I agree with Princess."

We turned to see Liza walking toward us. We'd been so deep into our conversation we'd missed her coming into the Barn.

"Because you want to break the news?" Cade asked.

"I think the two of you owe me a story," Liza said as she swiped a curl out of her face. She had on a lilac dress with matching sling-back heels. Unlike us, she looked rested and refreshed. "Besides, the voters need to know how you're going to address the theft of the aluminum at the Bin Dover Recycling. The metal you promised that would pay for the recycling program, and reduce our carbon imprint, has been stolen, and now the city budget is going to have to pay for a program you started."

This was the first I'd heard of metal being stolen at the recycling center, but from the look on Cade's face, he was well aware of the problems the plant suffered. I looked back at Liza. Only then did I see the cameraman hiding near the store entrance. Liza had brought the big guns in with her. This wasn't about an interview. This was about payback for last night, and I wasn't about to let her throw Cade's career away.

"Mayor Calloway has brought a wonderful recycling program to Hazel Rock. The program was designed to pay for itself while having a positive effect on our environment. We've had a run of events, tragic events that have set us back as a community. But with leadership like Cade Calloway's, Hazel Rock will come back stronger than ever. When time runs out in the fourth quarter, Mayor Calloway and Hazel Rock will be on top."

Liza looked like she wanted to knock my block off. "What are you going to do, Mayor? Help track down the metal?"

Cade, the politician, was back. "I have all the faith in the world in our county law enforcement to track down whoever is responsible for the crime. But I would ask our citizens to report any unusual activity they've seen at Bin Dover Recycling to the sheriff's office. As a community, we are at our best when we work as a team." He beamed at Liza. "Thank you for your time, Ms. Twaine." Then Cade went in the tearoom and closed the door in her face.

I had no doubt he could hear her repeated questions about if he was running for senate through the door and over the top of it as well, but he didn't answer her. Liza had lost her opportunity to interview the man I knew would be the next senator.

"I'm sorry, Ms. Twaine. The Book Barn Princess is closing for the day."

"Are you hiding more books in the tearoom that you're planning to burn, Ms. Warren?"

Liza's attack caught me off guard. I didn't know what to say. "Excuse me?"

With the discovery of Maddie's body, everyone seemed to have forgotten about my arrest. Not Liza. She was making sure Cade wasn't the only one who experienced her payback.

"You have a court date in a matter of weeks in regard to burning books here at the Book Barn Princess. How do you plan to plead considering we caught you in the act and have your crime on film?"

Cade was out of the tearoom in a flash. "Don't answer that ridiculous question."

Liza's smile was as sly as they come. A used car salesman couldn't have used a better con to sell a bill of goods. She knew Cade would stop me from answering.

"Are you representing her, Mayor Calloway? Doesn't that go against everything a green candidate stands for?"

"We have no comment for you, Liza." Even though Cade's anger was suppressed, I could still see it seething under the surface. I hoped the camera didn't pick up on it as well.

The front bell to the store sounded, and I wanted to throw up my hands and yell, *What now?* Instead I repeated what I'd told Liza. "The Book Barn is closed."

No sooner had the words left my lips than Tiny stomped into the store. "You may have gotten them released out of jail, but I'm not through making sure my sister gets justice." Tiny's fists were clenched and down at his sides. The cameraman immediately backed out of his way; his tall lean build was no match for Tiny's nose tackle frame.

Cade, however, had gone up against guys like Tiny for years. "The sheriff will get justice for Maddie. Leave it to him."

I didn't understand Tiny's obsession with coming into the Barn. The man had never stepped inside the Barn before Maddie died. Granted, he may have more time on his hands after being laid off from the recycling plant.

Tiny had been laid off from the plant. If anyone knew how to steal the aluminum from the plant, it would be Tiny. Standing in front of us could be the man responsible for all of Cade's headaches. "Did you steal the aluminum from the plant?" I asked.

Cade eyed me sideways, but he wasn't going to take all his attention off the man whose anger was like an active volcano ready to erupt. Tiny, however, gave me his undivided attention.

"What aluminum? I didn't steal any aluminum."

Liza pointed at her cameraman to continue to roll. The video wasn't my first choice for a witness, but I'd take it if it meant helping Cade's program rebound.

"You know the operation," I said. "I'd say you know it as well as the back of your..." I looked at his beefy fists. "As well as the back of your *scratched-up* hand." I thought of Maddie's injuries and wondered if Dallas was closer to the truth about what happened to Maddie than all of us. Maybe Tiny's anger over her death was all an act to throw the attention of the investigation in another direction, and now the man found himself without money. Cashing in on the losses of the recycling plant might seem like poetic justice after Dallas fired him.

Cade didn't know anything about Tiny's abuse, but he immediately caught on to my accusation.

"Lady, you're crazy. I didn't steal anything from the plant. Trying to steal the aluminum would be like going to the dump and wading through mountains of trash for something of value. Nobody's been sorting the recycling since I got laid off."

"What's happening to the recycling?" Liza asked.

I closed my eyes. My plan to help Cade had backfired. Things had just taken a decided turn for the worst.

Tiny ignored Liza's question, and asked Cade, "Mayor, I want to know something."

Cade didn't hesitate. He nodded to indicate that Tiny needed to go ahead and ask his question, but I could tell he was going to proceed with caution.

"Are you going to make sure Maddie gets justice?"

Cade's expression softened but showed a confidence that only came from telling what he believed to be the truth. "I can tell you this: We have the best sheriff's department in the state looking into your sister's case. Dedicated professionals who have sworn to investigate the case thoroughly and will do everything in their power to see that your sister's killer is brought to justice. That I can assure you."

Tiny nodded. He accepted Cade's word with a solemn trust I hadn't expected. I couldn't tell if it was an act, or if this was the side of Tiny that Maddie may have known—an earnest brother who just couldn't accept anything but the best for his sister.

Liza seemed as disappointed in Tiny's acceptance as Cade was pleased.

"How do you feel about Sugar and Dean being released this morning?" she asked.

Tiny leaned toward her and looked at her through squinted eyes. "I suggest you don't ask me another question, lady." He left as abruptly as he'd appeared, and I released the breath I'd been holding.

Relief flooding through my system. Then I turned toward Liza, who seemed to be a little bit shaken up by her nose-to-nose conversation with Tiny. I took advantage of the wobble in her knees. "Is there a purchase I could help you with? A book you would like to buy?"

"I don't have time for books right now!" Liza yelled in my face and did an about-face toward the door.

"Of course, you don't. Have a nice evening, Ms. Twaine." The door to the Barn swished closed as Liza and her cameraman exited the store, and I quickly locked it behind them.

"I guess I better prepare my denouncement speech of my candidacy tomorrow."

"Cade—"

Cade shook his head. "This is it, Princess. The end of the line."

Chapter 15

The crowd was gathered in front of the Barn, and my stomach was turning knots faster than a roadrunner escaping the hungry teeth of a coyote. I'd let everyone in town know they needed to be at the Barn at one o'clock, and they'd shown up in droves. The small announcement Cade had planned to make for the media about not running for senate had turned into all the people of Hazel Rock and countless others from Oak Grove and the outlying county showing up to hear the news. The crowd was packed tighter than the church on Christmas.

Scarlet patted me on the shoulder. "It's going to be all right. You're going to do great."

"How is it that I always end up in the middle of these media circuses?"

Scarlet smiled. "Because you're Charli Rae."

"What's that supposed to mean?"

"It means life is always interesting when you're around." Scarlet moved away, and Cade pushed through the crowd.

"What are you doing?"

"I'm trying to fix the mess that I made."

Cade's hand scrubbed the short hair on that side of his head, and I could hear the fine hairs bristling under the pressure. He was dressed in a navy-blue, tailored suit, a crisp white shirt, and a solid royal-blue tie. Every woman in America would stop and take notice—provided he didn't say something stupid. Which was not in his repertoire. It was in mine, and just thinking about that made me sweat.

"Princess, it wasn't meant to be," Cade said.

He was right in one aspect, but wrong when it came to his career. I gave him a sad smile; the pang of my heart was real. It was time to let go of our childhood dreams and move forward with our lives. "You're right Cade. Some things weren't meant to be. Your career isn't one of them. Your service to our community, our state, and our country is important. You're good at it, and it would be a major disservice to everyone if you gave up because of a few bumps along the way. This *is* the fourth quarter and the *final* game of the season. You're in position to win with a Hail Mary. Of course, it's a long shot, but you love a long shot. You love adversity. This is your time to prove it. So, when I hike the ball to Hazel Rock's golden-boy quarterback, I expect him to throw a touchdown. That's your destiny."

Cade stared at me, his eyes searching my face as if he was looking for the lie. I wasn't being dishonest. He had to see that. When his features softened, I knew I'd gotten through to him.

"As your attorney I can't let you do this."

"Fine. You're fired. You're no longer my attorney."

"Princess, you'll be hurting your case."

"There's no dispute about the facts, Cade. I did what I did, and I did it all by myself. No one else was involved. Not you, not Daddy. It was my decision, and I stand by that decision. It may have been the wrong thing to do, but I did what I thought was best. And I made a mistake. The consequences are mine."

When he started to object, I added, "And only mine. So, are you going to run for senator? We could really use you in office."

"Even with the failures my program is having?"

"Especially with the failures, because they haven't stopped you from seeing the program to a successful conclusion."

"They aren't at a successful conclusion, Princess."

"Yet. The key word is yet. You and I both know the programs you've put in place will be your legacy in Hazel Rock."

Cade laughed and ran his hand against the short hair on the top of his head. "I'll run on one condition."

"Wow, conditions. You learn fast for a man who professes not to have an interest in running for office." I grinned. "What's you're condition?"

"Will you be my campaign manager?"

That was the last response I expected. "What?"

"I need a campaign manager. I need someone who is willing to go out on the limb and make mistakes. Then come back fighting. I need someone with unshakable belief in me. You're the only one who fits that bill, and I trust you."

"You trust me?" I snorted. It was less than ladylike. "I'm the one who started this. I'm the running back on the team who fumbled the ball."

"Exactly."

I didn't expect him to agree so wholeheartedly. "Thanks." I turned to address the reporters, my irritation fueling me forward, but Cade stopped my progress.

"Let me finish." He dipped down to look me in eye. It was a long way to bend for a man of his height. "I need you to run the two-point conversion. Only then can we win the game. We make a great team."

I looked at Mateo standing at the entrance of the Barn. What would he think if I became Cade's manager? Would he be jealous? Would he be upset? Or would he support me one hundred percent, no questions asked? I was pretty sure I knew the answer.

"You want to put a criminal at the head of your campaign?" I asked.

Cade grinned. "This is politics. Today's criminal is tomorrow's leader."

"You don't really believe that."

Cade winked. "Let's just say I believe you can be rehabilitated and become a person who believes in helping the environment. Can I count on you?"

I grinned. "You had me when you made me running back. Let's go announce your candidacy for the United States Senate."

I stood up at the podium Scarlet had insisted we needed and addressed the sea of reporters and local citizens. I explained what happened the day a skunk entered the Barn and went into detail about how brave our sheriff was to sacrifice himself for Liza Twaine, who just happened to be standing in the front row.

Other reporters looked in her direction to see if my version of the story was true, and she confirmed it with a nod. I suspected the only reason she did agree, however, was that I didn't throw her under the bus and say she threw her phone at the skunk, but rather she tripped and dropped her phone and it bounced on the floor and startled the skunk. Nor did I mention that she stunk to high heaven when she left the bookstore. There were some things a woman wouldn't tolerate. Saying she stunk was one of them.

Mateo on the other hand would just look more brave and manly for his sacrifice. Period. He rolled his eyes.

The reporters were polite during that portion of my story, when I got to the cleanup of the store, however, their moods changed. They wanted the scoop that would bury someone alive—preferably a politician. I couldn't and wouldn't give that to them.

"Once we'd cleaned the bookstore, and I had collected the books that had been ruined along with the boxes we were storing for the mayor, I asked him for advice on how to dispose of them."

Liza Twaine was the first to jump on that statement. Her question sounding more like an accusation than a quest for the truth. "So, the mayor *did* approve of you burning his campaign signs?"

Other reporters followed, firing questions at me like bullets at the shooting range. I held my hands up to quiet the crowd. "Mayor Calloway sent me to Dallas Dover. His company, Bin Dover Recycling, holds the city's recycling contract, and the mayor firmly believed the problem was over."

"You never once told the mayor that you didn't recycle the books or the posters?" A reporter I didn't recognize asked.

I shook my head and looked at Cade. "No, I didn't. And that was my mistake. There were so many more options to take than the one I did. For that, I apologize, Mayor Calloway."

Cade gave me a gracious nod.

Liza wasn't satisfied. "What about the recycling plant? Why didn't Bin Dover Recycling take the books and posters?"

"I went to the recycling plant and spoke with Dallas Dover, but they weren't equipped to take contaminated products. They're still a fairly small operation, and their sorting facility couldn't take them inside. The stench would kill the workers. You can attest to that, Liza."

The reporters laughed and looked to Liza once more for any hint of my dishonesty. Liza had no choice but to agree. "The sheriff did carry that scent with him," she said.

Cameras turned and caught Mateo's left eyebrow rise above his sunglasses, and another laugh rolled through the crowd. There was nothing like making fun of a macho man and him taking it in stride. Mateo couldn't have played it better.

The reporters then started to wander off—a misguided book barn princess and a hot sheriff didn't make headline news. "If I could have your attention," I said. "The error of my ways is not the reason for this press conference." Most of the reporters continued to pack up their stuff, but a few, like Liza Twaine, weren't about to give up on the possibility of snagging the best story of the week, maybe the month.

"Ladies and gentlemen, please," I said. "I called this press conference to set the record straight because the public needed to know the truth. They needed to hear that the mayor of Hazel Rock was a good man. A man that can be counted on to do the right thing. To make decisions that are based on sound judgment and good decision-making skills. Not my level of decision making, mind you." A few reporters snickered, but most of them recognized the direction I was going and knew the story was just beginning. "But decisions that will take into consideration the concerns of the citizens, the costs to the environment, and the needs of the economy. Decisions you can trust to have been made from the heart and mind of a man we are proud to call Mayor Calloway and will be even prouder when we address him as Senator Calloway of Texas. May I present to you, the next senator from the Lone Star State…Cade Calloway!"

The snick of cameras aimed in our direction filled the courtyard but were soon drowned out by the whoops and hollers of the crowd. Reporters who had been ready to pack their bags and head for home were vying for the best possible position to get their questions answered. Liza fought for her spot in the front row, pushing and shoving and throwing elbows with colleagues who had much more experience in the political press pit.

I'm not going to lie, I enjoyed seeing Liza get pushed around.

I stepped back and let Cade take front and center.

"Mayor your disagreements with the incumbent Senator Jones have been widely publicized across the state. Are you running because of the rift between the two of you?" Liza asked.

I looked at Cade. I knew he didn't like our senator. I didn't know about any rift. I suppose the political scene wasn't exactly what I read when I was on the internet.

"A rift with the current senator would hardly propel me toward a larger role of service in our government. However, a belief that the people need better representation, a belief that our current leadership is not meeting the needs of the people, and a belief that I can do the job of representing the people of Texas at a higher level are reasons for me to run for Senator of the United States representing the state of Texas."

A large whoop went through the crowd, and I joined in wholeheartedly.

"You were very good at that," Daddy whispered in my ear from my left side.

I smiled. "It was kinda fun."

"Am I going to lose you at the Barn?" he asked.

I glanced at him and saw the worry on his face. He was trying to act like it didn't bother him, but the creases in his brow said otherwise.

"What do you mean?" I asked.

"I heard you agree to be Cade's campaign manager. You can't exactly do that and work at the Barn."

Fuzz buckets. I hadn't even considered that I'd have to give up my nine-to-seven day job. I loved the Book Barn Princess. It was my home. My life. My future. At least it had been, up until fifteen minutes ago. Now, I wasn't sure. What had I gotten myself into?

Those infamous decision-making skills had gotten me in another mess that I wasn't sure how to solve. On one hand, the job of being Cade's campaign manager had sounded new and exciting, with all kinds of potential. Yet I liked being at home—in Hazel Rock. My best friend was here. My dad was here. Not to mention my home and job and pet and boyfriend. Everything I wanted was here. So why had I said I would be his campaign manager?

The crowd had grown bigger with news spreading fast about Cade's announcement. Neighbors and business owners stayed to savor the moment they suspected could make history. Everyone in Hazel Rock knew Cade had something special. He was meant to do great things. We initially believed he was destined for greatness on a football field, because that was where his heart lay. But when life handed him a set of challenges to overcome, he did it with style and stamina. He was a born leader. Whether it was on the field or in the political arena, Cade brought the best out in others as well as himself.

He was focused and determined and that's what we loved about him. His desire to win was infectious. Everyone fell for it.

And that's exactly what I'd done. I'd jumped on the political bandwagon without considering my life, my prior commitments, or the people who depended on me on a daily basis. Cade had asked, and as usual, I had jumped.

What if he asked me to jump into the fire? Would I? Or had I already jumped into it and didn't even recognize my life was going up in flames.

Fuzz buckets. I'd done it again.

Chapter 16

"He's coming here!" Reba Sue came running into the Book Barn as if she was being chased by Princess's boyfriend. Her big blond hair was less than perfect, and her makeup looked like it might melt off her face in one large land slide.

"Who's coming here?" Daddy asked.

"You're never gonna believe it. I waited outside his trailer to talk to him, and he came!" She panted.

I joined them in the front of the store. "What are you talking about, Reba Sue?"

She braced herself with the palm of her hand on the counter. Every one of her fingernails were chipped. Something had happened to make her rush over and give us the big scoop.

"You've got to tell the mystery moms. They're going to die!" she exclaimed.

I looked at Daddy, who shrugged and grabbed a stack of books to take upstairs. "Tell me when you figure out what's going on," he said.

Reba Sue's mouth dropped open, and she gave him an exasperated look that may have said, *well, duh. Haven't you figured it out by now?* She turned her attention toward me, expecting me to totally understand where she was coming from.

I disappointed her. My expression was blank. I had no idea what she was trying to tell us.

Reba Sue raised both hands in the air to add a big *ta-dah* to her announcement. "Nathan Daniels is coming to our meeting Wednesday morning! Isn't that great?"

I wasn't thinking it was great. If anything, I was thinking, *well kiss my foot, that son of a beehive was capitalizing on Maddie's death.* But I kept my mouth shut, because Reba Sue was happy again and no longer thinking about having her granny panties exposed to the mystery moms, my daddy, Jessie, and Mateo. It was progress.

It was irritating, yet it stirred my curiosity. Other than a media stunt, what could motivate Nathan Daniels to return to Hazel Rock, Texas after having spent a week with us over the summer jotting down all our quirks and idiosyncrasies? Why would a bestselling author visit the Mystery Moms when he didn't even bother to stop in the Book Barn on his last visit? Granted, part of me was hurt that the Barn hadn't even made an appearance in his book. We had an app for Pete's sake. How could he leave the Book Barn Princess out of his bestselling thriller? It was a slap in the face.

Even Princess didn't make a cameo in the novel, which was ridiculous. The whole town loved my armadillo and treated her like the town mascot. Granted, she could be a pain, but in general, being obnoxious didn't stop people from becoming an American icon. My mama always said she loved Flip Wilson, but she didn't want to be married to a man who greeted her with four hand slaps, two elbow bumps, and two hip bumps while acting like Geraldine and preaching like Reverend Leroy. For a wife, that would be annoying. As a neighbor, he would be funny.

Princess had the same relationship with people in Hazel Rock as Mama had with Flip. No one writing about Flip's hometown would forget Flip. It wasn't done.

"How did he know about our meeting?" I asked.

Reba Sue's eyes nearly bugged out of her head. "Haven't you been listening to a thing I said?"

I debated if I should tell her I was actually thinking about my mom's favorite comedian, but then decided against it. "I guess I just missed something with all the excitement."

Reba Sue exhaled long and slow. "After Liza left, Betty and I stayed in Dallas. We just had to get him to agree to come to our meeting. We waited outside his trailer all night, and at first light, he came out!"

"You and Betty waited outside his trailer? Where was it parked?"

"At an RV park south of Dallas."

"Where did you sleep?"

"In the car. The park made us rent a spot."

They were sounding more and more like stalkers. I couldn't believe Nathan hadn't called the police. "Why didn't you just knock on his door?"

"We did, but he wouldn't answer. We caught him coming out to go for a run."

"He runs?"

"How else do you think he would keep in shape?"

I shrugged. I hadn't given Nathan Daniels's physical fitness much thought. He just didn't seem like the running type. Maybe the yoga type. No impact, no high energy. Tai chi. I could see Nathan doing tai chi.

Reba Sue continued to tell her story. "He said he was in Dallas and was heading home but could stop by on his way. I'm so excited! Maybe you could get him to do a book signing?"

We'd already had one copycat killer in Hazel Rock who'd modeled his killings after a mystery series by an author we'd had scheduled for a big signing and a party. I didn't think it was appropriate to invite someone Mateo might be looking at as the mastermind behind Maddie's killing to the Barn for a book signing. What if he was the killer? Would it be right to have him profit in the very town he'd committed murder?

Daddy saved me from answering. "That's wonderful news, Reba Sue. But we've only got two copies of *Woman Scorned* on the shelf—"

"Actually, I think I sold the last copy."

Daddy shook his head. "We had two copies brought in for resale this morning. I've already put them out."

Reba Sue didn't hesitate. "Oh, I need to buy one for me and one for my sister. I can't have him sign an e-book copy, now can I!" Reba Sue ran for the thriller section in the second stall on the other side of the Barn.

"—make that no copies." Daddy smiled.

"Problem solved. Thanks Daddy."

"Anytime, Princess." He lowered his voice. "Apparently, the mystery was rather obvious." He winked and looked over his shoulder to check on Reba Sue's progress before asking, "Do you think you should tell Mateo that Nathan Daniels is coming to town?"

"I was just going to ask you if you could watch the register, so I could go call him." The last thing I wanted to do was call Mateo in the store where anyone and their brother could hear. I had too many interruptions by people with cameras in the past few days to take a chance.

"We make a helluva team," he said, and I couldn't help but think of my commitment to Cade's campaign. He thought we made a good team too. I guess the question was what team I thought I belonged on.

Reba Sue returned with her two copies of the book.

"I'll see you and Nathaniel on Wednesday morning, Reba Sue."

"You're going to make the meeting special, right? Ask more people to join. Have fresh pastries and coffee?"

She acted like I was new to the business. This was my thing. Of course, there'd be other people invited—especially a man in brown who filled out his uniform rather nicely.

"We've got it covered. No worries," I told her.

Reba Sue smiled, and I finally saw what Cade had seen in her when they were dating. She didn't seem to be his type, but she was attractive.

I left and decided to get some fresh air on my way to my apartment. The skies were blue, the air had a hint of dust, and the town seemed empty. Kind of like a ghost town minus the tumbleweeds. Although we did have them from time to time. The Inn hadn't reopened, and the diner only had a couple of cars parked in front. I rounded the Barn and went through the gate that shut off the alley between the buildings from the courtyard and Main Street.

The ornamental metal gate was a bit rusty, but the patina seemed to add to the rustic charm of the Barn. Plus, it was the only thing to secure our backyard and the staircase leading to my apartment. I wanted to jump up and tap my mama's sign. I'd done it daily when I was in high school. I used to jump up and touch the sign to improve the height on my cheerleading jump. Now I wanted to say hello to my mom. As a teenager, it was a way for me to talk to my mom without looking like I was crazy if I went to her gravestone and talked to her there. Kids could be cruel that way, and I didn't want to be sent to a counselor just because I wanted to pretend my mom had my back even after her death. Just a *Hi, Mom. Let's see how high I can jump today.* Or *Today sucked but you would have been proud of how I handled it.*

Today, I felt the need to tap the sign and say hello. Eve's gate was my link to the past. The sign had been a gift from my daddy to my mom when they bought the Book Barn. It also signified the entrance to the family home where no one else was allowed unless invited.

I closed the gate, jumped and…my fingers caught air. I looked at the sign. Had Daddy raised it? I tried again and got nothing.

He had to have raised it. I was thirty, not fifty and I'd just done it a few days ago.

I backed up and gave myself a few steps running head start, leaped and… nothing. I landed on my feet with absolutely no satisfaction in my soul.

"Want me to lift you?"

I turned around and smiled, a little embarrassed by my childish desire to jump up and hit the sign.

Mateo sauntered up to the gate and came through. "You are trying to touch the sign, aren't you?"

"You know I am."

He leaned forward and greeted me with a kiss. The type of kiss no one would mistakes for a friendly peck between friends. I put my arms around his neck, loving the moment, if not the bulletproof vest and gun belt.

When we came up for air, I said, "I've missed you."

"How's the political arena treating you today?"

I sighed. I should've discussed my decision with him before I made it. I knew he was hurt by it, but he wanted to support me in everything I did.

"It's going good, but I need to talk to you about something else."

"What's up?"

"Reba Sue was just at the bookstore. She invited Nathaniel Daniels to the Mystery Moms Book Club meeting Wednesday morning."

The glint in Mateo's eyes was the only hint of his excitement. "Are you telling me he accepted?"

"According to Reba Sue, that's exactly what I'm telling you."

"I guess you can count on adding one more person to the Mystery Moms meeting," he said with a sly smile and a wink.

"Are you going to dress up like a mom?" I teased.

Mateo's lips met mine in a quick peck. "You're cute when you think you're funny."

"Did you read the book?"

"As matter fact, I did. I will be prepared to discuss the plot in its entirety."

I pulled back and searched his face. "Seriously?"

"Would I lie to you, Charli?"

That was one thing I knew Mateo would never do. Lying wasn't in his genes. It was as if that switch was turned off before he was born. Like the commandment *thou shalt not bear false witness* was literally tattooed in his makeup as *thou shalt not lie*. I wasn't sure he was even capable of a white lie.

Unfortunately for him, I didn't share that trait. It was a flaw in my makeup, but I also knew I wouldn't change it. Because the only time I'd lied to Mateo was when I was trying to protect him, or I was trying to find out the truth. Which seemed kind of ironic when I thought about it.

"That is one thing I will never expect from you," I confessed.

Mateo laughed. "You never know when people will surprise you."

Suddenly I began to doubt my ability to read him. "Are you telling me that you've lied to me?"

"I'm telling you, in this business, I've learned to expect the unexpected." He pulled away but left his hands around my waist. "Now, are you going to touch that sign or what?"

I grinned. "I'm going to touch that sign." I bent down, jumped straight up in the air, and tapped my mom's sign with Mateo's help. "Love you, mom," I whispered just before my feet hit the ground again.

I looked into Mateo rich chocolate eyes brimmed with eyelashes so long they were sinful, and said, "Thank you. Not many people would understand my need for that."

He kissed me again, and even though it was brief and not as full of passion as the first one, it was full of an emotion that felt a lot like love. "I'll be there at ten AM sharp," he said as he disengaged and grabbed the latch to the gate.

"We're not going to dinner tonight?"

"This case has me a little too busy. And Cade just advised me that he planned on meeting you to strategize for his campaign tonight."

Fuzz buckets. I'd forgotten all about that. "We could have an early dinner," I suggested.

"If you're asking me out for dinner, I'm going to have to decline."

My heart nearly stuttered to a stop. His message seemed the exact opposite of what we'd just shared.

"If, however, you're asking me to join you for dessert and breakfast, then I'll see you around midnight."

That warm tingly feeling returned. This was what we'd been building up to for months. "That's exactly what I'm asking for," I said.

Mateo's grin was full of satisfied male ego. "Then I suggest next time you make yourself clearer."

"I'll see you at midnight, Mateo."

"Yes, you will, Charli."

Mateo got in his car, and I went up to my apartment feeling better than I had all week. Finally, a conversation that had Mateo and me on the same page. We'd been struggling for so many days, I'd begun to doubt we'd get past it. But tonight, we were going to go back to the way it was before all this happened. Before life got all screwy, and my future seemed completely uncertain. Sometimes new adventures were exactly what I didn't want. And today, I'd been craving the past where my goal was to have a great sales day at the Book Barn, spend a little time with my friends, and have my boyfriend in my bed.

Lucky me, that's exactly what I was going to get.

Chapter 17

I met Scarlet for dinner at the Hazel Rock Diner. It was fairly crowded with people from the surrounding rural areas coming into town for the weekend. Sugar was working the Barn with Daddy who was leaving early for his bowling night in Oak Grove. We both had the night off. I'd thought Sugar would want to spend time with her family, but Dean was going out to spend the evening with Maddie's mom. They were going to make plans for Maddie's funeral, and Greta wanted to see her grandson—for the second time in the little boy's four years of life. That had irked Sugar, but she bit her tongue for Scotty's sake and bowed out gracefully since Sugar's face was the last one Greta would want to see.

I was betting Greta had invited Dean out to the house to ask him to pay for the funeral.

"What's your plan for tonight?" Scarlet asked.

I thought of Mateo coming over for dessert. "Nothing."

Scarlet looked at me as if I was one of my kindergarten students caught with my hand in the cookie jar. I took a bite of my chicken wrap. It was smothered with bacon, lettuce, tomato, avocado, cheese and ranch dressing. Nothing like having a mouthful of delicious food to help swallow a lie.

Cade slid into the booth next to me and stole some of my fried string onions. I scowled at him and pulled my plate away. "Those are bad for you."

He laughed, and his hazel eyes sparkled. "We're supposed to be talking strategy."

"We can talk strategy. You just need to order your own food."

"She hates when people steal food off her plate," Cade said as he took a drink of my sweet tea and snuck around my hand defending my plate to strip me of my onion rings like he was a linebacker running a stunt play to strip the ball from a quarterback. It worked like a charm.

I scooted away from him, and he grinned with my food in his mouth. Then he hailed the waitress and ordered a grilled chicken breast and fruit.

"You're not getting any more of my onion rings," I told him.

"That's okay. I feel my arteries clogging as we speak."

"Good."

Cade smirked. "Are you hoping I keel over, Princess?"

"I'm hoping you go sit with Reba Sue to eat your dinner," I said.

"O.M.W. you wouldn't seriously wish that on him, would you Charli?" Scarlet asked. She offered Cade the croissant that came with her salad. The one she never ate and usually gave to me.

I shrugged.

"I told you. She can turn vicious when you mess with her food," Cade said.

I rolled my eyes. "What did you want to talk about?"

"I've signed up a volunteer in Waco who has time tomorrow to put out signs. I need you to deliver the signs to her."

My eyebrows shot up. "Her?"

"I know what you're thinking, but it's not like that."

"If it was like that, he'd be delivering the posters himself." Scarlet winked, and I couldn't help but snort. She was right.

Cade ignored us. "She's a friend of my mom's, and she and her bible study group are going to hang signs tomorrow for me."

"Seriously?"

He nodded and pulled his hands out of the way as his food was delivered.

I thought of Mateo. "I can't do it."

"You can't?" he said.

"Why not?" Scarlet asked. "You just told me you weren't doing anything tonight."

"Well, I…" My brain raced for an answer. "I want to be at the store when Sugar closes. She's still pretty upset."

"That's not a problem. You'll be back in plenty of time," Cade assured me.

I thought about my apartment. I'd neglected it, and I wanted to make sure it looked nice and didn't smell like Princess or her little friend. I needed to shave my legs. "It won't work."

Cade set his fork down with the bite of chicken he'd been about to devour. He sighed heavily. "What's going on, Princess?"

"Nothing."

He turned in his seat, his face a mask of practiced patience. "It's not nothing. Have you changed your mind about working for my campaign?"

"Of course not!" Maybe.

Cade scrubbed the top of his head, his irritation obvious to everyone. I had that effect on him more often than not. "I'm trying to understand—"

"Mayor, is that your new car out front?" We all looked up at Liza and her cameraman. Scarlet and I groaned, but Cade smiled and stood up to address her. He politely wiped his mouth and hands before tossing his napkin on the table.

"As a matter of fact, it is Liza."

Liza pounced. "Senator Jones said a Tesla is hardly the car of a man claiming to be a running as the people's candidate."

Cade didn't miss a beat. He smiled that thousand-watt smile that had women falling at his feet. "I make no apologies for my family ties. Some say I was born with a silver spoon in my mouth." He quirked his eyebrows. "That may be true."

I closed my eyes. Even I knew that was not the right thing to say to the average American.

"But I am also from a philanthropic family who has given back to the community in more ways than Senator Jones could ever dream of doing. I've sponsored children's charities and retirement homes that provide health care for residents. I've started a green initiative for Hazel Rock, bringing recycling to town and getting businesses to think about creating a smaller footprint on our environment. I've accomplished more in the time that I've been mayor of a town that has the population of a little over two thousand people than Senator Jones has done during his eight years in office. And I've done it without questionable campaign donations from cartels south of the border."

"O.M.W.," Scarlet whispered.

I couldn't agree more.

Liza was salivating with the sound bite she'd just obtained for the evening news.

But Cade wasn't done. "In answer to your question, a representative of the people can drive a Tesla. In fact, it would be irresponsible for me to drive any other type of vehicle when I have long campaign trips to make. Especially when I can afford the greenest, most environmentally conscious car on the road."

Liza drew her mic back to ask another question, but Dallas Dover interrupted her interview. His hair was pulled back in a neat ponytail, and he held his hat in his hands.

I cringed. I'd kind of thrown him under the bus for not recycling the books the day before. If he was looking for retribution, now was the time.

"It's one helluva car, Mayor. I've been thinking about looking at one myself. Mind you it'd be the cheaper model."

Cade shook his hand. "Good to see you again, Dallas. If you'd like, I'll show you some of the features."

Dallas grinned. "Nothing like the state-of-the-art technology to make a man happy."

Cade agreed, and they talked about the pros and cons of the car. The only con I heard was that Hazel Rock didn't have any charging stations for him to plug into, but Cade was going to work on that. Sensing her interview was about to turn boring, Liza thanked Cade for his time, and she and her cameraman left the restaurant.

"I owe you one for that, Dallas."

Dallas grinned then turned expectantly toward me and Scarlet. Cade quickly included us in the conversation.

"You've met Princess...I mean Charli Rae and Scarlet, haven't you?" Cade asked.

"I've met Charli Rae, but I haven't had the pleasure of an introduction to Miss Scarlet."

Dallas held out his hand and shook Scarlet's before turning toward me.

"It's good to see you again, Charli."

I looked for a hint of animosity in his eyes, but there was none. If he'd heard the news conference, he didn't think poorly of my statement to the press. "Hi, Dallas."

He smiled and turned back to Cade. "Mayor, I wanted to apologize for not taking those books from Charli Rae. If I'd known she was going to burn them, I would have found somewhere on the property to put them, so the trash could pick them up."

Cade shook his head. "It's behind us. Just a matter of poor communication that we don't ever plan on having again. Right, Princess?"

I didn't like Cade's tone. It made me feel like a little girl too young to have good decision-making skills. Yet I wasn't about to undercut him; he was my boss.

"Yeah, it's my burden. Not yours, or the mayor's." Ready for the conversation to end, I took a bite of my chicken wrap.

"Well, if you need me to get you out of a bind, let me know. The last thing any of us need is more trouble over something we can fix," Dallas said.

I smiled and nodded at Dallas. "Thank you."

He walked away, and I couldn't help but think of Kid Rock. Dallas could stand in for him in a pinch.

Still irritated over his tone, I told Cade, "Do you know what the cartels will do to you?"

"Stay away from me and my state because they know I will come down hard on them?"

I looked around the diner to make sure no one was listening. "They will kill you."

"You worry too much, Princess. Now how about that trip to Waco?"

"I don't have a car. Tonight's dad's bowling night."

"Take the Tesla."

I choked on my chicken, and Cade patted me between the shoulder blades.

"O.M.W.," Scarlet said.

I took a drink of water and washed the remnants down. "You don't trust my decision making, and yet you're going to let me drive your brand new, fifty-thousand-dollar car?"

"It was a bit more than that," Cade mumbled.

"How much more?"

"Cade had the decency to look humbled. "Eighty-two."

Scarlet's eyes bugged as she took a sip of her sweet tea, but she kept her mouth closed.

"You're going to let me drive your *eighty-two-thousand-dollar* car?" I asked.

"It's the reason I bought it."

It was my turn to gulp down some sweet tea. "You bought it for me to drive?"

Cade's chuckle was genuine. "Not quite. I bought it for the campaign—"

"To look like a grown-up," Scarlet added with a smile.

"—to not look like I was still trying to hang on to my youth in the Camaro."

Scarlet's grin grew. We both knew he was still a kid, even if he did act more grown up than the two of us.

"But that doesn't mean I want to drive it all the time."

I shook my head trying to act grown up. "Of course not."

"Besides the signs are in the car, and Dean just texted me and told me he's done with the tune-up on the Camaro, so I've got two cars in town and one driver."

"I could take the Camaro." I'd always wanted to drive Cade's Camaro.

"No." That one word popped out so fast, I wasn't sure I heard him correctly.

"Excuse me?"

Cade had the decency to blush and lowered his voice. "No one drives my Camaro. You know that."

I did know that, but I thought since he was willing to let me drive the Tesla, the Camaro was fair game. "What about Dean? Did he drive your Camaro?"

Cade shook his head. "Dean is different."

"How so?"

"He's my mechanic."

"I'm your campaign manager."

"Exactly."

My eyes squinted. "What's that supposed to mean?"

"It means I trust you with everything—"

"Except the Camaro."

"Exactly."

"Fine. I'll take the Tesla to Waco and be back by eleven o'clock."

Cade grinned. He got his way, but I was going to be driving a Tesla and having dessert at midnight. I was the winner in my book.

Chapter 18

Driving Cade's Tesla was like driving a crotch rocket without the rumble between my legs and the bugs between my teeth. It handled like a dream, zigging and zagging through traffic like it wasn't a four-door sedan. I understood why he'd chosen the car. I'd probably choose the same—if I had the money. Although, if I had my druthers, I'd pick the two-door Roadster model. Now *that* was a car.

The stereo was also beyond anything I'd ever experienced. Especially when I Bluetoothed my phone, and my playlist tuned out everything but me, the luxury, and the road. It didn't hurt that I could go zero to sixty in 2.5 seconds. The car was so luxurious, it was insane. And I felt spoiled to be driving it. Too bad I'd wake up tomorrow morning and still have an empty parking spot in front of the Barn. But for tonight, it was mine.

I smiled. This job was turning out to be pretty awesome. I could get used to a job with perks like this. The drive to Waco had been all about getting used to the car and all its gadgets. The return home, however, was a different story. As soon as I'd hit the freeway, I had a hard time keeping my speed below seventy. I wasn't about to try to engage the Autopilot. I wasn't to that level of trust with the car…yet. No one who grew up with Linda Hamilton as their mom's hero could possibly trust a machine with artificial intelligence right off the bat. Machines could destroy us.

This one was destroying me for all other cars.

I passed several vehicles and felt the power seep into my psyche. It'd been like this the whole trip. After dropping off the boxes of signs and talking to Suzie Springer about where she was going to place them, I'd given her and her granddaughter a spin around the block that had turned into a race down Pioneer Parkway. It was just a minor setback in my time, and I thought I could afford it.

That was where I ran into my second hiccup on the trip—I got pulled over. Officer Buckholtz was ready to write me a ticket for racing down Pioneer Parkway, until he saw Ms. Springer's granddaughter's baby-blue eyes peeking out of the backseat. Apparently, the two had been flirting for weeks, and Ms. Springer told Officer Buckholtz it was time for him to start singing, or to get out of the choir, 'cause someone else was standing in line to put that choir robe on. I was pretty sure that meant he'd better ask her granddaughter out then or forget about her. Before Officer Buckholtz walked away with his full ticket book, the two had a date for Sunday brunch after church.

This trip had been too good to be true, and I was enjoying every minute of the ride. It was as if the car and I were linked. It was an extension of me, and I was a part of it.

The drive home was a dream…until I saw headlights closing in behind me from the three camera angles displayed on the digital dash. It had to be a cop. I look down at the speedometer and saw my speed had crept up to seventy-five miles per hour. I started counting the dollars that speed would cost me.

Fuzz buckets. This car would destroy my wallet too.

The headlights came closer, and I slowed to sixty-eight. The lights encroached on my space, to the point where I couldn't see them except through the cameras. Nor could I see the driver, despite the three different camera angles, who was bold enough to ride my tail like a like a second skin.

I pulled into the right lane. Giving him the opportunity to pass…or follow me and pull me over. He followed me, but not directly behind me. His headlights hit the side rear window right before I felt his bumper connect with the Tesla's left rear quarter panel.

"Holy crap!" The Tesla swerved after becoming the victim of what I could only describe as one of those pit maneuvers I'd seen a police cruiser do in a televised car chase. I fought the drag of the vehicle as it tried to spin out of control. The automatic breaking took over, but I had no idea how to handle it. I overcompensated. Tire tread burned. Smoke billowed. From where I had no clue. The grade of the shoulder made that *thumpity, thump, thump, thump* noise under the wheels that was supposed to wake me up if I'd fallen asleep.

I couldn't be more wide awake.

I gained control of the spin just as the driver's side rear window shattered behind me, and something hit the passenger seat. I instinctively knew it wasn't just bits and pieces of broken glass. This was much more powerful—deadly. I spit every cuss word I could think of out the broken window as glass sprayed the plush interior.

That was when I realized, I *could* be wider awake. Someone had just shot out the window! I gripped the steering wheel tighter and hit the gas pedal with everything I had. There were no emergency lights on that truck. It wasn't a police officer trying to get me to stop because he thought I was fleeing. This was a madman hell-bent on killing me.

And I wasn't going to let him.

I zoomed past a pickup and a sedan that appeared to be crawling at an ungodly speed. Three more cars were put behind me. I heard a horn honk as the breeze flowed through the interior of the car. Bits of glass riddled my hair, and I could feel tiny shards poking my back between me and the seat.

Cade was going to kill me…if I survived. Warning signals beeped at me that I was too close to the next vehicle driving in the passing lane. I flashed my lights as the Tesla slowed down. I looked in the mirrors but couldn't tell if any of the headlights behind me belonged to the shooter's truck or if he'd abandoned the chase and took the last exit. Several vehicles merged onto the freeway but all I could think about was creating more distance between me and whoever wanted to obliterate my existence.

I passed a Fiat with Kansas tags on the right when it refused to relinquish the passing lane and floored the gas pedal once more, kicking it even faster when I hit a straight away.

It was only then that I saw the curve. I should have remembered it. The state had vowed to fix it—make it less dangerous. My hands tensed on the wheel as I braked into the turn, and the automatic brakes engaged farther.

The yellow sign warning drivers to slow their speed to forty-five miles per hour flashed in front of me, and I could have sworn it looked like a smiley face emoji laughing at my stupidity. The automatic braking engaged farther, and a truck loaded with lumber loomed in front of me. I tried to pass him on the left, but with the curve, his load shifted. My wheels held… at first. Despite my speed, I saw the stack of lumber snap one belt in half, releasing just above the buckle with the top section whipping in the air. The second belt stretched and strained as the lumber fell off the back, landing like a stack of pick-up sticks being tossed across a table. The load tumbled end over end, snapping and twisting. A piece hit the windshield before I even saw it coming my direction and spiderwebbed the glass. I didn't have time to thank God it hadn't penetrated the windshield and skewered me to leather—the truck and the road swerved.

I hit the brakes harder and yanked on the wheel, but my reaction was too much, too frantic, and my fate was sealed. The car spun out of control. I hit the rumble strip running alongside the left lane faster than I had the last one. All four wheels spun across as the Tesla hit the median like Jimmy Johnson tearing up the infield after winning the NASCAR Sprint Cup series at the Texas Motor Speedway. Grass flew, and the car bounced over the rough terrain. I could see headlights coming at me from all directions, or maybe it was because I was spinning and seeing the highway through psychedelic sunglasses.

The car slammed to a stop, and three airbags hit me, filling the vehicle with smoke and powder. My heart lurched, then pounded when I began coughing. The stereo was muffled and sounded like a pillow had been pressed against each one of the speakers. Then again, the effect could have come from the pillows blocking my ears.

I released the seat belt and fumbled with door handle as I fought the airbags. I fell out of the car into a drainage ditch that ran down the center of the median and looked around from the vantage point of my knees as someone ran toward the car. If that was the man who shot at me, I was a sitting duck.

"Charli! Jesus, woman, is that you?"

I looked up from the snakeskin boots to the lanky man wearing them. "Dallas?"

The king of recycling reached down and grabbed my arm. "Are you hurt? Maybe you shouldn't move. I should call an ambulance."

"No!" I yelled over the noise of the freeway from the traffic going the opposite direction. The cars on my side of the road had come to a standstill thanks to lumber scattered across the interstate.

Dallas helped me to my feet, and I got a better view of the carnage. The Tesla was silent in the median, its rear driver's side dented and caved. The windshield wasn't just cracked like I thought, it had been speared by an eight-foot two-by-four that I hadn't even seen. My legs nearly buckled at the thought of that wood penetrating all the way to the passenger seat, but Dallas held on to me, steadying the Jell-O that had once been my legs.

He looked around and then pulled a large knife from his waistband. It flipped open with the push of a button, and I stumbled backward, but he wouldn't release my arm. Full of panic, I struggled against him until he stabbed the airbags blocking the driver's seat.

"Charli, I got you. Relax." His tone was smooth and calming as if he was coaxing a newborn calf to his side.

Another man ran up as Dallas closed his knife and eased me back into the driver's seat.

"Is she okay?" he asked. "I called the police. They're on their way." He paused and then blurted out, "She was driving this thing like a mad woman. She nearly rear-ended me!"

"You were driving too slowly to be in the passing lane," I argued but the man wasn't listening. He was checking out the totaled Tesla. I looked over the seat and saw Cade's extra boxes of campaign posters strewn across the back seat in a crumbled mess. "Cade is going to kill me."

"Cade?" Dallas squatted down in front of me and touched the bump on my forehead. His touch was gentle and caring, and after the horror I'd just gone through, I welcomed the tenderness. A tear slipped down my cheek, and he wiped it away. "It's going to be okay," he whispered.

I nodded, embarrassed that my emotions got the best of me, but unable to stop a second tear from falling. "This is the mayor's car. I delivered boxes to a volunteer in Waco. Just a quick trip there and back." I pointed to the rest of the posters in the back. "These were supposed to go to Austin tomorrow."

Dallas was sympathetic and a good listener. "We're lucky you're okay. That's what really matters."

"I need to call Cade."

"Cade can wait."

"No, you don't understand." I got up and tried to open the falcon wing back door, but it wouldn't budge. "Dagnabit." My head slumped. "This was supposed to be a good night."

Dallas's voice was gruff. "He doesn't deserve you Charli, if he's more worried about the car or his posters, or whatever you think he's going to be upset about."

Dallas didn't understand. I was bringing more drama to Cade's campaign. I was supposed to be helping, making things right, but I'd just brought more trouble his way. Who would vote for a candidate who continued to be surrounded by one disaster after another?

The voters would have to be crazy to back him.

Chapter 19

The first deputy on the scene asked if I'd been drinking. Dallas answered for me. Otherwise I may have taken his head off at that point. I was the campaign manager for a man running for US Senate. If anyone else at the scene got wind of Deputy So-and-so wanting to give me a breathalyzer it would create a scandal bigger than Cade would be able to handle. But he had kept me from calling Cade and giving him the heads up. My phone had gone flying in the middle of me doing donuts in the grass and since it was a crime scene, the officer wouldn't let me search through the car. I suspected he was hoping to find some type of illegal substance with my prints all over it.

The highway was a disaster, but the only fatality was the Tesla. The only injury was my pinky from the airbag deploying. Mr. Fiat told the officer I was speeding, and the truck driver confirmed it. Of course, he was trying to distract the officers from recognizing his crime of having an improperly secured load. Two straps for a trailer load of lumber—hello? In what world was that secure? He would have lost his load whether I'd been there or not.

An ambulance came, and paramedics checked me over, but I declined treatment. They wrapped my finger anyway and told me it was probably just a sprain, but if it continued to bother me, I should have it checked out.

Detective Youngblood arrived and told me that Cade and Mateo were en route to the scene. Then he called MacAlister's Auto Shop and had Dean dispatched to pick up the car. I wasn't going to let anyone else touch the car no matter what they said about it being a crime scene, so I was happy MacAlister's was on the list of approved city tow services for the Sheriff's Department.

Dallas had gone back to his car and got a jacket for me to wear, and I was thankful to have someone from Hazel Rock there with me. It wasn't that it was that cold leaning up against the trunk of the police car; it was that I was that shaken up. The unused adrenaline in my body kept my hands quivering and my kneecaps twitching. It was as if the synapsis between my nerves and my brain had shorted with the damage to the artificial intelligence in the car. The stupid thing had ruined me.

I saw an unmarked police car drive down the exit ramp and knew it was Mateo. I wasn't sure I'd ever been so happy to see that Dodge Charger.

"I can give you a lift home, if you'd like. It's no trouble," Dallas offered.

Before I could answer I heard Cade calling my name. I looked up and saw him running down the shoulder as if he had two linebackers hot on his trail. Before I knew it, I was off the ground being smothered in a bear hug.

"I can't breathe," I forced out.

Cade released me and set me on the ground and rubbed my biceps as if he was trying to warm me up. Then he saw the bandage on my hand, and something within him snapped. "You're fired."

"What?"

"That's it, you're fired."

"You're going to fire me because some...some..."

Mateo joined us. "Don't say it, Charli. There's no reason to get yourself all riled up."

"Riled up! He just fired me!"

Dallas stepped up. "I can take you home, if you'd like, Charli."

Mateo looked at Dallas like he was ready to throw him on the ground and handcuff him. That was the last thing we needed. "Thank you, Dallas. But I suspect I'm going to be a while, and I'm sure the sheriff will take me home."

"Yes, I'll make sure she gets home."

I started to take off his jacket, but Dallas stopped me. "Don't worry about it. I'll get it from you another time."

I reached out to shake his hand, and Dallas hesitated. He looked at my hand, and then enveloped me in a hug. It felt awkward, and I knew Cade and Mateo were watching, wanting to know what the heck was going on. But Dallas had been there for me when they hadn't been, so I couldn't deny him.

"If you need anything, just holler." He lowered his voice and said, "You're too good for him."

I pulled away and gave him a we-can-only-be-friends smile. He smiled back, and I wasn't sure the message got across before he turned and walked through the string of cars piled up in the traffic jam.

"What's that about?" Cade asked.

"None of your business."

Mateo's eyebrows rose, but he kept his mouth shut.

"Are you firing me because I wrecked your car?"

"Don't be ridiculous. I don't care about the car."

I'd care about the car. It cost eighty-two thousand dollars. How could he not care about the car? "Then why did you fire me?"

"Because you were driving my car when someone tried to run you off the road."

"And shot at you," Mateo added.

"Wait." I started calculating their arrival. Cade had arrived maybe a minute before Mateo, which meant that they'd probably ridden together... and got the 411 on their way to the scene from Mateo talking on the radio to the officers working the scene.

Angels may as well have started singing and playing their trumpets. The moment of clarity I had was that illuminating.

The two of them had planned and plotted how to handle me before they arrived. My lips pursed, and I was sure it wasn't very attractive. I didn't care. I looked at Mateo. "Did you tell him to fire me?" My question was more of an accusation that didn't need a response. The truth was written all over their faces. It couldn't have been clearer if it'd been printed in black Sharpie magic marker on their foreheads.

"It was my decision," Cade said.

"Well, kiss my foot," I told him then made sure they knew I wasn't just talking to Cade. "Both of you."

I turned and started walking toward Dean's tow truck that had just pulled up to the scene and was going to load the Tesla. If he couldn't take me to Hazel Rock, then I'd use the card Dallas gave me and call him back.

"Ms. Warren, my detectives still need to get a statement from you." Mateo's voice was smug. Like he had the last word.

I wasn't going to let him win. It wasn't in my DNA. "I'm going to get my phone out of the car. If your officers want to stop me, they're going to have to arrest me."

Because *that* wouldn't stir up trouble. These two were going to know exactly who they were messing with. Nobody, but nobody, told me how to run my life.

I heard footsteps behind me and was spun around facing Mateo before I knew it.

I folded my arms across my chest. "What?"

"You owe me dessert."

"I've lost my appetite."

"No, you haven't."

"How do you know I haven't?" Because really. The man couldn't possibly see how much I wanted to be wrapped in his arms.

"Because I've sat back and watched two men hold you in their arms and you looked about as uncomfortable as a cowboy in Central Park. You want dessert. You just don't want Cade to know about it."

That *was* it. I'd had enough of the back and forth. If I didn't know before, I knew the moment Cade hugged me, and I caught sight of Mateo walking up behind him. I'd just been too sidetracked by Cade firing me.

"Do you really believe that?" I asked.

Mateo didn't say a word, but his eyes held a sadness I couldn't fathom. He honestly didn't know where my heart was. He nodded in response.

I did the only thing I could. I kissed him in front of God and the whole world, Cade included. The heck with the onlookers. The deputies would get over it. Cade would survive and follow the only true love of his life, his career.

I wanted something else entirely. I wanted the man who wore an ugly uniform and made it look good. I wanted the man who waited quietly for me to make up my mind. I wanted the man who put me first. I wanted the man I loved—Mateo—and I told him so. But the sheriff was in control and not about to create a scene. For a split second I didn't think I'd gotten through to him. Until he took over and pulled me tight against his vest. Like me, he needed dessert and when this night was over, it was going to be the best meal of our day. Our week. No, our entire year.

Chapter 20

I rolled over and found the other side of my bed empty. I looked down at the floor, and Princess was missing from her bed. Then I smelled the heavenly scent of cinnamon rolls in the oven and grinned. I stretched and enjoyed the soft cotton sheets underneath me and remembered the events of the previous night. We'd gotten home late, but neither one of us had been tired.

I smiled again as I got out of bed and wrapped myself in my robe.

I knew the tasty treat was for me, and me alone. Mateo didn't eat sugar unless it came from fruit. I snuck up behind him as he leaned over my counter eating a bowl of oatmeal. Princess was next to him, staring up and blinking through tired eyes for a handout. She didn't normally get up until nine or ten.

"I could hear you purring from in here," he said before I reached around him and hugged him from behind. His hair was wet, and he smelled like he'd just stepped out of the shower. I breathed in his scent which was just as good as the rolls in the oven.

"I don't purr."

Mateo looked down at Princess. "She says she doesn't purr."

Princess snorted and walked away, her toenails clicking across the thick planked wood floors all the way to her bed in the bedroom. I liked the way he talked to my pet. He didn't discount her, or act like she was a piece of furniture, but rather a part of my family.

I kissed Mateo's neck and looked at his breakfast. Plain, simple oatmeal. With a banana. And a glass of water. No jumpstart for Mateo Espinoza in the morning. No sweet tea. No coffee. No soda. Not even a glass of juice. I think I would die if I had to survive on his diet.

The timer on my oven buzzed, and Mateo stood up to turn it off while I went to pour a glass of sweet tea.

"I know I didn't have a package of cinnamon rolls in my fridge. Did you make them from scratch?"

"I cheated. I went to the bakery and Franz had some ready to go in the oven. He told me to put them in the oven at three hundred and seventy-five degrees for seventeen minutes, and he guaranteed you'd wake up."

I stopped pouring my tea with my glass half full. "You told him they were for me?"

Mateo reached into the oven with my dish towel and pulled out a small, round cake pan stuffed with pillows of cinnamony goodness. "He was opening the bakery and saw me go out for my morning run. I asked him what you liked best and he gave me these."

"You asked Franz what I liked best?" My God, the entire town would know I was sleeping with the sheriff before noon.

Mateo put the pan on top of the stove and looked at me, a masked expression on his face. "I'm sensing a problem with Franz knowing that I spent the night."

"It's the first time!"

He waited for me to explain something I wasn't sure I could. I took a few deep breaths and tried not to show how panicked I was.

Drat the man. Some things were just meant to be secret.

"I just don't think it would look good for us to flaunt our...our..." I waved my hand at my bedroom. "Activity to the whole town."

"The whole town, or Cade?" Mateo asked. Again, he looked distant, closed off from me.

"I think our kiss in front of everyone should answer that." I finished pouring my tea and put the pitcher back in the refrigerator before going over and looking him in the eye to show how sincere I was being. "Last night was incredible. The beginning of something special between us. I don't want it tainted."

"You'd rather it was between us," he clarified.

I smiled. He got it. "Yes."

Mateo set down the blue-and-white dish towel on the counter. "I don't kiss and tell, Charli. But I also don't slink around in the middle of the night making booty calls. If what we have is *that* special, it's time to put up or..." He kissed me on the cheek and turned toward his gym bag sitting on the bar stool on the other side of the counter.

"Mateo..." I called after him.

"I'll see you at the meeting," he said without looking back. The door to my apartment closed behind him, and I was left with the heavenly scent of cinnamon rolls cooling on my stove and the sound of Princess snoring in the bedroom. Once again, I'd screwed up.

Fuzz buckets.

I finished getting ready for work and ate a cinnamon roll. Unfortunately, it had lost some of its heavenly flavor when Mateo had left. Daddy called and said he would stop by the bakery for treats, and I made sweet tea for the Mystery Moms. By the time I went to unlock the doors, there was a small crowd waiting to get in.

Everyone was so excited I could have put out cardboard cookies instead of the tray of gourmet treats Daddy had bought. They made their way to the loft, and Reba Sue was the woman of the hour. She was eating it up, and I prayed that Nathan Daniels showed up. Otherwise Reba Sue's thunder would turn into a gully washer of tears.

Scarlet arrived with Liza and her cameraman on her tail. I greeted Liza, but she made it clear she wasn't there for the meeting; she was there to work. I wasn't sure if she ever went anywhere without work on her mind.

"That's him!" Betty yelled, her blue hair bobbing as she tried to look out the front doors to see the author's truck pulling his dinged-up trailer behind it. Nathan pull up in front of the Barn and parked. Luckily, Daddy had thought to block off several parking spots that extended to the corner for the large trailer. Nathan made his way toward the door while all the women from the loft poured downstairs.

"Did you expect this kind of reaction?" Scarlet asked.

"Not for one minute. I don't think Mateo did either. He hasn't made it here yet."

"Well, I wouldn't miss it for the world," Sugar added. She was dressed in a jean skirt and a figure-hugging T-shirt that read *Eat Your Heart Out*.

I looked at her shirt. "Is there a message there?"

"Dean insisted I wear it. I agreed if he promised to stay away. I don't want him going back to jail." Sugar smiled mischievously. "I didn't tell him I planned to wear it all along."

Scarlet and I laughed. I started to go toward the door, but Sugar stopped me.

"I need y'all's help."

Scarlet stopped smiling immediately, and we both leaned in to form a small circle. "What's wrong?" Scarlet asked.

"Princess, I need to know if I can use the Barn the day after tomorrow."

I didn't hesitate. "Of course. Is it one of the kids' birthdays? We can have it in the loft—"

"Dean and I want to get married in the tearoom."

Scarlet squealed. Some of the women looked at us, but we ignored them. Especially Liza who moved closer to see if she could hear our conversation. We closed ranks.

"The tearoom still has a bunch of Cade's campaign stuff, and I'm not sure if I can get it all moved out in two days."

Scarlet wasn't daunted. "The girls and I will help, and I will be all over Cade Calloway like honey on a biscuit. That man won't know what hit him."

"There's one more thing."

I looked at her encouragingly, but I was really thinking what else could there possibly be? A wedding was as big as it got.

"I'd like for the two of you to be my bridesmaids." Sugar looked as if she thought we would deny her request. Her hesitation disappeared with Scarlet's squeal.

"Absolutely." Scarlet beamed. "We'd be honored."

"I couldn't agree more," I said as I gave her a hug. "What do you want us to wear?"

"Betty's making the dresses."

"Betty? As in Betty from Bluebonnet Quilts, Betty?" I asked. I could just imagine a quilted gown that looked like a bedspread.

"Yup. She said she knew exactly what to make, and she and I are meeting in just a bit to finalize the plans."

"Is she making your dress as well?"

Sugar laughed as if the question was funny. I didn't think it was funny. If she trusted her with our dresses, why wouldn't she trust Betty with hers? "No, silly. I've had mine picked out for a long time. I went and bought it this morning."

I knew some women looked at wedding dresses and loved all the pageantry surrounding it, but I couldn't imagine knowing what my wedding dress looked like before a man asked me to marry him.

"Betty will have the dresses made for the final fitting that morning. It will work out just fine."

I looked at Scarlet. There was a vast difference between my shape and hers and Sugar was like a combination of our best assets put together in one package. These dresses were going to be a nightmare.

"Is Franz doing the cake?" Scarlet asked.

Sugar glowed. It was like she felt no stress whatsoever. I'd be going bonkers in her place. "He is."

"What about decorations. Do you know what you want?" I asked, because really, I didn't have a clue.

"I hadn't really thought about it—"

Scarlet cut in. "I got this. Don't worry. Charli, you worry about that new job of yours, and I'll worry about the wedding."

I didn't have the guts to say I'd already been fired. If I did, they'd rely on me to decorate the Barn, and I really couldn't see that turning into anything but a disaster.

The crowd started getting anxious for Nathan Daniels to come inside and pushed toward the entrance.

"Congrats, Sugar. I'm so happy for y'all." I gave her a hug and excused myself as Nathan Daniels walked in with a calm, confident demeanor, but I could have sworn I'd seen a glint of pleasure in his eyes when he saw the number of women present and the camera there to record it all. I walked up and introduced myself.

"Welcome to the Book Barn Princess. I'm Charli Rae Warren. My daddy, Bobby Ray, and I own the store." Nathan shook my hand and then my daddy's. "We have a place set up in the loft for you to talk to our Mystery Moms Book Club, if that's okay?"

Nathan nodded and began to speak but a rumble from outside the store drowned out whatever he'd begun to say. The noise grew louder as the Barn doors suddenly opened, and a motorcycle came through. Several women screamed as everyone scrambled to get out of the way. Nathan Daniels, however, stayed rooted to his spot. Daddy and I immediately jumped in front of him to protect him from whatever was going to happen next.

The rider roared the engine, filling the barn with noxious fumes, before he came to a stop just feet from where we stood with our backs to him as we held our arms out as a protective barrier. What we thought our arms would do against a man on a bike that size, I have no idea. It just came instinctually to us to protect our guest. The engine growled one more time before Tiny Greer turned it off and put down the kickstand in one fell swoop as he dismounted. He was madder than I'd ever seen him, and that was saying something.

"You no-good, yellow-bellied sapsucker! I'm going to tear you limb from limb!" Tiny growled as he stalked toward Nathan. I turned my back to Nathan hoping Tiny would realize he'd have to go through me and Daddy first.

Daddy said, "Tiny, I understand you're upset—"

"Upset? He killed my sister! Upset doesn't begin to describe what I'm feelin'!"

Dressed in a leather vest with patches covering most of the front, I saw that Tiny had added something since the last time I'd seen him. Under his left eye was a tattoo of an outline of a teardrop that was a little puffy and red. It was brand new, and I wondered if he got it for Maddie. Yet didn't a tear drop tattoo mean the bearer had killed someone?

Tiny yelled at Nathan Daniels who was content to stay right where he was behind Daddy and me. "That was your plan, wasn't it?" He accused. "That whole time I was feeding you information about the people, the politics, and the history of this town dating back to my great-uncle Captain Jedediah Greer in the Civil War, you never said anything about killing off my sister and getting rich off it!"

I looked at Daddy. Were we protecting a murderer?

Tiny took advantage of our momentary distraction. He grabbed Nathan by his grungy Rolling Stones T-shirt and pulled him out from behind us. A look of pure panic crossed Nathan's face as Tiny wrapped the Rolling Stones logo of Nathan's T-shirt around one fist, as the other reared back to punch him in the face. The room filled with so much noise, I couldn't tell who was screaming, who was cussing, or who was grunting. Daddy pushed Tiny as I grabbed Nathan and pulled with all my strength. His shirt ripped from his body, and Tiny was left off balance with a T-shirt in his hands. But he didn't stop. He was ready to pulverize Nathan Daniels, and nothing was going to stop him.

Tiny moved faster than I thought possible. He came at Nathan like a freight train and swung again. His fist came so fast I didn't think anyone could defend it. Nathan saw it and did the only thing possible. He leaned back into me to avoid the roundhouse punch, and I stumbled away from him. Tiny missed his target, but I felt the air swoosh by my face.

A pink blur at Tiny's feet sent a panic through me. "Princess!"

Tiny saw my pet and tried to step around her, but the force of his swing hitting air spun him around, and he fell against Nathan with the force of well over three hundred pounds behind it. They crashed to the floor, and Nathan disappeared from sight.

A hush fell across the store.

Princess walked to her bed behind the register as if nothing had happened. I couldn't fathom her calm. She'd almost ended up at the bottom of that pile. As it was, I couldn't see one piece of Nathan. It was as if his body disappeared into the floor.

"Where is he?" Reba Sue screamed.

"I think he's under Tiny," Sugar said.

Liza was giving play by play to her cameraman who zoomed in on Tiny's face as he lay flat on his back with his arms splayed wide.

Reba Sue was in a panic. "Get off him!" She ran up to Tiny and pulled on his arm. Tiny blinked as if he was in shock as he looked up at the ceiling of the Barn. "There's a loft up there," he said. Then he wiggled his body and drew his eyebrows down as he tried to figure out why he was so uncomfortable on a floor that was lumpy, not smooth.

"Nathan Daniels is underneath you...you, you big oaf!" Reba Sue wasn't the least bit concerned about Tiny hitting her.

Tiny grinned, and I heard Nathan's muffled moan from underneath him.

"He's alive!" Reba Sue screamed.

"Not for long," Tiny said with a grin. He lifted his body ever so slightly and threw it back down.

Daddy leaned over and looked Tiny in the eyes as several women tried to pull him off Nathan Daniels to no avail. "Get off him, son. You don't want to kill him."

"Who says?" Tiny asked.

Daddy wasn't swayed by Tiny's comment. "Come on. Give me your hand."

Tiny's beefy hand wrapped around my daddy's, and I noticed for a second time that he had scratches and bruising all over the knuckles. It was the type of injury a man got from being in a fight, which wasn't a far stretch with a man who had a temper, like Tiny. It also wasn't a far stretch to believe he'd gotten them from punching a woman and shattering her cheek.

"Sheriff!" Reba Sue yelled. "He's killing him!"

Mateo squeezed through the crush of people gathered around and helped Daddy stand Tiny up. I wasn't sure the man could have gotten up without assistance.

"What happened?"

"I fell on him."

"You tried to kill him!" Reba Sue said from her position on the floor next to Nathan Daniels.

"I wasn't trying to kill him. But if he died, it would be no loss."

I had to agree with Tiny on that one, even if I didn't trust him. "Tell the sheriff what you said about him killing Maddie."

"He paid me for information on the residents of Hazel Rock last summer. He said it was for his research. Then he went and killed Maddie."

"You know that he killed your sister?" Mateo asked.

"He wrote about it before it happened, didn't he?"

Mateo looked at Nathan, who hadn't moved. Nathan almost looked like a miniature version of Tiny as he lay on the floor and tried to catch his breath. Reba Sue patted his hand and talked to him until Nathan sat up without assistance. He grabbed his ribs and moaned but didn't say anything.

"Detective Youngblood is on his way, Tiny. I'm going to need you to give a statement to him."

Tiny nodded but I doubted his interview would be as telling as what he'd said in the heat of the moment. Mateo walked over to Nathan and talked to him in a low voice that I couldn't hear. Nathan stood up, his pale thin chest glaring with the lights from the Barn. Reba Sue pulled his arm over her shoulder, insisting she help.

Like Princess, Sugar snorted and walked away. She didn't look back until she was standing in front of the pastries, eating an oatmeal-cranberry cookie and sipping on a glass of sweet tea.

I didn't blame her one bit for the eat-your-heart-out shirt or the matching expression she gave the author who had turned her life upside down. I just hoped Mateo found out what happened before someone else's life was put on the chopping block.

Chapter 21

Cade walked into the Barn and looked around at the empty lobby. "I missed all the action, didn't I?"

"Yep." I moved a box of books to the steps and set them down.

"Is that Nathan Daniels's trailer parked out front?"

"Yep." I reached for a second box, but Cade stepped forward and took it from my hands. "I get the impression you're not talking to me."

"Nope." I made sure he couldn't grab the third box by turning away from him and carrying the box all the way up the stairs.

Cade followed with my other two boxes. "Princess, someone tried to kill you. I don't want you to be targeted because you're my campaign manager."

"Did you and Mateo ever think that maybe I wasn't the target, but that you were the target?"

"We did, but either way, it puts you in danger."

I turned on him with my hands on my hips. "What about me told you two that I couldn't make up my own mind? That I couldn't worry about my own safety?"

"We just thought…"

"That's the problem. The two of you 'thought' without thinking of asking for my opinion."

I stomped down the steps, and Cade followed me. "Are you telling me that you still want to be my campaign manager?" Cade asked.

I stopped at the bottom of the steps. "Is the position still open?"

"There isn't anyone else I'd rather have."

"How much are you willing to pay me?"

"The same amount that you're making here."

"That's hardly worth my while." I wasn't about to let him off that easy.

"I'll double it."

He had my attention with that, but still... "Just a moment ago you didn't want me."

"You know you drive me nuts, right?"

"Fine. I'll take double and a half."

"You drive a hard bargain, Princess."

"But I'm worth it."

"Yes, you are." Cade turned away and grabbed the hand truck behind the register and started walking toward the back of the Barn while talking over his shoulder. "Since you're working for me, I need you to help me load up the boxes from the tearoom. My campaign office is ready to open."

I followed in his tracks. "What? You didn't tell me you had a campaign office?"

He slid the door open and asked, "What do you think all those renovations in the old barber shop were for?"

"I thought you were renovating it to rent out."

"I was. I'm my first customer. After the campaign is over, we'll see if I turn it into my office or rent it out to someone else."

"Oh, you won't be renting it out. That old barber shop will be your office for years to come. You didn't get rid of the barber pole, did you?"

Cade pushed the hand truck into the tearoom. "No. I kept it and had it refurbished along with one of the chairs."

I laughed. "What are you going to do with the chair?"

"It's a part of this town's history. I wasn't going to just wipe it off the face of the map." He stopped next to the side door and saw my overflowing bin of recycling. "What's this?"

"The recycling truck didn't come today. I called Dallas, but I haven't heard back from him."

"That's odd. You're the third person that has told me their recycling wasn't picked up. Normally Dallas is very responsive. I better call him and see if something is wrong at the plant." Cade pulled his phone out of his pocket, and I remembered what Tiny had said about no one sorting the recycling. I grabbed Cade's arm. "Ummm, we may have a problem."

I could tell Cade didn't want to hear what I had to say, but he asked anyway. "What?"

"I don't know if there's any validity to what I heard or not."

"I can tell I'm not going to like it. What is it?"

I sighed. Being the bearer of bad news was not my forte. "Tiny said that there hadn't been any sorting going on at Bin Dover since he was laid off two weeks ago."

"How would Tiny know that if he was laid off?"

"I don't know. I know that Dallas said he laid Tiny off because Tiny hit his sister."

"Maddie?" Cade asked.

"Yeah, and I noticed abrasions all over Tiny's fists too. You don't think that he killed his own sister, do you?"

"Why would he be going off halfcocked all the time and bringing attention to the case if he killed her?"

I didn't have an answer for that.

Cade frowned and tapped in Dallas's phone number into his phone. He stood there, not moving as he waited for Dallas to answer. I could see it on his face that something was wrong; then, he started talking. "Dallas this is Cade Calloway. I'm calling about the recycling. I've heard from a couple of the businesses that their recycling wasn't picked up this morning. If there's a problem with the trucks, or something is wrong, we need to talk. This program is important to our town. I also wanted to talk about the reported theft of the aluminum. Call me, and we'll sit down and get things worked out."

Cade hung up but he wasn't happy. "This isn't just bad for the town. This could break my campaign."

I punched Cade in the arm. "I'm sure there's an explanation for it. If there's a problem, we'll find a solution. Remember? I'm your running back."

"Then help me load up this dolly and take it out to the truck so we get that office opened for business."

"Yes, sir, Senator."

"Not yet. So far, it's just mayor. This time next year, you can call me senator."

"That's the Cade Calloway who stole my vote."

"Besides, if I didn't get these out of the Barn today, Scarlet said she'd shave my head the next time I came in for a haircut."

"She does have big plans for the tearoom."

"What's she planning?" Cade asked as he began stacking the boxes.

"There's going to be a wedding." I smiled because Dean and Sugar deserved their happily ever after. Cade didn't say a word, and we made thirteen trips to his pickup with me pushing a load on the hand truck and Cade carrying several boxes. By the time we were finished, the tearoom almost looked like new. Almost. Now I had to figure out what to do with the recycling.

Cade made me promise to come into the office the next morning to set up my desk and to help organize the office. Since it was my day off, it wasn't going to be a problem. He took off, and I began the process of cleaning the tearoom. Scarlet planned on coming over that evening to start the decorating. I wasn't sure what she had planned, but she said she had a Pinterest page set up and Sugar was pinning things she liked. My job was to make sure the tearoom was clean.

Easy peasy. I could handle that.

Princess walked in and squeaked at me. I looked over, and there she stood with her boyfriend looking for a handout. I froze, unsure how to proceed.

"Princess, you need to take him outside," I ordered.

She sat up on her hind legs and blinked at me. Her boyfriend looked at her and did the same thing. Then he blinked as well. If I hadn't seen it with my own eyes I wouldn't have believed it. As it was, no one was going to believe me when I told them.

Maybe I shouldn't tell anyone, just in case they were too scared to take a chance to come for the wedding.

The bell at the front of the store rang, and I nearly panicked. "Sorry, the Book Barn Princess is closed!" I called out. "We'll be open tomorrow morning at ten!"

The person didn't answer, the bell didn't ring again, and I got the crazy feeling that things on the other side of the wall were all wrong. I looked around for something to use as a weapon. I had a couple plates, a butter knife, a glass. Nothing that would protect me if someone was out there with a gun. Nothing except for a skunk.

"I advise you to leave. I have a skunk in here, and he's ready to spray whoever walks through that door!"

Princess got down and waddled toward the door. Her boyfriend followed. It was my chance to grab a frying pan.

"You're the only woman I know who would have a guard skunk," Mateo said from over the top of the stall wall.

I swung around and grabbed my chest. "Geez Louise, Mateo you nearly scared me half to death. Why didn't you answer?"

"Because it's five o'clock, and you were telling me the Barn was closed when I know for a fact it doesn't close until seven o'clock. Why didn't you just tell me there was a skunk in the store?"

"I didn't want to scare off a customer or tell someone who was coming to the wedding that there was a skunk, and I certainly couldn't risk someone making him spray in the store again. That would be a nightmare."

"How did he get back in the store?"

"Princess brought him in for dinner. I'm not about to feed a skunk and encourage him to come back."

"He doesn't look like he's going to leave if you don't."

The skunk had rolled up in a ball and was sleeping right in the middle of my aisle. I couldn't get out of the tearoom unless I used the side door and came around the front or back of the store.

"Princess you have lousy taste in men," I complained.

Princess sniffed and put her nose up in the air. I didn't think she cared what my opinion was. She was hungry, and they weren't leaving until she said so.

"God, you can be stubborn." I reached into the refrigerator and pulled out the container of mealworms I kept for Princess. I wasn't about to give them anything but organic food.

Mateo pulled himself over the wall of the stall with ease and hopped down on the floor.

"Is this the way you're going to be when your teenage daughter brings home a boyfriend?" he asked.

"Is that your idea of a tactical entry?"

Mateo laughed. "I've heard mother-daughter relationships can be volatile."

"I don't think they're any different than father-son relationships."

"You got me there."

Mateo put his arms around my waist from behind and hugged me tight. "I'm sorry for this morning."

I stopped fixing the food for Princess and her boyfriend and enjoyed the moment. "Me too." But there was one thing he needed to know. "I'm going ahead with the job as Cade's campaign manager."

Mateo stiffened, and I braced myself for the lecture. He turned me around and looked me in the eye. "I'd rather you didn't."

"I understand that, but you have to trust me to make decisions that I think are in my best interest and decisions that I feel strongly about."

He could tell I wasn't backing down. This was an important stage in our relationship. I didn't take orders from anyone unless I was working for them. And even then, there were conditions. He leaned his forehead against mine and closed his eyes.

"This is important to you?"

"It is. I believe in him, Mateo." To lighten the mood, I told him about my pay. "And I'll be making two and a half times what I make at the Barn."

Mateo smiled. "Well, if I knew you're going to be robbing Cade blind—"

"I resent that!" I said but laughed because the tension was broken.

Until he turned serious again. "I need to tell you something."

"That sounds like bad news."

"It's not good news."

I took a deep breath. "Spill it."

"I got the ballistics test on the bullet that someone fired into Cade's Tesla." Mateo stared into my eyes.

"And?"

"They match the round that the ME pulled out of Maddie's body."

"You're kidding."

Mateo shook his head. "I wish I was."

"Was it Nathan Daniels? Tiny said he killed Maddie."

Mateo shook his head. "We're still working on it. I have at least one piece of evidence that will tie the killer to the scene, but it's going to take some time to get our search warrants. I'm hoping my detectives will get a confession."

"What evidence?"

"I shouldn't tell you."

"But what if I know something about it and can lead you back to the killer. I've had a lot of contact with Tiny and the women have been talking about Nathan Daniels like crazy. I might be able to help."

Mateo sighed. "It goes without saying that you cannot tell anyone else about this." He waited for me to nod before continuing, "I have a rare coin we fished out of the water tank. I think it may have been on a chain and Maddie pulled it off her killer."

"A rare coin?"

"That's all I'm going to say about it. Do you know if either of these men collect or own rare coins?"

I thought about it long and hard, and although I felt like I should be remembering something, nothing came to mind. "I feel like I should, but I just can't place anything."

"Call me if you think of anything, okay? Don't go off looking for clues. In fact, I'd rather you didn't go running around tonight. I want you to go straight to your apartment from inside the Barn, and I want you to stay home."

"Mateo—"

"Listen to me on this one, Charli. Just give me a couple days. You can go to work and lunch, and even dinner. But I'd rather know you were safe at home at night until I catch this guy. I don't want him to hurt anyone else. Especially you."

I had to compromise. I knew I did. And Mateo had to compromise when he didn't like me working for Cade. It was a matter of being in a relationship and making it work. We were going to have to act like adults. Fuzz buckets.

"Fine."

Mateo grinned and then tickled me. Princess squawked, and her boyfriend grunted.

"I think that's their way of saying they're not going to wait any longer," Mateo said.

"I think you're right. The last thing Princess and I need are two irate boyfriends."

We finished pouring their food into a couple bowls, and I slowly inched toward the door. Mateo waited in the tearoom.

"Are you telling me you're not going to protect me from a skunk?"

"I think you can handle this one. He likes you better."

"You protected Liza," I complained as I made my way past Princess and prayed the skunk didn't decide to share his scent.

"I protected the skunk from Liza and he misinterpreted my actions. You and he seem to be on the same page."

He was right. Princess's man seemed to like me. He waddled after me with his nose in the air and ran out the back door as I opened it. I put the food down and slowly backed into the store.

Mateo was waiting for me. He reached around and locked the door. "That's the last time you go out back, promise me."

"Cross my heart." I meant every word of it.

Chapter 22

The next morning, I was at Cade's campaign office bright and early. I hadn't dressed as casually as I normally did at the Book Barn. Today I wore a skirt and blouse with a pair of dressy flats. Cade met me at the office and we spent the day arranging the it. A couple of desks were set up for volunteers even though we didn't have any yet, but there were a few people I had in mind.

I was just going over my schedule when I looked up from my desk and saw Dallas entering the hotel across the street by the side door. He wore his usual plaid shirt, jeans, and cowboy hat and looked like he was on a mission. I wondered if he was going to address the recycling problem we were having in town. None of the bins had been picked up that morning either.

The hotel seemed to have the most, which was a dual-edge sword. The recycling was there because the hotel was open and had guests filling the bins, but the full bins didn't bode well for a green hotel. Some people may have changed or canceled their reservations because of Maddie's death, but others recognized it wasn't the hotel's fault and appreciated the changes they'd made to the water filtration system. A system that had been further improved upon with electronic monitors gaging the purity of the water.

It was the second man coming out of the alley and following Dallas into the Inn that captured my attention even more. Dressed in jeans and his Sunday-best shirt and boots, Tiny edged out from behind a recycle bin and then ran to grab the side door before it closed. If I had to guess, I would say Tiny was following Dallas. What he did right before the door closed was a game changer. Tiny looked around, and then reached for the leather case on his waist that held his bone-handled knife. It was a knife big enough to scare the bejeezus out of me the first time I saw it.

This time, it turned my blood cold. "Did you see what I saw?" I asked Cade.

He turned from his desk with a stack of books in his hands. "What?"

"Tiny just entered the side door of the Inn across the street. He was following Dallas."

"Is that supposed to mean something to me?"

"He was looking around right before he entered the hotel. It was as if he was looking to see if anyone was watching him. Then, right before he went inside, he grabbed his knife. He's up to something, and I think Dallas is his target."

Cade rubbed his brow, and I was sure he was wishing he hadn't put my desk in front of the window. "I would have to agree with that."

I grabbed my purse and slung it over my shoulder. "Come on let's go."

"Where do you think we're going?"

"We're going to follow Tiny. Because he's following Dallas. And he looks like he's up to no good." I walked out the door before Cade could argue.

He caught up to me a few steps out the door. "Princess…"

I didn't wait to hear Cade's argument; it was a moot point. Something was going on and Tiny was up to no good. As I crossed the street, Cade was right on my heels. "What do you plan on doing when we get inside?"

"That depends on what they're doing."

"If they're fighting in the lobby?"

"Then we'll break it up."

Cade grumbled something that sounded an awful lot like it would be him breaking up the fight, not me, but we walked in the front door together, side by side. The old Victorian lobby was empty. Even the front desk appeared abandoned. The desk had once been a saloon bar made of mahogany with a solid brass footrest running the entire length. The piece had been restored to near mint condition with the dents and scratches of yesteryear adding to its character. In the middle was a silver domed bell. I approached it and rang for service.

"Where do you think they went?" Cade asked.

I'd only met the hotel manager once before at the grand opening. Now she came out from the back room with her hair in a neat coiffure and her maroon suit crisply pressed. She looked surprised to see Cade, and when her eyes traveled to me, her mouth rounded in a shocked *O*.

"Mayor," she said. "How can I help you?" Her professional demeanor slipped as she glanced in my direction and sized me up. Naturally, Cade was oblivious.

"You've got the wrong idea, Ms. Winters. We're not looking for a room," I said.

Cade looked at me sideways, then it dawned on him what Ms. Winters was actually thinking, and he quickly denied it. "No! That's the last thing on our minds."

I glared at him. He didn't have to go that far. Ms. Winters smiled and was the very definition of charming. I wanted to barf.

"Of course not." she shook her head and gave a polite laugh as if no one would ever think of Cade and me getting a room. If she said *bless your heart*, I wouldn't be responsible for what came out of my mouth.

"Did you just book a room to someone?" I asked.

"I'm sorry, ma'am, but we value the privacy of our clientele. You understand." Her tone was meant to cut me off at the knees. When someone did that, my legs grew back faster than a horned toad's tail.

But Cade beat me to it. He raised his hand to silence me and addressed Ms. Winters. "As a major investor in this hotel—"

Ms. Winters nodded in acknowledgment.

"—I need to know if you have a Dallas Dover as a registered guest." He didn't ask a question. He demanded the answer. It was a smooth move.

"Mr. Dover? As in Bin Dover Recycling?"

Cade gave a curt nod.

"We haven't seen Mr. Dover or any of his drivers in two weeks. It's becoming quite a problem for our recycling program."

"Two weeks? I thought Dover Recycling was supposed to pick up twice a week?" Cade was clearly shocked by her announcement, but the hotel wasn't the only business on Main Street that had missed their pickup this week.

"We don't have time to worry about the recycling," I told Cade and then addressed the clerk, "We need to know where Mr. Dover went. It's important that we contact him." I didn't tell Ms. Winters that it was more than just important that we contact Dallas. We needed to get ahold of Dallas before Tiny tore him to shreds.

"I'm sorry, but I haven't seen Mr. Dover," Ms. Winters insisted.

"You're sure Mr. Dover didn't come in?" I asked.

"I was in the back office. I didn't hear anyone come in, but I was running the shredder, so I could have missed it."

"Can you check to see if you have him as a registered guest?"

Ms. Winters hesitated, but Cade gave her that charming political smile of his, and she melted. She began typing on her computer and a moment later she said, "I'm sorry, Mayor, but he doesn't appear to be registered."

I was about to ask her to check for Tiny's name when she said, "Well, that's weird."

"What's weird?" Cade and I asked at the same time.

"The day after we closed, the sheriff asked us to program the system to alert us if Maddie's access card was used again since the police couldn't locate it. We did, and I just got an alert that the card was used to access the roof."

I looked at Cade. "Did Mateo tell you the card was missing?"

"No, but obviously it was...until now."

Cade addressed Ms. Winters. "I need an access card to the roof, now."

"I'm sorry Mayor, but I was told to contact the police if anyone use that card—"

"I want you to call the police, but right now it's extremely important that you give me an access card to the roof."

"Mayor—"

"As a major investor in this hotel, I demand that you give me an access key to the roof. Now, Ms. Winters." Cade wasn't messing around. He was the man in charge in this town. It was in his expression, his manner, and his body language. He was playing offense and he was unstoppable.

Ms. Winters didn't argue. She reached into her blazer pocket and pulled out a card key. "You can have mine."

Cade took the key with a curt, "Thank you," and no smile. The politician in him had disappeared, and a new Cade stood in front of me that I didn't recognize. His expression was serious, which wasn't different from his normal demeanor, but instead of the strong, understanding personality he normally had, Cade displayed an unyielding determination that was all about taking names and kicking butt. It was a very good look for him.

Until it wasn't.

"Stay here and tell Mateo I'm on the roof with the guy who stole Maddie's card key." He started to walk by me, but I stopped him.

"Ms. Winters can tell Mateo where we are." I pointed to the manager who nodded in agreement as she dialed the phone.

"I'm not going to argue with you, Princess."

"Good. Let's go." I was halfway across the lobby before Cade joined me.

That unyielding tone was back in his voice. "I go first. You stay behind me at all times."

I didn't argue. Anything I said would be a waste of breath. We entered the stairwell together, but Cade took the steps two at a time and made it to the roof access door before me. He didn't sound like he'd expended much effort at all, and I tried not to show how winded I really was.

I wasn't fooling anyone. My chest was heaving, and the adrenaline building in my system had my heart racing.

"Can I get you to stay here?" Cade whispered on the landing.

"Not a chance," I said between breaths.

Cade nodded, swiped the card key across the sensor, and we exited the stairwell onto the roof at a running crouch. The roof was the typical light gray material that looked and felt like a padded tumbling mat, but it was made of something much stronger. There were rows upon rows of large solar panels angled toward the sun for maximum exposure at approximately thirty-degrees. The door we came out was like an old telephone booth without windows sitting in the middle of the roof. It provided concealment, and it blocked our line of sight to the other side of the roof. We made it to a set of raised solar panels and squatted down behind them. Cade had to bend his head forward. We scanned that side of the roof but saw nothing beyond solar panels.

"They must be on the other side of the door, near the water tank," Cade said.

I didn't want to think about the water tank. "Or they're not here at all."

I ran back toward the door and hugged the wall. I made my way to the first corner before Cade joined me and pulled me back behind him. He peeked around the corner and came back quickly with his finger to his mouth telling me to be quiet.

"Tiny has a knife pulled on Dallas, and they're arguing. I'm going to go around the other side and disarm Tiny."

He started to move past me, but I grabbed his arm. "Do you know how to disarm someone holding a knife?"

"No, but I know how to throw a tackle."

Oh boy.

He disappeared out of sight, and I peeked around the corner of the building. Tiny's eyes had lost all their humanity, and his already volatile temper was on the cusp of bursting into a million pieces.

Then he saw me, and his anger disintegrated as if it had imploded into nothingness. My appearance was the distraction Dallas needed. He reached for a gun in the back of his waistband, and everything seemed to happen simultaneously.

Tiny yelled, "Charli, no!" and Cade tackled him from behind.

The knife went flying. Dallas raised his gun and fired but, Tiny and Cade were no longer there. They were airborne. Then they were slamming into a set of solar panels that shattered underneath their weight as they tumbled to the rooftop.

Dallas fired again, and it was my turn to yell, "Dallas, no!"

Startled by my voice, Dallas whipped around and pointed the gun in my direction.

I raised my hands and said, "It's…it's just me."

But Dallas didn't seem to register that I wasn't a threat. The gun waved back and forth between Tiny and Cade and me. His eyes darted all around as Cade and Tiny grappled for the knife. I slowly move closer to Dallas, inching my way as he became more and more distracted by the fight occurring on the other side of the roof. Frustrated with where to point the gun Dallas reached his breaking point. He fired into the air and yelled, "Enough!"

Tiny froze with Cade's fist raised above him as he straddled the bigger man. He was ready to throw a knockout punch. I moved closer to Dallas, but his eyes were wild, and I wasn't sure how to get them back to where he needed to be to drop the gun. To let Cade handle Tiny until Mateo could get there and take Tiny into custody.

But it was Tiny who changed the meaning of what I was seeing. "He killed Maddie!"

I looked to Dallas to see if any of that made sense. I expected to see his anger grow at being accused of a crime he didn't commit. But his features smoothed, and he shook his head. That calmness I'd sought to give him engulfed him. The change was as eerie as it was quick.

"You just had to go and put them in the line of fire as well, didn't you Tiny?"

"He's telling the truth?" I asked Dallas.

"Unfortunately, he is."

"Why?" It was the stupidest question in the world to ask a man who could do what Dallas had done. He'd shot Maddie, and then left her in excruciating pain to drown, knowing no one would find her.

"Because she cheated on me. I treated her like a queen, and she went back to him. She went back to the man who treated her like trash. It was like I recycled her. Made her new and shiny again, and she went back to him. How do you women do that?" It was a rhetorical question. He wasn't even looking at me when he asked it. He was asking the space above my head like some more powerful or extraterrestrial being would answer the question for him.

He didn't want my answer. So, I didn't give him one. Yet that seemed to irritate him. The sneer he threw in my direction told me I was the trash that couldn't be recycled.

I ignored his disdain and told him the truth. "Maddie didn't cheat on you with Dean. Dean and Sugar are getting married. It was all a big misunderstanding."

"She left me when I laid off Tiny. She said I was a failure who couldn't even be a good trashman. I spent money on her I didn't have. She was the reason I could no longer pay her brother and the other workers to sort the recycling. But I was making it right. I paid to have that trash hauled off to the dump, and I was starting to turn it around. Until you started digging around in my business." He shook his head as if I was a spoiled child too self-absorbed to see the good he was doing for me. "I tried to be nice and straighten you out.

"Look at you. You've gone back to the mayor, and all he's done is use you. He has no respect for you. He dumped you in high school, and he's going to dump you as soon as he reaches the Senate. He's got no time for a woman like you in his life."

His words would have hurt if I'd gone back to Cade, but I hadn't. I'd chosen a different path, and it was a route to love that I wanted to take. "I didn't go back to Cade. He's my boss. I'm just working on his campaign."

"I saw you with him. You were even driving his car."

"Do you mean his Tesla?" It suddenly hit me how blind I'd been. "That was you who tried to run me off the road." Dallas had been there when I'd crashed, but he'd been kind, caring even. "Why did you run me off the road?"

Dallas got a little kick out of that. "You ran yourself off the road darlin'. I may have hit the car, but it was your bad driving that caused you to leave the road."

"I was in a panic because you tried to run me off the road and shot at me! I'm a good driver when someone isn't ramming the car I'm driving and using the windows for target shooting." I wasn't sure why Dallas insulting my driving offended me, but it did. Yet it was the last thing I needed to worry about right then while looking down the barrel of his gun.

Dallas shrugged. "I thought you were him. I was trying to get rid of the man who treated you so badly. Maybe if I'd gotten rid of Maddie's ex, I wouldn't have been put in the position where I had to kill her. I tried to be her hero, just like I tried to be yours."

That was the angle I needed to use to buy Cade and Mateo time. Dallas wanted to be a hero. It was there in everything he'd done since I'd met him. I didn't know where Tiny fit in to all of this, but he definitely wasn't in the same role I'd had him in five minutes ago. I used the only angle I knew to use. "You were my hero. You were there for me—twice. I hope you'll be there again."

Dallas was unreadable. His face was as absent of emotion as a dead person's. He waved his gun and indicated that I should move over to Tiny and Cade. I went where he directed me. Not because I wanted to make it easier for him to shoot all three of us, but because I wanted him to believe I would do anything he asked.

"I need you to tie them up."

I didn't hesitate. "Okay. Do you have any rope?"

"Use their belts."

"How do I do that?"

"Tiny, get up."

Tiny did as he was told, but he didn't look happy. It was hard to believe this man was anything but a hardened criminal.

Once Tiny was on his feet, Dallas said, "Take Tiny's belt off his waist and hold the two ends together. Create a loop in the middle. And gentleman, if you try anything, I will put a bullet in Charli's back."

I did as he said, step by step, waiting for his approval or correction. But most of all, waiting for the moment to arrive that I could make a move.

"Fold that loop to the belt buckle and shove that loop through the buckle. That will create a double-layered loop inside the buckle. Then you need to put those loops around his wrists." When Tiny put his beef hands out side by side, Dallas chuckled. "Palms together, Tiny, with your fingers intertwined." Tiny did as instructed with a sneer that made me wonder if maybe there were three different factions on that roof. Cade and I were one. Dallas was another. And Tiny was a wild card.

"Enclose his hands inside the two circular layers."

"Don't do it," Tiny whispered.

"Shut up!" Dallas lunged in our direction as he yelled. I flinched, expecting to be hit or worse, but he pulled up abruptly when Cade moved.

"Don't even think about being a hero, Mayor. Your day has come and gone." Dallas continued with his instructions, "Now pull the end of the belt tight."

I did as he told me to, but not too tight.

Dallas wasn't going to fall for it. "I said 'tight' Princess."

It was the first time Dallas had used my nickname. It felt dirty. Subservient and all wrong. I pulled the belt tight and knew immediately that the improvised cuffs would hold all too well.

Fuzz buckets. The moments to save us were dwindling.

"It's the mayor's turn."

I moved to Cade and he began to stand up.

"Let's keep you on your butt, Mayor. I saw that tackle. You haven't lost your touch in the last decade."

Cade stayed seated on the roof with his legs out in front of him and bent at the knees. I removed his belt and tried to establish eye contact, but he refused. He stared at Dallas the entire time, as if the two of us didn't know each other, had never met. I created the loop once more, and Cade held out his hands with his palms together as I tightened the leather around his wrists. It was only then that he looked at me and he had forgiveness in his eyes.

That look was nearly my undoing. My hands shook as I realized Cade didn't believe we were going to get out of this one.

"Come over here, Princess," Dallas ordered. Again, I followed his directions without hesitation. I moved toward Dallas wondering when that moment was going to come that I could change our fate. When I got within five feet, Dallas raised his elbows and exposed his waist. "Time to remove my belt."

My heart began pounding so hard, I thought for certain that he could see it. There was only one person that belt could be for, and if it went on my wrists, we were all dead. Mateo wouldn't make it in time, and I would have blown any moment we had left. I removed his belt and tried to think of a way to knock the gun away, but he had his finger on the trigger, and the gun was pointed directly at Cade. If I messed up, Cade was dead. I unbuckled his belt, and Dallas seemed to get an inordinate amount of pleasure from that small gesture.

"You do that well, Princess."

I ignored the jab and waited for his next instruction when I had his belt in my hands.

"Go on. Make a loop and then place it around your wrists." He said. "You've become a master at this bondage thing. I think you kinda like it."

The only bondage I had a desire to see was Dallas Dover trussed up and hog-tied. I would *enjoy* that.

"Now, pull it tight with your teeth."

I did as I was told, still waiting for that moment to arrive when I could do something, anything. But the moments were disappearing before my eyes. I was beginning to feel that same sense of hopelessness Cade felt.

I looked down at the belt and recognized it from the first time I saw him at the recycling center. At that time, the front of Dallas's belt had two 1947 five-peso Mexican coins attached to the front, but today there was only one.

"There's only one coin on your belt."

Dallas paused. "Did you find the other?" he asked. He genuinely wanted to know if I'd found it. There was a hopefulness in his voice that I wanted to dash. I wanted to crush his dreams the way he was destroying ours.

Yet I wasn't sure if he'd known how long it'd been missing. Did he know he lost it the night he killed Maddie? Or was he uncertain which day and where it'd gone missing? If I didn't make it out of there alive, I wanted Mateo to be able to trace his belt, and if I told Dallas I didn't have it, he might think twice about leaving it behind. Yet if I did have it, that might make him fear it being traced back to him as well. I wasn't sure what to say. I went with my gut.

"What? No. I was just trying to say I couldn't get it any tighter because of the coin." I held up my hands and kept my eyes on the loose wrap twining around my wrists.

I could feel Dallas eyeing me, trying to see if I knew something about his missing coin. Then his misguided chivalry returned. "Here, let me get that for you."

Dallas shoved the gun in the back of his waistband, and a shot rang out. I immediately looked for Mateo near the door, but there was no one there. Dallas jumped and yelled. The smell of gunpowder surrounded us. He pulled the gun out to his side, and blood covered his hand and the gun barrel. He dropped it like it was poisonous and stumbled backward.

It was the moment I'd been waiting for. The moment my fate was finally in my hands. I screamed and ran at him with everything I had. My shoulder hit him under the chin, and his head snapped back as we flew across the rooftop. Dallas was laid out prone, bent at the knees with his feet underneath him—digging into the wound where he'd shot himself in the butt.

The noise he made was anything but heroic.

"Princess," he begged. "You gotta help me. I'm bleeding!"

I rolled off him to find Cade holding the gun trained on Dallas. His hands were still secured in front of him with his belt, but the look in his eyes was deadly. Dallas saw it at the same time I did.

"You can't shoot me! You're the mayor! You're running for Senate!"

"Cade," I said. "It's over."

But it wasn't over in Cade's eyes. "He killed a woman because he thought she was unfaithful. He was going to kill you."

"He didn't. I'm here. You're here. And Tiny's here. It's over."

Cade blinked and finally took his eyes off Dallas for just a moment to look me in the eyes. "You're okay?"

I smiled. "I'm more than okay. I'm great. You should know that by now." Thankful that Dallas hadn't had the opportunity to tighten the belt on my wrists, I slipped it off my hands.

Cade took his finger off the trigger, and the corner of his mouth twitched. It wasn't a smile, just a hint of one.

"Let me take that," I said as I reached for the gun.

"Don't put it in your waistband and shoot yourself in the butt," Cade said.

I laughed. He may not be able to smile yet, but his sense of humor was returning.

Sirens began echoing in the distance, and I suddenly felt better knowing that Mateo was close.

"He's a lucky man," Cade said.

I looked at Dallas who had rolled on his side and was trying to stop the bleeding on his backside while tears were streaming down his cheeks. "I don't think he would agree." I set the gun down well out of Dallas's reach and began releasing the belt from Cade's wrists.

"I wasn't talking about Dallas. I was talking about Mateo."

I looked up to find him staring at me in a way he'd refused to look at me when I was putting the belt around his wrists.

"Thank you," I said.

Cade leaned forward and kissed me on the forehead. It was almost as if he knew it was the last kiss we'd ever share. He smiled and walked toward Dallas. For a moment I wondered if I should let him, but he took his shirt off, balled it up, and put it on Dallas's wound. Then he placed Dallas's hand over the shirt and told him to hold it tight.

That was more compassion than Dallas deserved.

I walked over to untie Tiny, but he shook his head. "Leave it on. I was going to kill him for what he did to my sister."

"But you didn't," I said.

"I still will if you release my hands. As it is, I can't get my butt up to even kick him where it hurts. It's best if I just sit here and wait for the police."

I understood Tiny's pain. I didn't have a sister, but I had a cousin who was like a brother to me, and I wasn't sure what I would be capable of if someone had taken him from me.

"We'll wait until the ambulance and the police take him away."

"That sounds like the best plan I've heard all day."

I had to agree.

Chapter 23

Today was the day. My stomach was churning with nerves. The tearoom was decorated with yards of white organza material flowing down from the rafters. The panels were gathered and tied with white ribbon with a cluster of paper roses made from book pages. Each book rose had been painstakingly inked on the edges with the color pink to add a touch of flair.

A chandelier had been hung from the center beam, and I knew as soon as I saw it that I would make it a permanent fixture in the store. The tables had been taken out of the room and moved to the wide aisles in the middle of the Barn for the reception that was to follow. Strands of white lights had been draped from one side of the room to the other, adding another element of romantic ambience to the area. The tables still had their white, lace tablecloths and centerpieces of mason jars filled with bundles of white bulbs.

The sun was going down, which helped with the mood lighting in the room and I had to admit, the Barn made the perfect backdrop for a wedding. Not that I wanted to have another one, but this one time would make it special—for Sugar and Dean.

Mateo walked up to me and bumped my hip with his. "You realize, that we also met here?" he said.

"Shhh. Everyone is watching."

"But they can't hear over the music."

That was the one thing I'd completely forgotten about. Every wedding needed music. Unfortunately, Betty had been the one to step up and fix my error. She was playing her piano, which had been rolled in twenty minutes earlier. I wasn't sure if the piano had been out of tune before it came, or if the move had jolted things around, but whatever key she was playing in, I didn't recognize it.

"It's awful," I whispered.

"It's perfect for this wedding."

I looked at Mateo as we made our way down the aisle together. He wore jeans with a tan vest, white shirt, and brown tie. On our first date, he'd worn a jacket, but no tie. Tonight, was the first time I'd seen him wear a tie, and I had to say I liked it on him. Cade and my daddy had the same outfit on, but somehow Mateo stood out.

"You look beautiful."

"I think something's going to pop out," I said as I adjusted my pink strapless dress with the hem almost as short as my short shorts. There were more ruffles on the skirt than a party-size bag of potato chips. The only saving grace was my shoes. They were comfortable, and my confidence was bolstered by my *Unconquerable* combat boots.

Mateo's grin was pure male.

"If that happens, it won't be funny."

"I'll be there to catch it."

I swallowed back the laughter. "My daddy wouldn't approve."

"Your daddy has his hands full."

It was true. Daddy was going to be walking the bride down the aisle, and he was more nervous than she was. Sugar was ready to get this show on the road and start her new life as Mrs. MacAlister.

"Do you think a woman should take the man's name?" I asked.

"I get the impression I can't pass this test."

I couldn't help but smile. "With an answer like that, probably not."

We reached the end of the walkway just as Betty hit the wrong key, and Mateo leaned over and kissed my cheek. "Then I'll plead the fifth."

"Chicken," I said as we went opposite directions to our positions at the front of the tea counter where we would wait for the bride and groom.

Cade and Scarlet were already standing with the preacher and Dean. Scotty followed us. Carrying a pillow with two rings attached to it, he was walking in front of his two older sisters who dropped rose petals made from book pages. Scotty was leading a very special flower girl: Princess. Princess didn't seem to mind her rhinestone leash or her tulle, ruffled skirt. Between the two of us, I think she was more comfortable than me.

I had been skeptical when Sugar had asked for her to be in the wedding party, but she walked well, as long as we had the petals dropped behind her and not in front of her.

My daddy and Sugar made their way into the tearoom, and cameras
started clicking. Sugar's dress was similar to mine and Scarlet's, but in
white with a short hem in front and a long train in back. The bodice was
covered with gorgeous white beading, and the waist with gold-toned beads
that accentuated her small waist and matched the tan cowgirl boots she
wore with pride. It was as unique as it was perfect for a barn wedding.

Daddy handed Sugar off to Dean who looked like he might cry. His
attire was similar to the other men's, but his vest was off-white, and he
wore a brown tweed jacket. I couldn't help but notice their hands shaking
as one as they greeted each other for the first time on their wedding day.
We turned toward the preacher, and the ceremony began.

It was simple, yet romantic, and the crowd stood and cheered as the
preacher pronounced them husband and wife. It wasn't long before we were
cutting cake and tossing the garter belt. The men gathered like it was no
big deal, but the women were eyeing them like they were the last piece of
chocolate in the box. They were hungry.

"Please tell me I don't look like that," I said as I indicted the crowd of
women I wanted Scarlet to see.

"You don't look like that."

"You're sure?"

Scarlet pointed out the signs. "Are you licking your lips like Reba Sue?"

"No."

"Are your hands sweating as badly as Liza's?"

I looked at Liza who was wiping her hands off on a table napkin.
"Absolutely not."

"What about Betty? Are you giving your man goo-goo eyes the way
she is Franz?"

Franz looked terrified. I covered my mouth to hide the laughter. "No."

Like most of the weddings I'd been to, the garter belt toss was rigged.
Dean shot it straight to his little boy, Scotty who squealed with delight.

"Time for the bouquet!" Dean yelled, and Sugar walked up the staircase
toward the loft and stopped halfway up.

Scarlet and I stood next to each other, neither one of us real anxious
to catch the bouquet of book roses we'd made for Sugar. The piece had
turned out well, but it wasn't like I couldn't make another one. Like the
roses on the drapes, these were edged with pink ink but also had pale pink
ribbon and beads.

"I'm going to let one of Dean's daughter's catch it," I said.

"Then the other one will be upset," Scarlet whispered.

She had a point. The girls seemed to compete over everything.

"Let Betty catch it," I suggested.

"Franz might have a heart attack."

Franz was looking decidedly ill. "Well, we can't let Reba Sue catch it. Cade will have to leave town."

"Are you sure he'd want to?"

I rolled my eyes. "He's not that desperate."

"What about Liza?"

"No," I said.

Scarlet quirked her brow. "Why not?"

"Because she doesn't deserve it."

"It might make her change her attitude."

We looked at Liza who looked like she was going to fight dirty to get the bouquet. I scoffed. "You're dreaming."

Scarlet nodded in agreement. "Probably."

"One of us is going to have to catch it, and I think it should be you." I told Scarlet.

"Why me?"

"Because you've been dating Dalton longer. It makes sense that you're closer to the altar than I am."

"That makes no sense whatsoever. You should be the one to catch it. Your boyfriend lives in town."

I glanced at Mateo. He looked completely relaxed. It was as if it wouldn't bother him one bit if I caught the bouquet, but he was good at hiding his emotions, so it was hard to tell. Inside he could be down on his knees praying to the good Lord that I not catch the flowers. I shook my head. "Don't be ridiculous. I don't want to ruin a good thing with that kind of pressure."

A drumroll started on the tables. Hands pounded in a steady beat that matched my heart. All the men were eagerly waiting for Sugar to toss the flowers, so they could give some poor schmuck the ribbing of a lifetime. Sugar turned around and pumped her arm to the count of, "One! Two! Threeee!"

Liza pushed Reba Sue as the flowers went up in the air, and Reba went down on her knees. Betty, not wanting to be outmaneuvered, tripped Liza who face-planted at the bottom of the steps. Her only hope was to leap in the air. For a split second I really thought she was going to do it. Scarlet and I looked at each other. We both took four steps backward, and the bouquet dropped to the floor in front of us…at the feet of Princess.

Princess sniffed the bouquet, then bit into it as both of Scotty's sisters dove for it. Princess was gone before they hit the floor.

Scarlet patted me on the back. "Congratulations! You're going to have a son-in-law."

I shook my head. "She wouldn't do that." But as I said the words, I wasn't sure. Princess had given her heart to her prince, and who was I to stop true love?

Fuzz buckets.

I should have caught the stupid bouquet myself.

If you enjoyed *Killer Classics*, be sure not to miss all of Kym Roberts's Book Barn Mysteries, including

Running an independent bookstore in small-town Hazel Rock, Texas, doesn't sound like a high-risk pursuit. But when a fundraiser reveals a story with a truly killer ending, Charli Rae Warren will need to scramble to sort out the deadly plot...

Sponsoring the literacy drive to benefit the foster care system should be a feel-good endeavor, but one of Charli's helpers is definitely on another page. Charli's dad is distracted and keeping something secret, which Charli suspects is a harmless flirtation with an attractive county clerk who offered to lend them a hand. It's nothing to worry about—until the same clerk winds up dead...

When nosy locals begin pointing fingers, Charli finds herself entangled in a race to uncover the killer's identity—and to get to the bottom of a shattering family secret that could rewrite her history in alarming ways. Suddenly Charli is facing her worst fears and her childhood nemesis in order to unmask a murderer—before he silences her for good...

Keep reading for a special look!

A Lyrical Underground e-book on sale now.

Chapter 1

I knew better than to arrive at a bachelor's house early in the morning, but I'd been happily oblivious to the possibility that I might look like I was checking up on him—like I wanted to catch him in the act. I should have remembered that key word before I'd decided to surprise him with breakfast from the diner. He was a *bachelor*.

And the *last* person on earth I wanted to catch in the act.

Yet there he was…standing in his doorway wearing a T-shirt and jeans with his bare feet announcing to the entire neighborhood, make that the entire world, that he'd just rolled out of bed. The situation couldn't get worse. At least, so I thought. Until I noticed his hair was tousled and Ava James, with matching sex-mussed hair, gave him a tender kiss on the cheek.

I stood on the sidewalk, surrounded by the spring fragrance of the wisteria bush growing over the white picket fence around his front lawn, my mouth hanging opening. Our to-go order breakfast was in my hands as Ava turned around and saw me for the first time. She immediately averted her gaze and jammed a pair of sunglasses on her face. Their endearing moment over, I watched completely dumbfounded as her hand grasped at the neck of her button-down shirt, and her knuckles whitened as she held it together. I did not want to notice the missing buttons on the top of her blouse as she bowed her head in the traditional walk of morning-after shame.

We were all adults. We could handle this. It wasn't that big a deal. Their age difference wasn't shocking, nor was their potential of being a couple out of the question. It had just taken me off guard, and that was what I found most disturbing.

At least that's what I was telling myself.

Ava and I passed on the sidewalk and I tried to establish eye contact through her mirrored lenses. "Good morning, Ava," I said and smiled at the woman fifteen years my senior.

She mumbled a good morning without raising her head. I wouldn't have been able to see her eyes anyway, but I didn't want her to think I harbored a grudge. I didn't. They were consenting adults. I had no reason to judge them or be upset.

"Are you ready for the literacy drive for the foster care program?" I asked.

Ava nodded but kept walking right past me. "I'll call you," she said without looking back.

"Sure thing. Whenever you get a chance, I'm flexible."

I don't think I fooled anyone. I wasn't *that* flexible about any of this. I looked up at the door where he stood watching the whole scene unfold. His jaw was tight, and his eyes narrowed as he scanned the street to see if anyone else witnessed their indiscretion. Then his gaze returned to me, and I could tell it wasn't a proud moment for him. He sensed what neither one of us wanted to admit—he'd just fallen off the pedestal I'd put him on shortly after I'd returned to Hazel Rock, Texas, my hometown of 2,093 people.

That however, wasn't what I found most disturbing. There was something in his eyes that said *don't ask questions; don't ask for an explanation.* If I did? My inquiries would be ignored.

I reached the steps with the warm paper bag and two paper cups of sweet tea in my hands. "Are you going to let me in?"

He looked like he had no idea how to handle the situation. That made two of us, but from the look on his face, Ava James wasn't just a one-night stand. She meant something to him, and I needed to suck it up and accept the fact that the man had moved on. He stood back and held the door open for me to enter, but his gaze followed Ava as she walked down the sidewalk, past Mike Thompson, who had apparently started running to work off a few pounds, or fifty, before she rounded the corner.

"Daddy, you don't have to keep your love life a secret."

Bobby Ray Warren closed the door without saying a word, and by the time he turned around, he'd hidden that lost look in his eyes. "I'm glad you brought breakfast. I'm starved."

If he noticed the shudder he sent through my body with that comment, he didn't say anything. He grabbed the bag from my hand and walked into his kitchen without another word. I followed him into the perfectly designed kitchen of his old Victorian home. His last girlfriend, who had died the day I return to town a little over a year ago, had decorated and remodeled the century-old home.

Sometimes I wondered if he stayed in the house in memory of her. Today I wasn't so sure. After all, this was where he lay his head at night; it had his touches just as much as hers. Especially when it came to the industrial coffee station for his Colombian coffee he enjoyed so much. Most mornings he waited for a cup of joe until he got to the bookstore; on the days he didn't open the Book Barn Princess, he had a cup of fresh brew at home in his state-of-the-art kitchen.

I looked down at the two plastic cups of sweet tea in my hands and wondered why I'd bought two. Two empty coffee cups were sitting on the kitchen table. I set the tea on the table, picked up the coffee cups, and carried them to the sink.

Dad had just shared a cup of coffee with Ava after their night together—though I really didn't want to think about his night with Ava. But it was stuck in my brain like the sound of a greased pig squealing in an arena full of kids. Nipping at this end of my brain and screaming at the other, sending it straight through my right lobe into my left, it wouldn't shut up or disappear.

"So…is this the beginning of something new?" I asked.

"Are you planning to bring me breakfast from the diner every morning?"

I rolled my eyes at his attempt to hide what I'd seen. "You know what I'm talking about, Daddy."

"I think you're stepping into waters you don't belong in, Princess." My nickname rolled off his tongue with more than a hint of irritation.

I searched his face and could see he was dead serious. He wasn't going to discuss Ava James with me. I didn't know if that meant they were serious or if it meant they were less than serious. His face was a mask of discretion. He was not going to discuss her with anyone. Ava James had his ear…and more.

"You're right. I'm sorry, Daddy. I was out of line questioning you about your love life. When you're ready to talk about it, I'm here."

Dad reached over and squeezed my hand. "Now let's see what you brought for breakfast. At this point, I'm pretty sure I could eat the bag and think it tasted good."

We ate our breakfast of eggs, bacon, and waffles made out of Texas Toast while discussing our upcoming fundraiser for foster kids. Ava James had pitched the idea to my dad and he'd been all for it. I was too, but now I wondered how personal that pitch had been.

Ava had been a customer of our family bookstore for as long as I could remember. When I was a kid she used to come in every now and then with Isla Sperry, the old sheriff's wife. When I was a teenager, she was a dispatcher at the sheriff's office, working for the same sheriff who spouted scriptures every time I so much as breathed in the direction of trouble. When the sheriff brought me to the station after a wild night of leading a cheer from the top of the town's water tower, it'd been Ava James sitting at the one-person phone system in the sheriff's office who tampered down his lecture straight out of 1 Peter 3:3–4.

"'Women with unfading beauty of a gentle and quiet spirit are precious to God,'" Sheriff Sperry had said.

Ava had turned around and looked at him with one eyebrow raised. "You can't tell Princess to be quiet and gentle, then turn around and quote John 10:10 to me. Princess is literally stopping 'the thief who comes to steal and kill and destroy' by sharing her joy with the world. Remember? 'Jesus came that they may have life and have it abundantly.' Princess has life—abundantly."

At that moment, I'd felt like I had a big sister looking out for me. It was wonderful. I'd never be able to quote scripture in an argument. But Ava could, and she did it effectively.

The sheriff's authoritarian attitude had turned into a pained expression as he looked between the two of us. Even at my tender age, I knew there was something important hanging in the air between them. And when the sheriff walked down the hallway to his office, I'd dared to complain to Ava about the old coot.

That had been a mistake.

My big sister disappeared. Ava had practically raised her claws in his defense. He'd been like a father to her when she'd aged out of the foster care system. Without him, she wasn't sure what street corner she would have been sleeping on. It was the last time I'd complained about her boss. At least to her. It also explained why she went to work for Sperry when he became a judge, and it explained her passion for collecting the books we couldn't sell, to give to foster children every month.

My dad broke into my memories. "When are you leaving for Dallas?"

"Tomorrow evening after I get off at the bookstore. I'm going to stay for the weekend and do a little shopping."

Dad's lip quirked. "I hear Mateo has the weekend off as well."

"Oh?" I began clearing the table to avoid any further comments. The last thing I wanted to discuss with my daddy was Mateo Espinosa. Mateo and I hadn't told anyone that we were going to a concert in Dallas together. For him, it was a privacy issue. For me it was complicated. We were taking a big step I wasn't sure I was ready for. During the past month, I'd found myself questioning my intelligence. Mateo was the current county sheriff, and I'd already had one bad relationship with the lead law enforcement officer in town. What if things went south between the two of us?

Would he quote the Bible to me as well? Would he be there every time I went two miles over the speed limit? Come running when I didn't cross the street at the intersection and tell me I was jaywalking? Or would he focus on first-time offenses I hadn't been old enough to experience with the old sheriff? Like shake his head at the "wild girl" in town when I came out of the Tool Shed Tavern a little tipsy after a Monday night football game, then arrest me for public intoxication. Those fears were very real… to me, anyway.

When my thoughts went in that direction, breathing became difficult, and as the weekend drew closer, those moments of panic seemed to be increasing. I finished clearing the table as my dad leaned back and patted his belly.

"Is Ava still working as Judge Sperry's clerk?" I asked.

Dad stiffened, the way he always did when I talked about the county judge who used to be my archnemesis. Unlike Ava, my relationship with Judge Sperry didn't contain fond childhood memories. They consisted of the man who had been sheriff looking for every reason in the world to spout the Bible to me. If I breathed a hint of rebellion, I somehow ended up staring at the gold star on his chest, saying "yes, sir" and "no, sir" before I'd even made a nuisance of myself. It always ended with Sheriff Sperry telling me my evil ways would send him to his grave.

I never quite understood why. Maybe that type of tough love had been a saving grace for Ava. For me, it'd been a pain in my backside and his nickname "the Judge" seemed to fit very well since the man had been evaluating my behavior since I stepped into town at the age of eight.

"Yes, but that may change soon," Daddy answered.

"Why?"

"Ava said Isla Sperry's Alzheimer's has taken a dramatic turn for the worse in the past month. She keeps wandering away from the nursing home and making wild accusations about the people she cares most about. The Judge is thinking about retiring."

"What? I had no idea she was suffering from Alzheimer's disease. I'm sorry to hear that. Isla Sperry was always good to me. I hate that she's going through that."

Dad cleared his throat, and I could have sworn there was a shimmer of tears in his eyes before he stood up and turned toward the hallway. "Me too. Me too, Princess."

As he walked down the hallway I couldn't help but wonder if I was missing something once again, but then his voice turned loud and clear when he said, "I'm going to take a shower. You better get to the store and open it. We don't want the customers busting down the Barn door."

We both knew there was no threat of our customers breaking down our doors. We also knew that something was bothering him, and my daddy wasn't about to talk about it...yet.

About the Author

Three career paths resonated for **Kym Roberts** during her early childhood: detective, investigative reporter, and…nun. Being a nun, however, dropped by the wayside when she became aware of boys—they were the spice of life she couldn't deny. In high school her path was forged when she took her first job at a dry cleaner and met every cop in town, especially the lone female police officer on patrol. From that point on there was no stopping Kym's pursuit of a career in law enforcement. Kym followed her dream and became a detective, which fulfilled her desire to be an investigative reporter, with one extra perk—a badge. Promoted to sergeant, Kym spent the majority of her career in SVU. She retired from the job reluctantly when her husband dragged her kicking and screaming to another state, but writing continued to call her name, at least in her head. Visit her on the web at kymroberts.com.

When kindergarten teacher Charli Rae Warren hightailed it out of Hazel Rock, Texas, as a teen, she vowed to leave her hometown in the dust. A decade later, she's braving the frontier of big hair and bigger gossip once again...but this time, she's saddled with murder!

Charli agrees to sell off the family bookstore, housed in a barn, and settle her estranged dad's debt—if only so she can ride into the sunset and cut ties with Hazel Rock forever. But the trip is extended when Charli finds her realtor dead in the store, strangled by a bedazzled belt. And with Daddy suspiciously MIA, father and daughter are topping the most-wanted list...

Forging an unlikely alliance with the town beauty queen, the old beau who tore her family apart, and one ugly armadillo, Charli's intent on protecting what's left of her past...and wrangling the lone killer who's fixin' to destroy her future...

Charli Rae Warren is back home in Hazel Rock, Texas, spending her time reading, collecting, and selling books—at least, the ones that don't get eaten first by her father's pet armadillo. Running the family bookstore is a demanding job, but solving murders on the side can be flat out dangerous...

The Book Barn is more than just a shop, it's a part of the community—and Charli is keeping busy with a fundraising auction and the big rodeo event that's come to town. That includes dealing with the Texas-size egos of some celebrity cowboys, including Dalton Hibbs, a blond, blue-eyed bull rider who gets overly rowdy one night with the local hairdresser... and soon afterward, disappears into thin air.

Dalton's brother also vanished seven years ago—and Charli is thrown about whether Dalton is a villain or a victim. After a close call with an assailant wielding a branding iron (that plays havoc with her hair), and some strange vandalism on her property, she's going to have to team up with the sheriff to untangle this mystery, before she gets gored...

KYM ROBERTS

A BOOK BARN MYSTERY

PERILOUS POETRY

BOOK BARN

UNDERGROUND

Charli Rae Warren doesn't plan on striking it rich as the owner of an independent bookstore in Hazel Rock, Texas—especially one with a pink armadillo as its mascot. But when an ingenious advertising campaign puts her business on the map, it ropes in some deadly publicity...

Charli can't believe writer Lucy Barton has agreed to promote her latest Midnight Poet Society novel at the Book Barn Princess—or that there's only a week and a half to prepare for the signing. It's all because of The Book Seekers, a smartphone app created by her cousin Jamal exclusively for Charli's bookstore, which sends fans on a virtual scavenger hunt around town for a chance to meet the best-selling author. But as soon as it goes live, people turn up dead...

Someone's using the Book Seekers to track victims and copycat the fictional Midnight Poet Society homicides, and horrified locals suspect Jamal could be the mastermind behind the crimes. While Charli readies the Barn for a stampede of new customers, it'll take true grit to shelve the culprit before her brainy cousin gets locked behind bars, Ms. Barton backs out of the visit, and she finds herself up a creek—with a serial killer holding the paddle!

Printed in the United States
by Baker & Taylor Publisher Services